MURDER BY SERPENTS

MURDER BY SERPENTS

THE MYSTERY QUILT

BARBARA GRAHAM

FIVE STAR

An imprint of Thomson Gale, a part of The Thomson Corporation

Detroit • New York • San Francisco • New Haven, Conn. • Waterville, Maine • London

LIBRARY OF CONGRESS CATALOGING-IN-PUBLICATION DATA

Graham, Barbara, 1948–
    Murder by serpents : the mystery quilt / Barbara Graham. — 1st ed.
        p. cm.
    ISBN-13: 978-1-59414-590-2 (hardcover : alk. paper)
    ISBN-10: 1-59414-590-3 (hardcover : alk. paper)
    1. Police—Tennessee—Fiction. 2. Sheriffs. 3. Clergy—Crimes against—
Fiction. 4. Snake cults (Holiness churches)—Tennessee—Fiction. 5. Tennessee—Fiction. I. Title.
PS3607.R336M87 2007
813'.6—dc22
                                                                        20070

First Edition. First Printing: November 2007.

Published in 2007 in conjunction with Tekno Books and Ed Gorman.

Printed in the United States of America on permanent paper
10 9 8 7 6 5 4 3 2 1

For my father.

ACKNOWLEDGMENTS

Thanks to Ken Fink, who was gracious enough to let a rattlesnake bite him and to describe it for me. Additional thanks go to his wife Sherry, whose talents with shovel, tree pruning tool and bucket prevented the rattler from becoming a repeat offender.

More thanks to Michelle Quick, who tests my patterns, laughs at me and turns her deaf ear to my whining.

Special thanks and love to my husband and sons, who continue to love me in spite of my quirks and obsessions.

All errors and omissions are mine.

SPRINGTIME IN THE SMOKIES
A MYSTERY QUILT BY THEO ABERNATHY

THE FIRST BODY OF CLUES:

Finished size is a lap or crib size top, approximately 45 1/2" × 35 1/2". All fabric requirements are generous and based on standard widths of approximately 44 inches. The instructions assume familiarity with basic quilt construction and an accurate 1/4" seam throughout.

Fabric (A). This is the main or theme fabric. Select a print— floral or novelty—on a medium background. The print should contain several different colors and motifs should measure in the two to three inch range. Cutting and construction does allow use of directional fabrics.

Fabrics (B), (C), (D), (E). Select "interesting solids" (prints that appear to be a single color) of colors found in the main fabric. (B) and (C) should be very light or very dark. (D) and (E) should be medium.

Yardage
- (A)—2 yards of print
- (B)—1/3 yard of very light or dark
- (C)—1/3 yard of light
- (D)—1/3 yard of medium
- (E)—5/8 yard of medium

Cutting Instructions
Be sure to label cut pieces with fabric letter and size
- (A)—from the 2 yards.
- Cut 2 strips 3 1/2" by width of fabric

Cut 4 strips 2 1/2" by width of fabric

Cut 2 strips 3 1/2" by <u>length</u> of fabric (approximately 3 1/2" by 55")

From remainder—Cut 2 strips 8 1/2" by width and subcut into 17 strips 8 1/2" by 2 1/2" and

Cut 4 strips 4 1/2" by width of fabric and subcut into 48 rectangles 4 1/2" by 2 1/2"

(B)—from 1/3 yard of very light or very dark. Cut 48 squares 2 1/2"

(C)—from 1/3 yard of light. Cut 54 squares 2 1/2"

(D)—from 1/3 yard of medium. Cut 48 squares 2 1/2"

(E)—from 5/8 yard of medium. Cut 4 strips width of fabric by 1 1/2" and set aside and

Cut 3 strips width of fabric by 4 1/2" and subcut into 48 rectangles 2 1/2" by 4 1/2"

CHAPTER ONE

"Beware the Ides of March." The words circled in Theo Abernathy's brain until she wanted to scream. Events over the past several hours gave Theo a healthy aversion to prophesy. She wondered if Julius Caesar felt the same when he realized his fate.

The day didn't begin well.

She overslept. Then, her naturally curly hair went haywire on one side, giving her a punk rocker look. The males in her family thought it was funny.

No coffee. That was more serious than the hair but it was still a mere irritant.

She dealt with each problem with reasonably good humor and kept smiling.

When her minivan didn't start, she stopped smiling. It still wouldn't start when her husband Tony hooked jumper cables to it. After giving her a kiss and unnecessary instructions to call the mechanic, he loaded their sons into his green and white Blazer.

At least the boys were happy. They loved to ride like prisoners in the official vehicle of Park County's Sheriff. Separated from the front seats by a wall of steel mesh, they pressed their faces close to it and made desperate moaning sounds.

Theo interrupted their little drama. "Don't forget to go to your scout meeting after school."

Jamie's blue eyes sparkled as he blew her a dozen kisses.

More subdued, as befitted his big brother status, Chris adjusted his new glasses and blew just one. She managed a merry smile for the boys. At least they weren't too grown up to blow kisses at their mother.

"I'll drop them at school on my way to work." Tony kissed her again. "Call me when you know something about the van."

Theo nodded. Silersville, Tennessee, boasted two mechanics. Brothers. Frank and Joe. She dialed the garage number from memory.

What she really needed was a new car.

Minutes later, she watched Joe, the smarter of the brothers, stare into the engine. The expression on his face was not encouraging. Theo wondered what this would cost. Her anxiety increased. How would they pay for this?

"I don't rightly know what's wrong with her." Joe tried several things but failed to start it. He chatted amiably as he attached the towing cable that swung from the crane on his vintage truck. "But she's sure dead as a stump, ain't she?" A flick of a switch tightened the cable and soon the rear end of her boxy van rose into the air.

Joe offered to drive her to work.

Without thinking it through, Theo accepted. But, in order to ride in the cab of the tow truck, she had to squeeze between a greasy toolbox and an even dirtier door. A newspaper served as a makeshift seat cover. After a jolting ride, Joe dropped her in front of Theo's Quilt Shop. He gave her a jaunty wave as he pulled away.

The relief created by a safe arrival dissipated the moment she walked inside.

Chaos reigned in her quilt shop.

The drawer on the cash register jammed shut and she had to pry it open with a screwdriver. Now it was jammed open. Customers milled around while Jane, Theo's mother-in-law and usually a levelheaded, dedicated worker, spent the day cooing into the phone like a lovesick dove.

No coffee here either.

Worse, no chocolate.

The computer dedicated to the Internet side of her business caught a virus, threw up and then died, taking several unfilled orders with it. Word trickled in that Theo's computer wizard was spending his vacation on a tropical beach, drinking fruit drinks with umbrellas and lots of rum in them.

Theo hoped the man was being ravaged by sand fleas and sun poisoning.

It wasn't just the computer.

Maybe it was the lack of caffeine or maybe the anxiety brought on by the rest of the day but Theo's brain wasn't running on all cylinders either. With the floor of her office littered with scraps of ruined fabric, she decided that her carefully written pattern instructions for a new mystery quilt read like gibberish. She needed to find a better way to describe the construction sequence or she would have to add a picture—a move that would eliminate the "mystery" from the pattern.

She glanced at her watch. Surprised that the endless day was hurtling to a close, she realized that she had only fifteen minutes to get to the garage before it closed. Even if she took the shortcut over the hill, she would be lucky to get there in time. She ran to the back door, pulling on her patchwork jacket as she left.

If mountains had tendrils, the ridge that cut through town was a tendril of the Smoky Mountains. She nervously glanced at the path that zigzagged up the hill. Everyone in Silersville used the shortcut from Main Street over to the garage and Ruby's Café on the highway side. Although recent snows meant that footing might be treacherous, she told herself that she'd be fine. Wet leaves covering slippery red mud might send her falling if she wasn't careful.

It would be completely dark soon.

In minutes, she crested the ridge and paused, taking a deep breath. Below her stretched the highway that connected them to the rest of East Tennessee. A tangle of trees, rhododendron, honeysuckle and kudzu surrounded her. She heard voices of others walking the same path. Behind her was the town of Silersville and to her east the Smoky Mountains crouched, an obsidian presence under a darkening sky.

Welcoming lights glowed at Ruby's Café. Theo took a step forward, beginning her descent, but her right foot tangled in a vine. Emitting a soft cry, she pitched forward, automatically reaching to break her fall. She never hit the ground. A pair of long-fingered hands grasped her shoulders and Theo grabbed the owner's thin forearms for balance.

"Nothing like some old vines to trip you up, is there Miss Theo?" A man's soft words, accompanied by putrid breath, came to her in the semi-darkness.

Theo recognized that voice and smiled at her tall rescuer. "Thanks, Quentin." Standing below her, he seemed close to her petite height for a change. When she regained her balance, she released his arms and examined his face. Never a handsome young man, Quentin Mize looked thinner and paler than usual. Sores dotted his face. Shocked by his worsening appearance, she struggled to find words.

A second man stepped forward to stand next to Quentin, distracting her.

"Who's your little friend, cousin?"

Theo had never seen the man before, but she found something about his face and demeanor repellent and automatically stepped back. Shorter than Quentin, he glanced up at her and the fading light caught his eyes. Freaky eyes. The irises were dark, probably brown, and too small, leaving the whites of his eyes visible all the way around. As if to emphasize that trait, the eyelashes weren't longer than an eighth of an inch and had blunt tips, like they'd been cut to that length.

Uneasy, Theo wrapped her arms across her chest.

"Aren't you a pretty little bitty thing?" The man with the odd eyes leered at her and his tongue darted out between his lips, like a reptile testing the air.

Her stomach tightened in disgust. Theo looked away from his face and noticed that he had a snakeskin-patterned handkerchief sticking out of his suit coat pocket. She felt like running but forced herself to remain still.

Quentin stepped between them and faced Theo. "You'd best be getting on down the hill now. It'll be full dark soon." Clearly, Quentin had no intention of introducing his companion. In fact, he reached a skeletally thin hand around the man's bicep and pulled him up the path and further away from her.

"You leave her be. She's my friend." Quentin's soft words reached her ears. They were filled with anger. "Not only that, but she's the sheriff's wife. He's a big man and very protective, if you catch my meaning. You mess with her and he just might kill you."

Still disturbed by the encounter, Theo shivered and stepped forward again. Below her, the lights went dark in the garage. It didn't matter. Her car wasn't going anywhere tonight. She groaned. Her minivan still dangled from the tow truck like a giant catfish.

One foot slipped and she almost fell. Slowing down, she reached for her cell phone and pressed Tony's number. When her husband answered on the first ring, she felt her eyes fill with tears.

"You're late." Tony's voice boomed through the tiny phone. "Where are you?"

"I'm fine." Theo's uneasiness made her sassy. "Thank you for asking."

"Okay. I deserved that." He lowered his voice. "You're late, my darlin', love of my life. When last seen, your chariot was busted. Might I inquire as to your current whereabouts and when I might see your lovely face and golden dandelion curls again?"

In spite of her efforts not to, Theo snorted. "Chariot is hanging on the truck. They haven't touched the van yet." She stepped into the empty overflow parking lot behind Ruby's and glanced around. It was empty. "Can you pick up the boys from scouts and meet me at Ruby's?"

"Sure." Tony's voice was calming now instead of teasing. Some of her distress must have filtered through her voice. "What happened?"

"I just thought that maybe we could all have some dinner before I have to go back to the shop."

"Tonight?"

"I'm afraid so." Theo looked up, searching for stars in the darkening sky, but she saw only clouds. "I'm supposed to meet the backup computer wizard at eight. If we don't do it tonight, he can't come until after four tomorrow."

"We'll be there in just a bit."

Theo slipped her phone into her purse and stared at the kudzu that grew like a black curtain against what she knew was a wall of red dirt. Light from the café reflected in a pair of eyes that stared at her. Before Theo could scream, the owner, a large raccoon eased onto the pavement and waddled past her.

CHAPTER TWO

The next morning, Park County Sheriff Tony Abernathy sat at his desk, trapped in his own office. He considered sticking his fingers in his ears and humming so that he could block out the mayor's voice. Calvin Cashdollar had a whine like a dentist's drill, and he'd invaded the sheriff's office to "chat" about the upcoming tourist season. Tony's young sons, Chris and Jamie, used the plugged-ear technique and it seemed to work for them, but Tony decided that would just make Calvin talk louder. Almost as annoying as hearing the mayor was being forced to watch him. Calvin twitched each time his dull blond hair flopped into his eyes, which, considering the way he twitched had turned into a vicious circle. The man was practically convulsing.

Tony knew he couldn't continue to watch the mayor without either strangling the man or laughing in his face. Caged between his desk and a row of four drawer file cabinets, he shifted his eyes to the wall quilt that hung behind the mayor's oversized head. As a tribute to his desire to write Wild West adventure books, Theo had used fabrics with cowboy motifs to make the colorful decoration and had given it to him on his last birthday.

A shrill ringing came from somewhere on his desk. Blessing the interruption, Tony shuffled stacks of papers as he searched for the telephone. Undeterred, the mayor continued to babble. At last, Tony located the missing object and pressed the receiver to his ear. "Sheriff."

A blast of high-pitched sound poured from the receiver and ripped into his brain, threatening to exit through his eyes. Tony immediately recognized the source—Blossom Flowers was in another flying purple panic. He sighed.

"Slow down, Blossom." He moved the receiver away from his throbbing ear. Not certain of everything she had said, Tony was sure that he had picked out the words "dead" and "snake," but the torrent of words, accompanied by the whooshing sounds of panting, was otherwise unintelligible. He sighed again, unconcerned. Blossom had at least one emergency a week. It hadn't been long since she had called, hysterical, because her dog was lost. The mutt had eventually been located under her bed, sound asleep. Tony felt another sigh working its way up toward the surface. He forced it down. "Take a deep breath and tell me again what you saw in the parking lot at Ruby's Café. Where are you now?"

Rising from the chair that faced Tony's desk, Mayor Cashdollar balanced his bony frame on his size sixteen feet. Tony noticed that his black suit pants ended a good two inches above his shoes and exposed skinny ankles in white socks.

"We'll talk later, Sheriff." Clutching a steno pad and a yellow pencil in one huge hand, he tiptoed toward the door.

Watching Calvin in motion, Tony couldn't suppress his grin. His fellow citizens had elected a walking cartoon character and put him in the mayor's office.

As Calvin crossed the threshold, he paused, turned, and gave Tony a childish wave goodbye.

Turning his full attention to what Blossom was saying, Tony didn't return the wave. She switched from panting to emitting a bone-piercing screech. He feared the sound would make his skull explode. In self-defense, he interrupted her. "I'll be right over."

Massaging his ear, he checked his watch. It was only nine

o'clock in the morning and he already wanted to go home. Dealing with the mayor and Blossom in one week was enough to increase his perpetual heartburn. He thought that dealing with both of them before noon might just kill him. His stomach rumbled and he reached for the king-size jar of antacid tablets that was the centerpiece on his desk.

He was still chewing several tablets as he pulled his brown nylon jacket from its hook by the door. He dialed Wade Claybough's cell phone. As usual, his eager-beaver chief deputy answered on the first ring.

Tony spoke without preamble. "Meet me at Ruby's Café. I'm not sure what's happened, but Blossom was shrieking into the phone like a banshee on speed. You know how she gets, but I'd say that whatever is in the lot behind Ruby's must be pretty ugly. I'm sure I heard about something dead and snakes." He pulled on his jacket before opening his private door into the parking lot. "I'm leaving now."

Tony drove his official green and white Blazer around the side of Ruby's and noticed a few onlookers milling around the café end of the upper parking lot. In spite of the mist, he could make out the form of a dark green car at the far end. It blended into the kudzu-choked hillside.

In the center of the lot stood what looked like an orange haired manatee wearing a yellow slicker. It gestured at the small gathering with a blue and white golf umbrella, while it talked on a cell phone. As he got closer, it became clear that this was not a manatee but an exceptionally large woman with tufts of traffic-cone orange hair. Tony felt himself smile. This was classic Blossom, the youngest of the myriad Flowers sisters. Whatever else might be said about her, the word timid was never mentioned.

From what he could tell, Blossom was doing her best to protect the area from sightseers even though she created a fearful scene in the process. Tony pressed on the horn. At first, that had no obvious effect on the gathering. Just as he was about to flip on the siren, the people moved aside and let him pull forward, where he stopped, blocking the entrance into the upper lot.

Seconds later, Wade pulled his patrol car to a stop next to the Blazer.

Spotting his arrival, Blossom flipped her cell phone closed and, with a flourish, dropped it into the green tote bag dangling from her elbow. She jogged her way toward the car and, considering her bulk, moved quite briskly.

Tony climbed out of the Blazer and opened the passenger door so that she could sit. As she climbed in, her tote bag slammed into his knee. He glanced down at fifty neon green frogs with brilliant red eyes. They all smiled at him.

While he waited for Blossom to get settled, he studied the car. From where he stood, it looked like an ordinary, small, dark green station wagon. Beads of water covered the car, but the pavement under it looked dry.

It had started drizzling very early that morning and now the falling moisture was more than mist and not quite rain. The whole world seemed to be dripping as Tony lifted his face and sniffed. The air smelled like the damp earth of early spring, more promise than fact, and it was chilly enough that he welcomed the warmth of his nylon jacket with "Sheriff" emblazoned on the back. It usually made him feel like a target, but it came with the job.

"I'm going to take a look, Blossom. You just sit here and try to relax." With a gesture of his hand, he signaled for Wade to stay behind.

Some sixth sense, or maybe Blossom's frantic call, made him walk carefully. He looked for anything out of place but saw nothing. However, as he approached the car, he felt heat coming from it like it had been baked in an oven. It literally dripped with sweat. Fat droplets ran down the sides and splashed onto the pavement like rain.

Tony couldn't see through the driver's window.

Condensation both inside and outside, combined with tinted glass, completely obscured the interior. He glanced back at Blossom, wondering how she had been able to make out anything.

"You got to look in the windshield. Over there." Blossom's strident voice carried through the thick air and a chubby finger indicated the passenger side.

Tony followed her directions. At first, all he could see was a shapeless form. From this angle, there appeared to be dark blotches on the inside of the windshield, like something sticky had been thrown against it. He blinked again and a cluster of water drops slipped down the glass and revealed what appeared to be a human form and, seen quite clearly, the brown and black geometric markings on a fair-sized rattlesnake. Coiled, rattles held high, it sat on the person's lap. The rattles vibrated, making its warning clear. Cold, dark eyes stared into Tony's and made him flinch. Was it guarding the car?

Tony peered through the driver's window again and tapped on the glass, searching for signs of movement, of human life. Only the snake moved. Tony pulled the flashlight from his duty belt. Shining it into the car, he was able to see that the body looked like that of a man dressed in a short-sleeved shirt. Mouth open, eyes staring, his head rested against the driver's door window, and the only visible foot was on the passenger seat.

Still crouched near the window, Tony pulled on a pair of purple, latex-free gloves and reached for the door handle. Seeing his movement, the snake countered with a lightning quick strike at the glass that separated them. With his eyes a quarter of an inch away from the interior of the open mouth, Tony got a chilling look at the fangs gleaming pink in the subdued light.

"Damn!" He jerked upright, his heart pounded in his chest and his guts tightened. His movement, or maybe the snake's, caused a reaction inside the car and a second snake writhed into view. As it twisted around its companion, Tony recognized the reddish brown and cream bands of a copperhead.

Snakes made his skin crawl. He considered what he had seen. Two types of poisonous snakes loose in one car? What were the odds of that happening by accident? He knew the answer. Slim and none.

Tony stepped back and surveyed the area around the car. Within seconds he decided there was no way those snakes had gotten into the car without a lot of help. Equally obvious, there was no way that he could shoot them without shooting the man.

"What's in there?" asked Wade. He stood a bit behind Tony and below him in the parking lot of the Thomas Brothers's garage. Curiosity burned in his dark eyes.

"There's definitely a person in here. Looks like only one and he can't be alive, but I have to make sure." Tony didn't mention the snakes but searched the area for a forked stick to use to keep them away while he checked for a pulse. He considered having Wade come help but discarded the idea. It would probably be safer for him to do this alone. Getting shot by his deputy while they were both snake-dancing around the parked car would not improve his deteriorating mood.

"I want you to get Doc Nash and an ambulance. Then get someone to help tape off this whole area and start taking your photos." His gesture covered a large part of the parking lot. "There's something damned suspicious about this whole setup."

Nodding, but clearly curious, Wade turned to go.

"Wait."

The young deputy pivoted. A hopeful expression crossed his face.

"Look up the number for the snake guy and give him a call first. We'll need him before we need the doc." Tony knew that no one assigned to animal control would handle snakes, and he didn't blame them. It would take all of his nerve just to open the car door wide enough to check for a pulse. Dodging snakes while removing the body was out of the question.

Wade backed up a step. "The snake guy?"

Tony could see the color leach out of Wade's handsome face as he stared at the car. The high cheekbones seemed sharper than usual and against the sudden pallor, his thick hair looker even blacker. "Yeah, you know, Stan-the-Snakeman."

"There's a snake in there?" There was a definite quaver in Wade's voice.

Tony grinned. With the door closed, he managed to seem unconcerned. "Yep. At least two of them. Tell Stan that I saw a rattlesnake and a copperhead." He turned his attention back to the car. There were shapes in the back that looked like cages but he couldn't see them well enough to know if they were occupied. Reluctant to disturb the snakes, he knew that his first priority was to check the body for signs of life. He pulled the handle. It was unlocked.

He hadn't found a stick so he opened the door just wide enough to slip his right hand inside. A wave of scorching, fetid air hit him, surprising him, and he gagged. It smelled of blood, vomit and excrement. As he touched the neck, he held his breath. It only took a moment to verify what he already knew. The man was dead.

A warning rattle sounded in his right ear. He threw himself clear of the car at the same time that he slammed the door shut. Standing with his hands braced against his thighs, he gulped in deep breaths of cool, clean air and concentrated on the car.

The exterior seemed to be in good shape. There were a few minor scratches near the back passenger door that might have been fresh. The tires were new. He didn't remember seeing the car around town, but it bore a Tennessee plate.

In fact, the plate had Park County emblazoned right in the center. Since Park County was so tiny that it all but vanished on the map and the town contracted his department to supply law enforcement, Tony guessed that he'd seen every vehicle. There were lots of pickup trucks but probably only about a thousand licensed automobiles, so it surprised him that the car was unfamiliar to him. Until they could get inside it, he didn't see much more for him do here for the moment.

He jotted down the license plate number and made his way back to Blossom. She still sat in his car with the door open. As usual, her expression was as adoring as a spaniel's. Her fingers toyed with her watch. It looked like the band cut into her flesh but she seemed not to notice.

"I told you it was ugly."

"Yes, you did and you were right." Tony braced a hand on the Blazer's roof and looked around. The rain had stopped and the small knot of onlookers had grown. It looked like half of the county was there, standing in groups behind the line of yellow tape.

His eyes returned to Blossom. Her sparse but vivid hair stuck out in all directions, but her cheeks were rosy and her skin didn't look as pasty as usual. She appeared excited but not frightened as she reached into the frog-festooned bag and pulled out a king-size Snickers bar, peeled down part of the wrapper and took a dainty bite, leaving a touch of chocolate clinging to one corner of her mouth.

"What made you look inside? Do you know who drives that car?" said Tony.

Her head moved from side to side. "I was on my way to work." Suddenly she slammed a hand over her mouth. The force of the blow jiggled her chins, loosening a crumb. "Oh, no!

I'm so late now that I just know I am going to lose another job." She wailed like a baby. Tears welled in her bulbous eyes and overflowed, cascading down her cheeks before splashing on her bright pink T-shirt.

He patted her soft shoulder and thought that it felt like fluffing a down pillow. "I'll vouch for you, Blossom. If you get into any trouble at work, I'll just tell your boss that you were helping me with my investigation." Tony kept his tone gentle. "Where are you working these days?"

Her sobbing stopped in mid-breath as if a switch had been thrown. Tears balanced on her stubby eyelashes even as she began to giggle. She sounded girlish and surprisingly musical. "I work at Ruby's. Didn't you know that?"

Tony lifted his eyes and looked at the back door of the café. Breakfast smells still floated in the damp air. He took a deep breath and could identify the aromas of sausage, bacon grease and biscuits. His stomach growled. "I've never seen you in there."

"I come in and make the desserts." Another sweet giggle escaped. "That warm apple pie with the special crumb topping is one of my granny's best recipes. Miss Ruby told me that it is one of your favorites." Coquettishly, she batted her eyes.

At the mention of that delectable dessert, his stomach growled again, this time with more force. That pie tasted like a little slice of heaven.

"It's wonderful." Tony agreed. His mouth watered just thinking about it. "What else do you cook?"

"I bake all the pies and the cakes for Miss Ruby. Sometimes she has me make bread or rice pudding and even, sometimes, gingerbread." She sighed loudly and fanned herself with her little hands. Ringless, the fingers were thick and soft. Pasty white, they resembled marshmallows stuck together. "At least today's Thursday and not Tuesday. I'd never get it all done if I was this late getting started."

Tony's eyebrows pulled together. "Why is that? What is so different about Tuesday?"

An amused expression brightened her plain face. "Tuesdays, that diet group meets over at the Baptist church and then they all come over here for dessert, so I have to bake twice as much on Tuesdays. I don't know why they don't just skip that boring old meetin' and just come on and eat. That's all they are interested in anyways. Mostly something chocolate. Didja know that your Aunt Martha is one of the regulars?"

Tony grinned at that bit of news, knowing that eventually he'd use it. "Maybe it's their reward for good behavior. I'm sure that Ruby will understand why you are late and I'll vouch for you if it's needed." The look of adoration on her face made him take a step back. At last, she seemed calm enough to question. "Just tell me what you saw this morning."

Just then, Ruby stepped out the back door and looked around, a look of concern distorting her beautiful face. When she saw Blossom and Tony, she waved. "Is everything okay?" The petite brunette approached. "I was in my office doing paperwork when one of my customers came in and told me that Blossom had been attacked or something. He didn't seem too certain about anything." Her dark eyes searched their faces but she seemed to relax when she saw their expressions. After a quick glance at the half-eaten candy bar, her smile widened as if seeing it reassured her that Blossom was just fine.

"Morning, Ruby." Tony turned to face her. "I just need to ask Blossom a few more questions and then she'll be ready to go to work. She seems to be worried that you'll fire her for being late."

He watched as Ruby's eyes widened. His words clearly surprised her. Many of the locals referred to her as Little Ruby. Old Ruby had been the previous proprietor. The name went along with the business. This particular Ruby was officially Maria Costello, a Mediterranean rose blooming in this Scotch-Irish garden. Even with her hair tightly corralled into a chignon and wrapped in a sparkling white apron that covered her almost to her toes, her beauty haunted many masculine dreams. Tony knew that Deputy Mike Ott was in love with her.

"Nonsense." She smiled at Blossom. "You come in whenever you're ready. That's fine with me." Hesitating, she eyed both his Blazer and the green and white patrol car parked next to it. She watched Wade stringing the yellow crime scene tape and the small cluster of observers keeping their vigil from the side. She frowned and craned her neck, trying get a better view.

"I can see that Blossom is fine, but obviously there is a problem back here. Is it something I should know about?"

"Actually, I'm glad that you came outside. Do you recognize that dark green car?" Tony pointed to it. "Do you remember seeing it around here?"

She stepped up on the Blazer's running board to see more clearly. "No. I'm sure that wasn't there last night when I locked up and went home about ten. There were no cars at all in the lot. I drove through it before I left like I always do." She looked puzzled. "Why would anyone park way back there anyway, when there are so many close spots open?"

"I don't know that yet but I do know that there is a dead body in the car." He paused at her shocked expression and quick intake of breath. "I'd rather not say more for the time, but I'm sure that once Doc Nash arrives, this whole back area is going to be crowded and out of bounds for a while."

Ruby nodded but didn't seem to be taking it in. "In my parking lot? Someone is dead in my parking lot? What happened?" Her dark eyes searched his face.

"We don't know that yet and I suspect that it is going to take awhile to find out." Tony opened his notebook to a clean page.

"While you're here though, can you tell me who arrived first this morning?"

"That had to be Pinkie," said Ruby. "She opens at four-thirty at the latest and works alone until Red comes in at five."

"Pinkie Millsaps?" Tony thought that was good news. He could see Pinkie's motorcycle parked nearby and knew that the sixty-year-old woman would remember if the car had been there when she arrived. As he wrote a note to himself, he smiled. Pinkie, Ruby and Red all worked in one café. What were the odds of that?

"I think that I'll go back inside if you don't need me." Ruby looked dazed, and she shook her head as if to get her thoughts moving again. "Should I send Pinkie out?" At Tony's answering nod, she turned away. "Let me know if you need anything else."

Thinking that there was something odd about the whole conversation, Tony turned his attention away from the retreating young woman and back to Blossom. "Start from the beginning."

"Well, I was on my to work and I was a little late, so I took the shortcut down the hill and I just got to the front of that car when I saw something moving in there. You know how it is. Don't you always look inside a parked car, just to see who's in there?" She didn't wait for an answer. "Anyways, I looked in and that there snake was on the seat next to something that I couldn't see clear, but it looked really ugly. When I tapped on the windshield, it opened its mouth and hissed at me. Then I saw that guy—I guess it is a guy—an' I called you."

The arrival of Pinkie interrupted their conversation. Tony stepped away from Blossom to chat with the stately gray-haired grandmother of twelve whose arms and neck were covered with tattoos of unicorns and flowers. Under her white apron, she wore a black leather vest and pants.

While he talked with Pinkie, Blossom rummaged in her frog-coated bag and came up with a tissue and a stick of chewing gum. A quick blow of her nose into the tissue sounded like the honk of a goose. Seconds later, she started chomping away on the gum, chewing with her mouth open. Blossom looked happier than he had ever seen her before.

In response to his questions, Pinkie said that the car had definitely been there when she arrived shortly before four-thirty, but she didn't recognize it. Nothing about the morning seemed out of the ordinary. The early morning shift had been quiet until about six. Red had arrived at five as usual, and to Tony's question about strangers, she had stated that all of the customers were regulars.

"Did you see anything else unusual this morning?" Tony addressed his question to both women but as he looked around the empty area, he knew the answer already.

There was nothing to see but a quiet parking lot behind a small-town café. From here, not even the car with the snakes looked odd.

On the other side of the parking lot, he saw Theo. The arrival of his wife meant that word of some disaster had already traveled on the gossip chain as far as her fabric shop. He'd give the rest of Silersville about ten minutes to complete the transfer of information. He groaned. That aspect of small town life drove him nuts.

Theo's blond hair gleamed in the morning light and he watched as she pulled the lapels of a brightly colored patchwork jacket up around her throat and stepped aside to let the arriving ambulance pass. His wife's expression looked strained, at least until she spotted him. He had been a cop in Chicago when a hopped up junkie shot him. Since then, she had trouble dealing with her fears. Not long after that incident, retiring Sheriff Harvey Winston had suggested that Tony move his family back to Silersville and run for the job as his replacement. Theo still owned the house that her grandparents left her. Returning had seemed like a good idea at the time.

Since the move, Theo still worried about him, but not as much. Now that she could see his evident good health, she smiled and waved.

A canary yellow pickup truck equipped with a sporty camper top drove in front of her and stopped, blocking his view. The painting on the door depicted a coiled rattlesnake. It was a very detailed, realistic painting surrounded by the words, "Stan-the-Snakeman" and a telephone number.

Reinforcements had arrived.

CHAPTER THREE

Stan-the-Snakeman didn't take his face away from the car window, but Tony could sense his excitement. He positively quivered. There is nothing like a man who loves his job, and Tony had to admire his enthusiasm. Stan was short and round and everyone's first choice to play Santa because he knew how to have fun. Clean-shaven now, he would start letting his beard grow out again on Labor Day, and by Thanksgiving he would be ready to play his favorite role.

"That sure is one mad looking snake, Sheriff. That's the rattler, looks like a Timber rattler. You said that you saw a copperhead as well?" Stan didn't look up and he didn't wait for an answer. "Those wooden crates in the back look like cages. I guess there are more of them in there, but I don't think I can tell you any more than that without getting inside. Can you open the door for me? Slowly. We don't want to scare the poor thing." As he spoke, he slipped his hands into long, heavy leather gloves, a smile of anticipation lifting the corners of his mouth, exposing a gap where he once had two lower central incisors.

Tony massaged his bald scalp as he peered in at the driver. The windshield was drying as the clouds dissipated, making it easier to see inside. There was no way that the guy had been alive for quite a while. It looked like he, if it was a he, had been hit with a bomb. Blood and vomit spattered most of the front portion of the car interior.

"Maybe I'll go away on vacation until this can be cleaned up.

They should probably just bury the whole thing." Tony silently gave thanks that it was not his job to do more than head the investigation if the death was deemed unnatural. This would not make Doc Nash, the coroner, a happy man. In addition to his ceremonial job as mayor, Calvin Cashdollar was the area mortician. He wasn't going to be happy either. That thought *did* bring a smile to Tony's lips.

"You think that something suspicious caused this?" Wade held the snake man's extra bags and a set of forty-inch tongs. "It has to be an accident. After all, it looks like the guy carried his own zoo around with him." The way his eyes kept moving, he couldn't have looked less comfortable if he had been forced to perform a striptease at a revival meeting, with his mother seated in the front row.

"Wait a minute. What's that?" A flash of something silver caught Tony's eye. He leaned forward trying for a better view. At the same moment, a ray of sunshine penetrated the gloom in the car. Suddenly, they all could see what had been hidden. Handcuffs. Steel handcuffs secured their dead guy to the steering wheel. Someone made sure that he stayed in the car.

"Now *that* looks as suspicious as hell." He looked over at Wade. "Escort Stan back to his truck and park him there while you get your stuff. I need you to do a little fingerprint work before we touch those handles. While you're at the car why don't you run these license plates. Maybe they'll tell us who this is. Give me the camera, and I'll take some pictures."

Seeking reinforcements, Tony stabbed the numbers on his cell phone with more force than necessary. He would have to get a couple of deputies started canvassing the area. He might even have to wake up the night shift.

Stan's curiosity was clear. He swiveled his head around as he followed Wade but he didn't seem to understand what caused the increased excitement.

As they moved away, Tony could hear Wade talking to Stan. They weren't making any attempt to be quiet.

"You might as well get comfortable, but don't go anywhere and don't say anything to anyone," said Wade.

"Kin I at least get a cup of coffee at Ruby's?" Stan's lower lip extended in a pout.

"Sure you can as long as it's take out." Wade frowned as he opened the trunk of the patrol car and took out an aluminum suitcase and set it down before he climbed into the car to run a check on the plates. "I doubt the sheriff wants you sitting at the counter flapping your lips." His frown had deepened when he climbed out and hurried back to Tony.

"As if I know anything to flap my lips about." Stan continued talking to himself as he dropped his tools onto the open tailgate of the truck. Soon he crossed his arms over his round belly and clearly settled in to wait. From his post, he would be able to see Tony and Wade setting numbered markers in the parking lot and taking lots of pictures. An uncustomary frown pulled the corners of his lips down.

His words traveled to Tony's ears. "I am gonna be an old man when y'all are done." His eyes sparkled as he watched Theo walking toward him. "At least I git to snuggle with that little lady."

That morning, Theo had barely arrived at her shop when a customer said there was some trouble behind Ruby's. The familiar fear that came to her whenever she heard the words "dead" and "sheriff" in the same sentence pulled closer. Memories of Tony bleeding buckets of blood and so nearly dying in Chicago would always haunt her. Coming home to Silersville had eased her fears. Even as she told herself that if something bad had happened to him, someone would come tell her, she barely dared to breathe as she had hurried over the hill.

She spotted Tony standing by a dark green car. One good thing about being married to an oversized man was that he was easy to find in a crowd. Almost six feet four inches tall and broad shouldered, he looked even bigger in his dark brown jacket and khaki pants. Not even the dark brown ball cap with the sheriff's insignia on the front could disguise the fact that he was as bald as an egg. Tony didn't enjoy being called "Mr. Clean," like the cleaning products, but the appellation fit him like a glove.

Theo did her best to keep her fears locked away, but sometimes they crept out like hungry mice. Now that she saw Tony in obviously good condition, she relaxed. She spotted Stan next to his truck. Her eyes were drawn to the logo on the door. "There's a snake in the car?"

Stan turned to face her. "Yes ma'am." He looked like he might have said more if he hadn't seen the local newspaper reporter coming toward them like a heat-seeking missile. As he inserted a cigarette into the gap between his teeth, he hissed like one of his snakes. "That woman from the paper is coming this way." He pulled a wooden kitchen match from his pocket and struck it on his thumbnail. It flared to life. Cupping one hand around it, he lit his cigarette.

"You don't like her?" Eyebrows lifted, Theo took a step backwards, dodging the smoke that burned her nose and made her eyes water. "I thought you liked everyone."

"Humph, people think snakes are bad, but they're not. That woman is meaner than any of 'em. Wouldn't surprise me if she gets arrested some day."

Theo watched the object of their discussion, Winifred Thornby, reporter and editor of the newspaper. Winifred had graduated from high school with Tony, but the last twenty years had only soured her and aged her prematurely. From her frumpy clothes to her already deeply wrinkled face, she looked closer to sixty than forty. As her eyes met Theo's, it looked like she would like to talk, but she swerved away before she reached them. A glance at Stan's face revealed his expression of absolute triumph. She wondered why Stan disliked Winifred so much and was about to ask when he cut her off.

"Now, I do have a complaint about you, Theo. I don't know if you meant to, but you've about ruined my life," said Stan.

"Me? What did I do?" Theo's mouth dropped open. She was absolutely baffled. Having been born and raised in Silersville, she had known Stan all of her life and he had always treated her like she was about as dangerous as a ladybug.

"Why? Because you went and taught my wife to quilt, that's why. I never had any idea that you were so cruel." The laugh lines deepened in his face and his pale eyes twinkled. "I haven't had a hot meal in months. Why just last night, she stayed in her sewing room picking out fabrics for your new mystery quilt instead of cooking my dinner. I had to go to the Food City myself because I couldn't even make a sandwich. There wasn't even a crust of stale bread in the house." The corners of his mouth turned down and he rubbed his stomach. His customary paunch still existed, but it did seem a bit smaller. "She used to be a wonderful cook and now I'm gonna waste away. At this rate, I'm gonna be a skinny Santa."

Full of pure joy, the laugh that burst from Theo attracted all eyes. Some of the onlookers moved away as if thinking that the sheriff's wife and the snake man knew that there was nothing to see. They didn't appear to be discussing anything serious.

Standing near them, Doc Nash could overhear the conversation. He leaned over to join in. "That's nothing, Stan. She taught my wife to quilt and now we have to go into every fabric store we come within a hundred miles of, and that's with two closets full of the stuff at home. I'm surprised she hasn't filled my golf bag with it." He braced his fists together and sagged

35

against the side of Stan's pickup. "After our last girl left for college, the missus started talking about storing our dishes in the garage and using the kitchen cabinets for fabric storage and the counter for her cutting space. It got so bad, I began to fear that I would have to keep my Cheerios in the refrigerator. In self-defense, I had that big room added on to the back of the house. Her sewing room is bigger than the garage."

Theo's grin showed no sign of guilt. "I'm just doing my part to keep the economy moving."

Tony joined them, but he didn't have a reason to smile. With his jaws clenched, he could feel the scowl that creased his face. It wouldn't be long before he developed a pounding headache. Headaches and indigestion were not his favorite part of the job, he thought as he searched his pockets for antacid tablets. He found some in his shirt pocket but left them for later.

The pressure in his skull increased with Wade's news about the license plate. It had been stolen. And not just stolen, for pity's sake. It belonged on Queen Doreen's beige Volvo. Tony could hardly wait to ask the mayor's wife why she had not reported the theft.

He and Wade photographed and made notes of everything they could think of about the outside of the car. There wasn't much to see except a couple of tire tracks and footprints that remained in the damp lot. The footprints most likely belonged to Tony.

When the last of the clouds dissipated, the sun quickly dried things. Not even a drop of water remained on the car windows. Maybe it had something to do with the difference in air temperature, but he could swear there had been more heat around the car when it was first discovered than now with the sun shining on it.

The sunlight also illuminated Theo's wild blond curls. He

grinned. He didn't tell her that it made her head look like dandelion fuzz—at least he didn't this time. The last time he'd said that, his dinner had been pasta from a can for three nights in a row. Who knew she'd be so sensitive about her tangled halo?

This morning, though, she smiled at whatever Doc and Stan were discussing. To his eyes, she still looked more like the little girl he'd first met in Sunday school than the mother of two, business owner, author and quilt pattern designer that the rest of the world knew. Seeing her smile eased some of his tension and he moved to stand close to her, inhaling the clean scent of her shampoo. He addressed the men.

"Okay Stan, if you are still ready, let's do this. Wade has finished fingerprinting the door handles. Let's get those snakes out of there. Then we can deal with the body."

Stan looked less eager now. "I hope they've had plenty of fresh air."

Tony sighed deeply, removed an antacid from his meager stash and popped it into his mouth and looked at the doctor. "I don't think you'll have to wait much longer, Doc, but I sure don't envy you this one." At the his lifted eyebrow, Tony just shook his head. "Come on along and you'll see."

Sunlight reflected from Theo's glasses as she turned to face him. Instead of speaking, he fluffed his wife's hair, winked at her and accompanied Stan to the car. She followed, standing with the doctor, well out of the way.

Tony watched as Stan slipped his hands into his gauntlets. All business now, Stan handed a pair of long tongs to Wade and lifted a large hook on a short handle. A cotton bag appeared in his hand like magic. To Tony, it looked a lot like the laundry bag that he had taken to college. The drawstring on it hadn't lasted very long. He could only hope that this one was better quality.

The three of them stood near the car and adjusted their

gloves. Armed with their weapons of a laundry bag, a vaudeville hook and barbecue tongs, Tony guessed they resembled the Three Stooges more than they did anything else. Behind them, Doc Nash made a hissing sound. Tony frowned. He recognized the sound. Doc was laughing.

"Where do we begin?" asked Wade. He shifted his weight back and forth, foot-to-foot, pacing in place.

Tony eyed the slumped figure in the driver's seat. It blocked access to the rest of the car. "The passenger door." Stepping up to it, he tested the handle. This door was locked. Without hesitation, Tony unlocked it with the ease of a professional thief. "We can at least see this snake, so I'll open the door on your call, Stan."

"Now." The softly spoken command focused everyone's attention.

Stan held the hook in his right hand and a snake bag in the left. He was all business as he focused on the first snake. "Okay, let's do it, but slowly. We don't want to scare the poor baby."

Praying that Stan moved quicker than the snake, Tony worked the handle and pulled. He eased the door open. Even though he expected it, the hot air, carrying the aromas of death, seemed to rise as a cloud and hover around him until he turned his face into his left shoulder. The nylon smelled cool and sweet in comparison.

Next to him, Stan's complexion turned green and gray, but he managed to concentrate long enough to lift the rattlesnake from the seat with the hook. With a gasp, Stan backed away from the car even as he tenderly eased the writhing serpent into the opening of the bag. He whispered sweet endearments to his prize. "Close the door."

Tony did. The moment it shut, the men moved away, sucking in great gulps of clean air. Without a word, Wade turned and hustled over to a patch of weeds where he threw up what had to be both his breakfast and previous night's dinner. He returned almost immediately, even though Tony thought that he did not appear to be a healthy young man.

"That's the most awful . . ." Stan started to speak and had to stop. Suddenly he jogged away, holding the bag aloft, and his breakfast joined Wade's.

When he returned, his face seemed less green but was still ashen. Tony watched the way his hands trembled as he wiped his face with a handkerchief before he tightened the drawstring on the snake bag and placed it on the ground.

"That can't be normal." Stan's eyes watered and he wiped with the sleeve of his jacket.

"Oh, yeah?" Wade managed a one-sided grin, but his complexion was far from his usual shade of tan. "I do it all the time."

"Not that, you big lout." Stan punched the much larger, much younger man in the arm and grimaced and moaned as if he had broken his hand. "That." He pointed to the car.

For his part, Doc Nash, who had followed only to watch the procedure, looked like he was thinking of early retirement, starting immediately. Any amusement on his part had vanished when the door opened. He began easing farther from the car.

"Hey Stan, your bag is on the move," said Wade.

Tony guessed that his own color wasn't normal either, but he was undecided whether it was from the aroma inside the car or from watching the bag with the rattlesnake in it moving toward him. It didn't require a rocket scientist to see that a cotton laundry bag would provide no defense against fangs.

Stan lifted the bag as if it contained a treasure and moved it to the other side of the car. "Let's get that copperhead, and then we can see if there are any more loose in there. If I wait much longer, I'll never get my nerve back up. The snakes don't bother me, but whatever is making that smell liked to do me in." Taking a deep breath, he picked up his equipment.

The second snake proved to be harder to catch. They thought they saw it slip under the back seat, but then it couldn't be found there. After several frustrating minutes that seemed much longer because of the smell, they decided to start emptying the car, hoping they would see it before it saw them. The first things they removed were a couple of latched crates that held other snakes, mostly rattlesnakes. Careful to keep them latched, the men stacked the boxes where they could keep an eye on them. One crate on the back seat was empty.

"I'll bet this is the rattlesnake's box." Stan cast a professional eye over it and ran his hand over the smooth wood slats before he nodded his apparent approval. He lifted the unlatched lid of the crate next to it. A copperhead coiled and its tongue flickered busily. Closing it quickly, Stan latched the lid.

"You think it went back into its box?" Wade asked as he lifted that crate, holding it as far away from his body as he could manage, and placed it with the others.

"No way. Look, there it goes!" Stan dived back into the car like a duck going after a water bug. His voice was muffled as he said, "It went under the seat."

Tony and Wade took one step back with drill team precision and watched the show. Hanging out the open door, Stan's ample rear end wagged from side to side.

"Gotcha, you pretty baby." Crooning endearments to the reptile, Stan backed away from the car before he stood and showed them his prize. Forgoing the gauntlets, tongs and hook, he held it just behind the head with his bare hand. Its body and tail wrapped around his arm.

Watching as Stan held the snake aloft like the winner might hold a golf trophy, his eyes glistening with love and joy, Tony cringed, fearing that Stan might plant a kiss on its face. To his own eyes, the snake was a deadly mixture of brown and cream.

The way it writhed and twisted until Stan got it into a separate bag made Tony think that it wasn't a very happy snake.

Wade stared at the crates and fluffed the fine fiberglass brush that he used to dust surfaces, looking for fingerprints. His pained expression earned him Tony's most sympathetic look while Stan checked the car for other snakes.

"You have to at least fingerprint the latches on those crates," said Tony. He surveyed his motley little team. "Doc, I think you can do your thing now, but Stan, I want you to stay on the hunt for a while just in case 'pretty baby' has a friend."

Stan nodded his agreement, but his expression seemed to be less enthusiastic than it had been. Armed with his hook, he stood on guard, but upwind of the vehicle.

Doc Nash backed up one more step before he pulled himself together. Exuding professional competence, he stepped to the open door and looked intently at the corpse. "I'd say that he died right there." He made little snapping sounds with the wrists of his gloves. Judging by the expression on his face, curiosity had taken over and he carefully examined the body. He paused with his gloved hands resting on the corpse's torso. "This body is warm. I mean really warm, you know, like he's been baked." With the flair of Harry Houdini, he produced a thermometer. When he withdrew it, he squinted at the number and frowned. He turned to look up at Tony. "Was the car sitting in sunlight?"

"Nope." Tony shook his head. "Darkness followed by a cool mist. The sun just became a factor a few minutes ago." Peering over the doctor's shoulder, he couldn't read the thermometer. "I thought the car exterior seemed hot when we first got here but then it seemed to cool down."

"Not much, I'd wager. It looks like it is still over a hundred degrees in there and that is after Stan's pursuit of our legless companions." The doctor shifted the body a little bit and suddenly jumped backwards, clutching his chest.

41

"Damn it all to hell! I'm not interested in being coroner any more." A wisp of snakeskin-patterned silk lay at his feet. "I thought that was real."

Stan's shoulders fell. An aura of disappointment surrounded him as he wandered around the car.

Tony snagged it and bagged it before it had a chance to get muddy. "Not exactly my style handkerchief." He made his notes on the evidence envelope and glanced up to see Theo staring at his hands. Her face had lost all color.

"I saw him last night," Theo said. She sounded like she'd swallowed a bug. "The man with the handkerchief. He was with Quentin up on the hill."

"What time was that?" Doc Nash turned to face her.

"It just turned six." Theo shivered and looked around. "I ran into them as I headed down."

"Was this car here?" said Tony.

"No." Theo's eyes searched the parking lot. "There were no cars at all back here, just a fat raccoon."

Tony moved to stand behind her, one arm wrapped around her waist, keeping her close. Her shivers increased.

He balanced his notebook on her shoulder and stared into the doctor's eyes. "Is there any way that the heat killed him?"

"Not directly." The doctor returned to his examination.

Tony released Theo. "Go back to your shop, sweetheart. The gossip ought to flow like rain for the rest of the day. See what you can learn."

Doc Nash waited until Theo was up on the path, out of earshot.

"Okay, Sheriff, I can tell you that the heat is sure going to screw up my calculations for time of death. There's no question that a snake bit him, but until we get him out of here, I won't be able to tell you much more than that." His bright brown eyes speared Tony. "And just how are we going to do that?"

42

"We have lots of photographs. Do you want us to leave him attached to the steering wheel?"

"Not if we don't have to."

With his forearm braced on the roof of the car, Tony studied the handcuffs. They were definitely not toys. In fact, one of the two pairs that he always had attached to his belt was the same brand and style. They were not only the stronger pair, but because the edge of the bracelet was sharper than that on other handcuffs, he used them on the more violent arrests, usually those that involved drug users. In his mind they were the "bad boy" handcuffs. He handed the doctor a small key. "See if this one will open them."

Careful not to touch the surface of the handcuff and disturb any fingerprints, Doc Nash complied. The key worked and the blood-encrusted handcuff dropped open releasing the victim. Doc turned to look at Tony, one eyebrow lifted, "How did you know?"

Tony produced the matching handcuffs. "I have a pair just like them."

The doctor jerked around, hitting his head on the doorframe. "Mmf." He massaged his bruised scalp. "Is this man a cop or did a cop do this to him?"

Tony considered the question. "He isn't one of mine, but until we can get to his wallet and find out who he is, we won't know." His focus shifted to his own handcuffs and he idly twirled them around. "You don't have to be a cop to have a pair of these, you know. Even your wife could have ordered them on the Internet. We might be able to trace them through the serial number." Tony beckoned to the waiting ambulance driver. The man might be half-asleep now, but he was about to get a rude awakening. "Let's get him out of there."

Stan stepped forward, blocking Tony's way. "Say, Sheriff, what do you want me to do with those boxes of snakes?" He

43

picked something out of his ear with his little finger and examined it. "Are they, like, evidence or anything?"

"Yeah." Tony glared at the boxes, but they were silent. "I am not taking them to the station. That's for sure. Can you take them home with you or to wherever and care for them? The county will pay."

Stan nodded.

"Do you know if they are valuable?" said Tony.

"You mean like money or environmentally or what?" His tone and expression said it all. Stan was tired of dealing with people who didn't share his enthusiasm for the reptiles.

"I mean like money. Would someone want to steal them to make a quick profit?" Fists on hips, Tony stared at Stan. Santa or not, his attitude irritated him.

"No." Stan lit a cigarette. "You know, though, the timber rattlesnake is protected. I don't know where he got his snakes, but they are not all local." He pointed to one of the crates. "That snake comes from the western desert around California. It is really bad news. It is short tempered and extremely toxic."

"He probably ordered them on the Internet." Tony turned to Wade. "Did you find any usable prints on those boxes?"

"I tried, but there were only smudges on the latches and tops." He looked at Stan. "If you empty them and give them back to me I'll be able to dust the whole thing."

"I'll wear gloves. I promise." Stan continued to study the boxes, an odd expression on his face. "Those boxes are strange, though." Without waiting, he trotted closer and looked them over carefully.

"How so?" Tony couldn't see what the man found disturbing, but then, he didn't think that he had ever seen snake boxes before. To his eyes they were rectangular wooden boxes constructed of narrow slats and held together with metal brackets and finished with a hinged lid. "How are they special?"

Clearly bewildered, Stan shook his head as he lifted two of the boxes and headed toward his truck. "I can't quite put my finger on it but if it's important, I'll call you."

"Okay, Doc, explain it to me. If the only apparent holes in the guy came from a pair of fangs, or several pair, where did all of that blood come from?" Tony and Doc Nash stood upwind of the car, watching the paramedics puking in the weeds. Tony wondered idly if he should have the fire department come out and hose down the area. "It looks like something exploded in there."

The doctor nodded. "If I'm right, something did." He looked from the sheriff back to the car. "It's an extreme reaction but if he was bitten, say at the base of his thumb, the venom could travel quickly through his system causing blood blisters which could burst. Different snakes produce venoms that create different types of reactions." He pointed out the deep injuries to the dead guy's wrists. "Off the record, I am guessing that one of those snakebites created some intense swelling, and I would guess that he struggled like crazy to get out of those handcuffs. He probably didn't even notice that his wrists were bleeding. Mix that with the excessive heat, which might have caused the violent vomiting, and you have our fragrant little scene."

"So if he had been wearing long sleeves, especially a coat, there wouldn't be so much of a mess?"

"Exactly. It's a hellish way to die." Doc Nash crossed his arms over his chest and watched with sympathy as the ambulance crew maneuvered the body into a body bag and then onto the gurney. "Speaking of hell, why do you suppose it was so hot in there?"

"I'm guessing that he had the heat cranked up in the car for a long time, but who knows if that is what he intended." Tony rolled his shoulders, making them pop and snap to release some of the tension. The specter of those license plates haunted him already. He sincerely hoped that he wouldn't have to talk directly to Queen Doreen. A conversation with her would triple his heartburn. "I'm going to have the car checked out, and the heating system is just one part of it." They both leaned over the body. Doc Nash stared at the man's wretched condition even as Tony removed the wallet and flipped it open.

A clear plastic window framed a Tennessee driver's license belonging to John Mize. The address on it was in nearby Maryville, but a piece of masking tape attached to the back bore a Silersville address, that is, if "Care of Quentin Mize" could be called an address. There were no credit cards, but Tony counted two thousand dollars in hundreds and another eighty in small bills.

"I'd say that this guy is definitely not a cop." Tony dropped the wallet into an evidence bag. As they went through pockets, he added only a handkerchief wrapped around a comb. For the moment, he left the keys in the ignition, and stepped away.

"He's all yours, Doc." Tony's eyes lifted and he saw the expression on Wade's face. Witnessing an autopsy would provoke another bout of upchucking. He decided to let his deputy off the hook. "Let me know when you are ready to do the autopsy and I'll come down."

"You don't want to send Wade?" The doctor snickered as he zipped the bag closed. "It always adds a little something extra when he faints."

"He's got plenty to do here with the car and in the meantime, I'm going to find Quentin and break the news to the next of kin. Maybe he can shed some light on what happened to this guy."

CHAPTER FOUR

Tony knew Quentin Mize. Not only had he been born and raised in the area, the man was more than slightly familiar with the Park County jail facility. He claimed that it had superior food and what he referred to as "the amenables." Tony wasn't sure that he wanted to know what those might be, but he assumed it had something to do with the fact that they gave him aspirin for his inevitable headache. Quentin was usually intoxicated when he arrived, and by the next afternoon would be holding his head in both hands and howling like a coyote.

They supplied him with aspirin in self-defense.

No street address followed Quentin's name on the makeshift address label, but Tony knew where his home was. He lived so far up the mountain and in the backwoods that it didn't have mail delivery. Actually, Quentin had no mailbox, and no mailbox meant no home delivery.

To get there, Tony drove east out of town, up and down several narrow, winding roads, through a tiny settlement of homes and then onto a dirt road consisting of a pair of ruts running between the trees.

Tony flinched when the Blazer met encroaching branches. When the dirt turned to mud, he had to slip the vehicle into four-wheel drive. The mud was as slick as ice. Up here on the mountain, snow still lay on the ground in the shady spots. There might even be some ice mixed in with the mud.

Accompanying him was Deputy Sheila Teffeteller, Park

47

County's solitary female deputy. They did not usually work closely together, but he had left Wade fingerprinting the interior of the car. An attractive woman, only twenty-five, with thick blond hair neatly braided up on the back of her head, Sheila was the most efficient of his deputies. Her paperwork was a pleasure to read. Tony knew that she had grown up in an impoverished area much like the one they were driving through, and it had not stopped her from achieving her goals. "What do you know about Quentin?"

"You mean besides the fact that he is a dedicated drinker and drug user?" Sheila's eyebrows lifted and she smiled. She looked as radiant as a bride. "I know that he would rather be naked in that car with all those snakes than be anywhere with me. I beat the snot out of him when I was thirteen. The advantage to growing up with so many brothers was that I knew just where to kick him and I did. Hard. Several times." At that memory, she giggled.

Tony didn't say anything but he smiled at the merry sound.

"My brother Vernon even took a few swings at him after I had him down in the dirt." She reined in the merriment, but her eyes still twinkled. "Not long ago I picked him up for public intoxication. The poor man climbed into the back seat and begged me to let him put the handcuffs on himself."

As she finished her story, they came around the last curve and stopped in front of Quentin's home.

It had started out as a white mobile home with charcoal gray shutters and trim. That had been many years ago, and the ensuing years had not been kind. It still surprised Tony that someone had ever managed to tow it up that miserable road without breaking it in half along the way. He could only believe that the road had been better in those days.

Some years later, the Mizes made a series of "improvements" to the original structure. They painted everything that had been gray a hot pink. Everything that had been white was painted khaki green. When they added a wooden porch, they painted it hunter orange. A few years later, they "found" enough corrugated metal to cover the porch. It had rusted nicely, achieving a wholesome shade of burnt sienna. The whole thing snuggled under a canopy of dead trees and kudzu like a slug under a bucket.

A slight distance behind the trailer stood another structure created with more corrugated metal. Tony guessed it would be called a shed, but that word implied more strength and design that it deserved. Kudzu was about to swallow it whole. Off to one side was an outhouse. Against common practice, someone built it uphill of the house and then painted it hunter orange to match the porch.

A brand new black Ford pickup with a locking cover over the bed stood in the center of the clearing. Someone had professionally decorated the front with flames. Someone, presumably Quentin, kept the four-wheel drive vehicle polished to a gleaming brightness. No dust had been allowed to settle on the surface. It was obviously a thing well loved and well cared for. Only some mud in the wheel wells kept it from being spotless.

The same could not be said for the yard. If grass had ever grown there, it had been killed off. Refuse of all kinds littered the open area. Most easily identified were the various brands of beer cans. Quentin did not appear to have a clear favorite. Piles of empty Sudafed containers were everywhere. Interspersed with them were pizza boxes, potato chip bags, empty food cans and what looked like the front half of a motorcycle. It had no handlebars. A vicious looking speckled rooster with a bald patch on his back proclaimed that a hideous orange and black three-legged armchair belonged to him.

Tony and Sheila cautiously climbed the four steps to the porch. Each board sagged under their weight, threatening eminent collapse. From inside came the sounds of dogs barking. Tony and Sheila paused, then knocked. The dogs began howling.

Next to the front door, five water-filled one-gallon plastic milk bottles hung from a frayed yellow nylon rope. Tony guessed that the water from his well was not fit to drink and that this made up Quentin's supply of fresh water. He probably filled his bottles at the gas station in town.

Quentin and a pair of spotted hounds answered their knock. He didn't invite them inside but slipped out onto the porch. That suited Tony. When Quentin joined them outside, the quality of the air plummeted and if the aroma coming through the screen was any indication, Quentin's housekeeping was like his gardening. It didn't smell like wholesome sweat or even garbage, but had a more chemical aroma. Peering through the dirty screen, Tony could see someone moving in the house, obviously female by shape, but Tony didn't recognize her. He presumed that the aromas from Quentin or the air in the house did not offend her.

Squinting his eyes seemed to help Quentin focus. He started to smile until he recognized Sheila and then he quickly jumped over the porch rail and stood in the yard.

"I'll welcome your visit, Sheriff, but if you don't mind . . ." He indicated Sheila with a tip of his head. "I've got nothin' to say to her."

Tall and bone thin, he appeared incapable of remaining still. Standing in front of them, he practically vibrated. Years of chemical abuse had given him a series of tics and twitches. Although in his early thirties, acne covered his sallow skin, and he seemed to be losing his teeth. Tony considered it a toss up whether Quentin looked worse than he smelled or smelled worse than he looked.

Tony followed him into the yard.

"That woman is plumb crazy." Quentin watched Sheila like she might pounce on him at any time.

Tony knew that the man had some experience with "crazy," but it did not mean that he could recognize it in others and so he did his best to ignore Quentin's raving. "I may have some bad news for you."

At that, Quentin jerked to face Tony and teetered on a moldy pizza box, almost losing his balance. "News?" Quentin appeared to be having trouble processing the word. "What do you mean?"

Tony saw no way around the blunt approach. "Have you got a relative by the name of John Mize?"

"Sure do." His smile exposed all of his remaining teeth and gums, Stained brown, they were embedded with smokeless tobacco. "Got me a cousin John." For some reason he found that vastly entertaining and started to laugh, spraying brown droplets from his mouth. "He's been stayin' with me, but he ain't here right now. What do you want with him?"

Realizing that he was barely out of spit range, Tony took another step backwards. "What does he drive?"

"He's got one of those itty bitty station wagons, you know what I mean?" His gesture indicated something the size of a shoebox. "I think it's kind of a sissy lookin' thing but he says it's better for the snakes than a truck."

"Snakes?" Sheila managed to look horrified. She even managed to put a bit of a squeal in her voice. "He has snakes? What kind of snakes?"

Quentin crossed his arms over his chest and leaned back as if the venomous creatures didn't faze him, but he couldn't disguise the hint of fear in his eyes or the quaver in his voice. "Rattlers mostly. He uses them in his church services. That man sure does love his snakes and they love him." Quentin slapped at some invisible insects.

"Maybe not." Tony mumbled to himself as he remembered

the sight in the car, "Are you saying that he's a preacher? A snake handler?" Tony had heard only vague rumors that a small group had started up church meetings in the area. It had been a long time since the last congregation of snake handlers had been in Park County. For the most part, the county citizens were conservative and considered the snake handlers to be a little too far off the beaten track.

"Yep, he's the preacher all right." Quentin looked surprised that his family had produced one.

"He didn't grow up around here," Sheila said with total assurance. "How close a cousin is he?"

"Dunno. He's kin to my mama or something like that." Quentin shot a quick glance in Sheila's direction but was careful to keep his eyes away from her chest. Cautious, he moved back another foot, putting him well out of range of her feet. "He come here from Atlanta and asked for a place to stay and I give it to him." He scratched his neck and left little trails of skin showing through the ground-in dirt. "That's what family does. What's it to you?"

"When did you see him last?" Tony wasn't sure that Quentin knew the current year and month.

"Yesterday evenin'. He was loading the snakes in his car, getting ready for his church time." Quentin pointed to the porch. "I was sittin' right there when he left."

"What time was that?"

"Dunno."

"When does he usually get back?"

"All hours." Quentin licked his dry lips. "He didn't come home last night, but that happens a lot."

"Why's that?" said Sheila.

"Sometimes that little car can't make it up here and sometimes, although he don't name any names, I think he gets a better offer." Quentin smirked and punched Tony's shoulder.

"If you know what I mean."

Tony stared into Quentin's red-rimmed eyes and couldn't help but wonder if everything that Quentin saw was tinted that shade. "Did he call?"

Quentin shook his head.

"Any idea about who the better offer might be?" At Quentin's second shake of his head, Tony inhaled slowly and released the breath. "There's no easy way to say this but I think he's dead. The body is with the coroner now but we have his wallet and he was found in a little station wagon. You may have to come in and identify him."

"Don't say?" Quentin lifted his eyebrows but he didn't actually look interested. Years of alcohol and drugs had aged his body and destroyed a lot of brain cells, and he hadn't started with a full set. "Run off the road?"

"No. Definitely, not that." Since Tony didn't have a good idea what had happened to the man, he was not going to speculate about it with the cousin. "Where's he been doing his preaching?"

"Huh?" Quentin blinked several times while he processed the question. "Oh, yeah, you know that old motel out on the highway, just past the road towards Townsend? Well, they've been using the office building."

"Is he married?" Sheila asked. "Or is there someone else who can identify him?"

"Naw, John ain't never married. I can do it just fine." He scratched again, dislodging more grime. A jaw-cracking yawn released a puff of putrid air. "Want me to come along now?"

"No, not now. If you have a phone, we can call you and let you know when." Tony doubted that Doc Nash had the body cleaned up enough to make any kind of identification possible and he would just as soon not share the Blazer with Quentin if it wasn't necessary.

"You bet. I'm in the book and everything." Quentin stayed in the yard and waved to them as they drove away. A wide smile illuminated his homely face.

Using the mirror on her door, Sheila watched Quentin until they made the first turn. "I wouldn't say that Quentin is exactly broken up by the possibility that his cousin is dead, would you?" She didn't pause but continued musing. "I wouldn't even say that he seemed all that surprised, either."

Tony nodded without taking his eyes from the treacherous road. "Not only was he *not* all torn up by the possibility, but I've never known anyone to be that eager to identify a body. It's not something that I would expect him to enjoy."

"Maybe he doesn't like his cousin." Sheila turned to look out the back window. "Do you suppose that the snake handling cousin does the same drugs that Quentin used today? If so, he might not have realized that he had been bitten."

A shrug of his shoulders was Tony's initial answer, but he frowned. "Whatever Quentin is taking now is powerful stuff. If he keeps on, it is going to kill him."

Back on the county road, he returned to two-wheel drive and looked at the houses in the little settlement. Everything looked normal, but if something turned up in the autopsy, he would have all the residents interviewed. "Most of those preachers are so fundamental that they won't even touch anything that isn't in the Bible."

"I guess that rules out a lot of vices." Sheila pointed to a narrow drive. "There's a shortcut." After they made the turn, she looked at Tony. "What bothers me is that the last I heard, the stealing of license plates is not encouraged in the Bible either."

CHAPTER FIVE

Theo watched the influx of the curious into her quilt shop. Even the air seemed to buzz, sending Theo into hiding in her studio. After the excitement in the parking lot at Ruby's, a wave of gossip seekers descended on the shop. She hoped that they were buying fabric and not just talking down there.

The shop's main room was large enough to accommodate several thousand bolts of fabric plus a couple of large cutting stations. The back room served as classroom, meeting room and what Tony referred to as "gossip central." Built to Theo's specifications, the spacious room had fantastic lighting, skylights and fixtures, plus a kitchenette. The electrician she hired to install the myriad outlets on several circuits maintained that NASA didn't need that much electricity to track a rocket.

At one end of the room, chairs surrounded a quilt on a full-sized frame. Anyone who wanted to work on the current quilt for charity was welcome. Theo supplied free coffee and most of the regulars had their own mugs. Luckily, Jane purchased a large supply after the previous day's drought. They would use a lot today.

At all hours, a small cluster of women and the occasional man stitched on it. As far as gossip, well, one woman summed it up with, "we have to talk about something."

Theo's studio filled the large upstairs room. Visitors were not welcome. A large sign posted on her door made sure that no one was in doubt of that fact.

Jane Abernathy, Tony's mother, ran the retail end of the shop. With a couple of part-time employees, she cut fabric orders and chatted with customers. Theo helped out when needed, but she usually let Jane handle the counter while she designed patterns in her studio.

Today seemed no different, except the telephone would not stop ringing. For some perverse reason, many of the county's citizens seemed to believe that Theo would have additional information and be prepared to share it. Every two minutes, Jane's voice would come through the intercom telling her that someone wanted to talk. Desperate, Theo told Jane to leave her alone and turned off the intercom. She loaded a stack of CDs into the player and turned up the volume.

"Do they think I share a brain with my husband?" Theo complained, talking to herself again. Sometimes the habit concerned her, but most of the time she believed it helped her think. With a laugh, she shoved a pile of fabric off her worktable and into a laundry basket.

To her amusement, Zoe, a kitten recently adopted as the official office pet, chased an empty thread spool to the basket and then abandoned her game in favor of the pile of fabric.

"Theo?" Jane pounded on the studio door. "Can I come in? Please?"

"Are you alone?" Frustrated by her inability to get any work done, Theo was past caring about hurt feelings. She had a deadline with her publisher. Three quilts scheduled to be in the book hadn't been started. At this stage of the process, she wondered why she had ever wanted to design quilts. Maybe it wasn't too late to learn how to type. She could work at some nice "normal" job. Surrendering, she lowered the volume on the music and called out, "You can come in if you are alone."

"I hate to bother you." Jane opened the door just wide enough for her to squeeze into the room. "I know that you are running behind schedule, but the members of the bowling group want to know if tonight's meeting is on as usual?"

"Why wouldn't it be?" Distracted, Theo stared at her mother-in-law. She had not seen Jane today except to wave across the room to her. From this distance, Jane's hair seemed to be turning more blond than gray and her eyes were sparkling with mischief. It even looked like she had applied mascara and a touch of makeup. She opened her mouth to ask about it when Jane's statement cut her off.

"I won't be there tonight." She fluffed her hair with her fingers. "I have a date."

That statement caught Theo's full attention. "A date?" Theo didn't think that in the years since her husband had died Jane had come closer to dating than sitting next to a single man at a carry-in supper at the church. She had been a widow for over ten years, in fact, just few months longer than Tony and Theo had been married. Growing up in the same small town, they had known each other, but it wasn't until Tony came home for his father's funeral that they had started dating. Only a few months later, they had married and she had joined him in Chicago. Theo raised her thumbs, showing her approval. "It's about time. Who's the lucky guy? Does Tony know?"

A tinge of pink colored Jane's cheeks. "Not that it is any of your business, or his, but Thomas Smith and I are driving over to Knoxville to see a play at the Clarence Brown Theatre, you know, at the University. We've been planning it for a couple of weeks." Jane grinned.

"Since when could you keep a secret for a couple of weeks?" Theo thought that maybe it wasn't just the hair color that was making her mother-in-law look younger. Jane's choice for a date surprised her, though. Thomas Smith was the morning cook at Ruby's and everyone but Jane called him Red. A nice man in his late sixties, he and his wife had moved to Tennessee from

Georgia the previous year. Theo had known the couple for several years starting when Red's wife Raeleene had taken Theo's beginning quilting class on one of their annual visits. The couple had moved permanently right after he retired. Soon after their move his wife became ill and had succumbed to cancer only a couple of months later.

"It hasn't been that long since poor Raeleene died," said Theo.

"We are just friends and we both wanted to see the play." Jane patted her hair into place even as her blush deepened. "At least that's all it is, for now."

"Am I allowed to talk about this or is it a secret?" Theo was accustomed to keeping information to herself. While it was a challenge in Silersville, she was experienced. As the wife of the sheriff, she sometimes heard things that had to stay private.

"You can tell Tony, but I'd rather you not tell the group." Jane lifted her eyebrows as if to remind Theo of her original reason for visiting.

"Say yes, of course, to the bowlers." Theo snatched a rectangle of fabric away from the kitten. The kitten retaliated by meowing and going after the spool again. Both women grinned at its antics. "You know that they are going to want to know why you aren't there. You never miss a meeting and there are few secrets that last around that group." They had named their group of quilting friends the Bowlers to appease the husband of one of the older members.

"I know, I know." Jane gave her daughter-in-law a hug. "Just tell them that I went to the play. They don't need to know that I have an escort."

"Deal. I'll do the best I can." Theo pushed the older woman to the door. "Go. Work. Have fun. Stay away from me." Theo latched the door firmly behind her. "Let's get back to work, Zoe." Grabbing her rotary cutter and a length of crimson batik fabric, she started to work.

Zoe blinked a couple of times, her golden eyes flashing like caution lights, then turned and bounced onto the window seat and settled down for a bath and nap.

It didn't take Tony and Sheila very long to reach the location of John Mize's temporary church. The motel office sat on a dead end road just off the highway. Over the decade or so since the motel had stopped operating, it had been used for many things. At one time the twenty units, which were built like tiny cabins, had been offered as individual low cost housing. Poorly insulated and poorly constructed, they were only comfortable in the summer. No one stayed past the first frost.

Looking more like a bunker than a church, the office building was a flat-roofed cinderblock rectangle squatting under some old, large tulip trees. If an architect had been involved in the project, it was one with zero imagination. At one time the cinder blocks had been painted white. Now the paint was peeling but the basic structure remained sound. The trim was painted robin's-egg blue, complete with speckles.

A sign propped in the front window announced the building's new use. Written in crude block letters on a sheet of neon yellow poster board was an invitation. "Join our Church of Divine Revelation. Mon thru Fri 6:30 p.m., Sun 9:30 a.m. All Welcome." There was no phone contact.

The windows gleamed. Using his hands to shield the glare, Tony could see through the spotless glass and into the room. Devoid of all furnishings but a double semi-circle of metal folding chairs, it looked absolutely uninviting but spotlessly clean. Even the battleship-gray linoleum floor had the shine of fresh wax.

Sheila walked around the building, checking the doors and windows. She reported to Tony that they were tightly locked and the area around the building had been cleared of trash. The bare dirt showed signs of being recently raked. "Who owns this place?"

Her question echoed his thoughts. "I'm not sure, but it won't take Ruth Ann more than thirty seconds to find out." He grinned at his deputy. "That is, of course, if her nail polish is dry. If she still has to apply a top coat, it might take her five minutes."

Sheila's exuberant laughter proved to Tony that she, like everyone in Park County law enforcement, knew that Tony's incredibly bright and efficient secretary virtually ran the sheriff's office. She had when Harvey Winston had been sheriff and it didn't change when Tony was elected.

Since Tony was basically lazy, it worked out well for both of them. Ruth Ann was anything but lazy. She worked full time for his office and studied law in the evening. Theo told him she thought Ruth Ann stayed so busy because of her mother-in-law. After an accident at work rendered Ruth Ann's husband Walter partially disabled, the older woman had come to help and stayed on.

The two women barely tolerated each other.

Everyone at the station also knew that Ruth Ann allowed nothing to interfere with her manicures. One drawer of her desk was dedicated to her fingernails. She owned innumerable bottles of polish in every imaginable shade, and a few that Tony thought should not have been imagined much less bottled.

"It's lunch time," said Tony. "Let's go back and see if Wade has had any luck with his project. I can't say I envy him spending more time with that car."

Sheila turned to follow him.

Tony thought that he saw movement in one of the windows and paused, looking back at the units.. It might have just been his imagination, or not. "Wait. Let's see if any of the cabins show signs of being lived in. Maybe this is where Mize stays when he doesn't go back up the mountain."

They started with the unit nearest to the road. Nothing. No door. One glance inside showed that even the bathroom fixtures were gone. The next two looked about the same. In the fourth one they found signs of occupation. A family of raccoons had taken it over. When the door opened, their little black masked faces turned to check out the intruders, but they did not appear frightened.

Only the next to the last cabin showed signs of recent human habitation. It was still in fairly good physical condition. The door worked and the windows were intact. With the exception of a plastic grocery bag half-full of empty sardine tins, the floor was surprisingly free of debris. Three unopened sardine cans balanced on the narrow windowsill. Wadded into one corner of the room was an old down sleeping bag, leaking feathers. It looked like a pair of chickens had been fighting in that corner. The air in the room made their eyes water. The vile aroma suggested that some little creature, probably a skunk from the smell of it, must have died somewhere in the building and started to decay. That aroma, mixed with the sardine scents rising from the bag, rendered the air in the space intolerable.

Wordlessly, Tony and Sheila quickly backed out of the cabin.

Tony wiped his eyes on the sleeve of his jacket. "Has it occurred to you, Sheila, that we have made our way from stench to stench this morning? Have you had enough yet?" He could see that against the pallor of her face, her freckles seemed darker than usual.

Sheila grinned at him, even as she wiped her own watery eyes. "I can take it if you can, Sheriff." She breathed deeply through her mouth and the muscles of her throat moved under her creamy skin. "I'm one stench behind you because I didn't get to smell the car this morning, you know." She managed a chuckle. "If you think that we need more, we could always go out to the dump and chat with Marmot-the-Varmint, you know, just for fun. I'll bet something out there stinks."

"Yeah, it's usually Claude Marmot." The corners of Tony's lips turned up. "Sounds like more fun than I can handle today. Let's go see what Wade has accomplished, maybe compare aromas, but first I think I'll snag an empty tin. I'm curious if there are fingerprints on it besides those of our furry friends. Maybe we can match them to our dead guy."

"Do we need a warrant?"

"To pick trash off the ground? I sure hope not." Reaching into the room, Tony used his pen to lift an empty tin that had fallen from the sack onto the floor. He slipped it into a small plastic evidence bag that he dragged from his pocket.

Tony managed to hang his jacket on the hook before Ruth Ann dropped the bomb. The gentle smile on Ruth Ann's coffee-colored face would normally have warned him. Any display of merriment on her part usually signaled a problem on his, and he knew that all too well. The compassionate expression in her deep brown eyes lulled him into a false sense of security. Without invitation, she settled onto one of the industrial strength chairs that faced his desk and sat blowing gently on her raspberry colored nails. Her smile widened.

Too late, warning bells clanged in his head. Ruth Ann was being way too pleasant. "What's wrong?" Tony settled onto his chair and gripped the edge of his desk with both hands. He knew that he was about to be shelled. He didn't know whether to duck or to run.

"I happen to know who owns that old motel. I don't even have to look it up." Ruth Ann paused while she checked her nails.

As a dramatic pause, it was powerful and effective. Tony

sucked in a deep breath and held it.

She did look at him then, but the hint of tears glistening in her eyes alarmed him even more. Her expression could only be called sympathetic. "It belongs to Martha Simms."

"Martha Simms, as in my Aunt Martha?" Tony groaned and reached for an antacid tablet.

Ruth Ann coughed, giving him a discreet warning before she continued the bombardment. "Actually, it is owned jointly by Martha Simms and Jane Abernathy."

Tony's hand stopped without touching the jar. "My aunt and my mother?" Tony searched Ruth Ann's face to see if by chance she was making it up. She wasn't. "When did they buy it?"

"They filed the deed maybe a month ago. I'm sure that it couldn't have been much longer than that because the sale hasn't shown up in the newspaper yet. I've been watching for it." Ruth Ann sat up straighter. "I do know that they are forming some kind of partnership. They asked me to read through the contract, but since I haven't finished law school yet, much less passed the bar exam, I told them to check with a real lawyer. I suggested that they call Carl Lee Cashdollar."

"If I give you my gun, will you promise to shoot me with it? Please?" His head spun. "How did that pair of women decide to buy that old motel, not to mention why? Are they nuts? Neither one of them has any business experience. They could lose everything they own and end up without a pot to . . . to . . ." He couldn't finish that thought.

Flinging himself out of his chair, he began pacing but the size of the room didn't allow a man his size to go very far. He came to an abrupt stop in front of his secretary. Ruth Ann didn't flinch but sat calmly, watching him. "Do you have any idea why they decided to buy that dilapidated piece of weed and skunk infested property or how they ended up having a makeshift congregation of snake handlers meeting in the office?"

Shaking her head, Ruth Ann's eyes widened. "All they told me was that they had big plans for it and asked me to keep it quiet. They said that they wanted it to be a surprise when it was ready but I don't know any more than that." Her shoulders moved in an eloquent shrug. "It is a matter of public record, so I guess the cat's out of the bag now."

"I'd say so." He heaved a great sigh. "I'd better go have a chat with them."

With those brave words, he plopped down behind his desk and picked up a folder. He couldn't focus on its contents, though; his brain spun. No way would he go over to the high school and pull his aunt out of her English class to ask her about this. The prospect of tackling the subject with his mother sounded like a good reason to consider moving.

Maybe he could find a job herding sheep in Montana or Wyoming. He could call it research for the novel he worked on in his spare time.

"Any word yet on what killed the snake guy?" Ruth Ann rose to her feet and headed toward the door then paused, turning to face him. Genuine sympathy radiated from her. "I heard about the inside of the car. It sounded like a mess."

"That's an understatement. I'm still waiting to hear from Doc Nash and Wade." He shot her a pained glance. "That is, unless they find my mother's fingerprints on the handcuffs. If that happens, I think I'll join the French Foreign Legion."

"Do they still exist?"

"I don't know. Maybe when you finish painting your nails you could find that out for me. You know, just in case I need to leave town in a hurry." Tony could have sworn that he heard her laughing as she left the room. He spoke to the open doorway. "It's hard to get good help."

CHAPTER SIX

Moments after Ruth Ann departed, Wade arrived.

Strolling into Tony's office, he said, "Doc had to leave and deliver a baby. He told me to go away and that he would call when he is ready to get back to dealing with the dead." He carried with him a notebook and a two-liter bottle of ginger ale.

As he watched his deputy lower himself into the chair Ruth Ann had recently vacated, Tony thought that Wade's complexion had not quite returned to normal.

"Why don't you just sit there for a moment and get rehydrated. I'll get Sheila and Mike to come here for a confab."

With a grateful smile and a nod, Wade broke the seal on the large bottle and lifted it to his lips.

Within minutes, Sheila and Mike joined them. Mike dragged a chair in from the hall and Tony sat on the edge of his desk. Sheila sat in the chair next to Wade. Except for Darren, this little group was Park County's day shift. The night shift was smaller.

Tony looked at Wade. "Tell us about the car. Did you find any usable fingerprints?"

"Not on the outside, I didn't, at least not good ones. I only found some partials on the driver's side door handle and a fairly good smudge on the roof. All that rain sure didn't help any." He finished the first third of the two-liter bottle. "I'm guessing the owner of the smudges had oil or grease on his fingers or there wouldn't be that much left."

Barbara Graham

Tony moved behind his desk and made a note in the file. "What about on the inside?"

Wade shuddered and took another swig. "The handcuffs were totally clean. I mean I couldn't even find a hint of a fingerprint." He looked at his notes. "There were lots of clear prints on the dash and the inside surfaces of the doors. We found magazines, pop cans, a Bible, and one of those soft leather briefcases." He looked at Tony. "It was empty, by the way. I haven't had a chance to check those things for fingerprints." Clearing his throat, he looked disillusioned and a tinge of red rose on his face. "I can tell you that for a preacher, he had pretty raunchy taste in reading material. Real rough stuff."

"How about our dead guy?" said Tony. "We're you able to get his prints?" The picture that formed in his mind of a preacher with a stolen license plate and violent pornographic literature made him uneasy. It had to be bad to make the former Marine blush.

"I did my best. The left hand was too swollen and messed up to get any good ones but I got a couple of partials from his right." He paused to take another long drink. "With those, I'll be able to make a match if he's in the system somewhere. I'll send them out as soon as I can. You just never know."

Mike took the floor. "You wanted to know who came by that parking lot this morning. That's easy. Every single resident. I swear that the entire population of Park County was there. No strangers. We did find something odd, though." Apparently thinking about it amused him and he chuckled. "Like nothing else is odd about this case. The key was in the ignition, right?" He waited until everyone nodded. "The key was still turned and the car was in 'park.' The only reason that it was not running when we arrived was that the car ran out of gas. I mean it was bone dry."

When everyone had absorbed that, he continued. "The heater

was set on warmest heat setting and the fan on maximum. That's why Doc is having so much trouble with the time of death and why it felt like an oven in there. No telling how much gas it started with or how long it had been stopped. I'm guessing that it ran for several hours."

"For heaven's sake." Tony couldn't believe his ears. "Were the headlights on or off?"

"Off." Mike answered.

"Fingerprints on the key?"

"No, sir." Wade swallowed more ginger ale and stifled a burp. "I found a few smudges but no real prints."

Tony thought that his color was improving.

Wade continued his report. "It was the only key on the ring with one of those little remotes. There are a couple of smudged and partial prints on the remote. Again, it is going to take a while to see if we have a match."

Ruth Ann knocked on the doorframe before strolling into the office with a couple of papers that she handed to Tony. "I ran the vehicle identification number. You'll love what came back on that VIN."

Tony reached for the paper and scanned it, surprised. It didn't take long to read. He could feel his frown deepening. "Thanks, Ruth Ann." He glanced at the curious faces that watched him. "Ruth Ann ran the VIN on the Focus. It seems that the vehicle is part of an inventory of cars that belonged to a dealer in Atlanta. The cars were impounded or something because of a pending bankruptcy hearing. According to the report, that car should still be locked up in Georgia. They were surprised to learn that it had been stolen."

He looked back up at his secretary. "Will you contact Atlanta and see if they know any thing about John Mize? A man who drives a stolen car probably knows it. Quentin did say that his cousin came here from Atlanta and he must have moved there from Maryville."

She nodded. "Can you believe how many people have moved here from Atlanta? I'd say that most of our new residents come from there. It's almost turned into our population base."

Tony started to nod when he was distracted by Ruth Ann's fingernails. They now sported tiny white polka dots on the raspberry background. "Did you check with the mayor's wife?"

"Oh, yeah." Ruth Ann's tone remained light, but the tension lines carved into her face said a lot about the other woman's attitude. "Queen Doreen told me that she was not aware of the license plate being off her car, and then she went on to say that she leaves all the car stuff to her husband and who was I to be interrupting her bridge game anyway?" Her dark eyes blazed and her lifted chin promised retribution. She stalked back to her desk just as her phone began to ring.

Tony turned and faced his deputies. He didn't try to hide his grin when he noticed that each of their expressions suggested that the mayor's wife had better come to a complete stop at every single stop sign and that her annoying little apricot-colored frou-frou dog had better be on a leash in the park. Ruth Ann might be a pain in the backside, but she was theirs. He cleared his throat and waved the papers.

Ruth Ann reappeared in the doorway almost immediately. She looked directly at Wade. "Doc Nash says that the newest resident of Park County has been born and if you don't want to miss the fun of an autopsy, you should get to the morgue right away." Her eyes twinkled. "He sounded even crankier than usual."

Wade swallowed the last of the ginger ale in a single giant swallow. A deep rumbling belch followed. The sound echoed in the quiet room. A self-deprecating grin blossomed on his face. "I really hate upchucking without something in my stomach to begin with. I'm ready to go."

Tony felt a surge of almost fatherly pride. It was a measure of the respect and friendship that existed within this group that no one made a comment. Everyone knew that Wade was tough enough to eat his cereal with battery acid, but the sight of a dead body was guaranteed to produce his last meal. The morning's combination of a hideously messy body and widespread blood spatters had tempted each of them to join him.

Tony considered asking Wade to stay behind to do his computer work on the fingerprints pulled from the car and snake boxes, but he knew that it would not be what the younger man wanted or needed. Wade wanted to be a detective. A good one. One way or another, he would get through the autopsy, even if he had to hold a bucket the entire time.

Tony rose to his feet. "Okay, let's go. I want to be there too."

He reached for his jacket. "Mike, stay on that car. I'll bet that we can learn something else from it. I'm really curious about how it came to be in our little town when it is supposed to be in Atlanta and why it has that license plate.

"Sheila, find out what Quentin's been up to lately. I doubt that he would know the truth if he sat on it, but make sure you have backup if you go out there. I wouldn't be surprised if he won't be so welcoming on your next visit." He remembered Quentin's attitude and grinned. "I would like to talk to that female in the house with him. She might have all kinds of information."

As autopsies go, Tony thought, it was uneventful. No bullets or knife wounds turned up in the body. The worst part was watching Wade try to obtain a set of fingerprints from the corpse. The fingers simply weren't cooperating.

After a single bout with the bucket, Wade observed the rest with apparent interest. Tony wondered if Wade's system could be getting stronger.

According to Doc Nash, nothing obvious indicated that any cause other than the snakebites was responsible for the death. He seemed to think that because of the severity of the reaction that the man would have died even if he had gone directly to the hospital.

Doc Nash wouldn't be through for a while.

Tony decided to go home. He left Wade there.

CHAPTER SEVEN

Theo couldn't believe her ears. The sounds coming up the stairs and through her door sounded like the mob storming the Bastille. "For heaven's sake, Zoe. Maybe I better go help Jane. I'm afraid they'll be calling for the guillotine."

She hadn't seen this many women in the shop at one time since Super Bowl Sunday. On that day, it had been the promise of great sale prices, door prizes and food that had created the excitement.

"Theo!" Several women shouted her name at the same time. "Do you know who died?"

Theo could only shake her head. Even if she had known, she wouldn't tell anyone until the news was announced. The relatives deserved to know before it hit the gossip lines.

"I know."

All eyes turned to the speaker. Nellie Pearl Prigmore stood near the front door. The old woman was an avid gossip but not a quilter. "I saw that little car speeding past my house all the time. A lot of the time there was another car following it."

"Whose car?" Theo wasn't surprised that she saw speeding vehicles pass her house. After all, she did live next to one of the busiest roads in the county.

"Well, how would you expect me to know? It's not like I keep track of my neighbors." The crotchety old lady cast a venomous glare at a young woman, who let a snort of dissension escape. "It's always going too fast."

"So who's the dead man?"

"Don't know his name but I can tell you that he's a foreigner."

Theo knew that only meant that he hadn't been born in the county. It didn't mean that he came from any place more exotic than the next closest town.

She stepped behind the cutting table. Maybe they would sell enough fabric today to make up for the orders that the computer lost.

The backup wizard had worked late into the previous night. He managed to get the system up and running, but so far hadn't been able to restore all of the files.

Jamie and Chris called to tell her that they would be at a friend's house. That was fine with Theo. They had their own area in the studio, but playing with a friend was better.

After a long afternoon, she closed the shop at the regular time and walked to the house.

Tony dragged his body over the threshold. It had been a long day, and he felt more like he expected to feel at eighty—and he wasn't even forty. He paused in the narrow foyer of their old house. To his left, he could see Daisy, the family golden retriever, sleeping upside down on the living room couch, her front paws folded against her chest. Gravity pulled her lips away from a formidable set of teeth. She snored softly.

Following the sound of voices, he took two steps down a short hallway toward the kitchen. The large room doubled as the family room. A pair of recliners faced the dark red brick wall that held both a raised fireplace hearth and the television. A sturdy rectangular table separated the family area from the cooking area. An old wood-burning stove shared another brick wall with the electric range.

Theo believed that comfort and history should win all decorating decisions. Small quilts hung on the walls, side by side with family photographs.

When he approached the room, he saw that near the television, Theo was trying to separate six-year-old Jamie and almost eight-year-old Chris. From his vantage point, it looked like Jamie might be winning the battle but if Tony read his wife's expression correctly, the little boy was about to lose the war. Rather than get involved in the dispute, Tony backed away and went upstairs.

Their house had the distinction of being the oldest brick house in Park County. It actually belonged to his wife. Theo had inherited it upon the death of her grandfather who had been a direct descendant of Amoes Siler, the town's founding father.

It had undergone frequent remodeling and additions over the last two hundred years or so. One enterprising family member had decided that the large sash window in the master bedroom was big enough to climb through. He constructed a narrow, private veranda just under the window. The base of it rested on the roof of the true veranda. Barely large enough for a pair of chairs and a tiny table, Tony loved it. It was almost as much fun as a tree house. Tonight it felt like an escape, like running away, as he climbed through the window and settled onto a sagging wicker rocking chair. Sighing deeply, he closed his eyes.

On any normal evening, he would lock his gun in the downstairs safe and change clothes as soon as he returned home. Tonight he believed that would take more energy than he possessed. He hadn't decided whether or not to wear his uniform when he left to attend the evening service at the Church of the Divine Revelation. Knowing the way news traveled through Silersville, all of the members of the congregation should already know about Mize's death. There might not even be anyone in attendance tonight at the motel office. Those thoughts brought up the question of what his mother and aunt wanted with the old motel.

Using his cell phone, he dialed his mother's number. Her voice on the machine chirped, telling him to leave a message. He didn't bother, but sat back gazing out at the community that he'd promised to protect.

Relaxing in the soft darkness of evening, he thought that everything in his little town looked so peaceful. In the park across the road, the trees were preparing for spring, coming back to life. Tony could almost smell the changes in the air. Soon the magnolias, redbuds and the remaining ancient oaks would provide welcome shade. A stand of dogwoods grew directly across the street from their house. In only a couple of weeks, the small trees would be covered with clouds of pale pink blossoms. So far these trees had not succumbed to the deadly anthracnose that had started decimating dogwoods several years ago, moving like the plague through the area.

In the cultivated flowerbeds, the tulip bulbs were sprouting. The Park County Garden Club, in a joint project with the Chamber of Commerce, had purchased and planted the bulbs. He knew where they grew even though it was too dark to see the long green leaves and fat buds.

In his head, he could hear the complaints already. The deer loved the tulips as much as the gardeners hated the deer. Every year, one crabby garden enthusiast would come to him and order him to shoot the deer when he saw them in the flower-beds. Ridiculous. Tony always said that they should plant daf-fodils because the deer did not like to eat them.

Although the small creek that ran along the side of the house and then cut diagonally through the park was normally lazy, it increased in size and strength with each day of melting snow in the higher elevations. This winter brought more snow than usual. If spring continued the trend of increased moisture, they would have to keep an eye on the creek and make sure it didn't overflow its banks. A couple of years ago, it had flooded about twenty homes in the lowest area of town.

Theo joined him on the veranda. "Are you okay? You looked a bit pale when you got home." She carried a tray and set it on the small table at his elbow. "I thought you might need a snack to hold you until dinner. I ordered from that new pizza place, and I'm not sure when dinner is going to arrive."

Surprised that she had seen him, he smiled at her. It felt like the first time that he had smiled all day. "Thanks, sweetheart. It's been a long day and it's not over yet. If I had lunch today, I don't remember it, and I have to go back out in a little while." He examined the mini-feast of crackers, cheddar cheese, sliced summer sausage and two mugs of hot cider. Using more force than necessary, he speared a slice of sausage with a toothpick and dipped it in a puddle of mustard before slapping it on a cracker. He popped the whole thing into his mouth and chewed as he reached for the cider.

Theo nodded. "I guessed that. You always lock your gun away as soon as you get home." Picking a slice of cheese from the plate, Theo settled on her chair and nibbled the edge, holding it with both hands like a mouse. She adjusted her glasses with the back of her hand and inspected him. "At least it's a nice evening."

"I'm afraid that it's lost on me tonight." He had another loaded cracker in his mouth when he started to talk, and little crumbs flew out, landing on her pale blue fleece shirt.

Theo glared at him and swiped a hand across the front of her shirt, sending the crumbs to the wood planks at her feet.

"Sorry about that." He finished his cracker. "With the fine mood I'm in, I have been sitting here thinking about diseased dogwoods, flooding creeks and old man Ferguson calling and wanting me to shoot the deer." He heard Theo snort. The inelegant sound was like music to his ears, forcing him to smile.

"If that stubborn old coot wouldn't insist on planting those little lavender tulips every year there would be more flowers and less controversy." Theo warmed to the topic, stabbing the air with her toothpick. "He absolutely refuses to admit that those bulbs are more expensive than the others are even when it is written out in black and white. I think that they must make sweeter flowers, too, because the deer always eat those first and then often leave the less expensive red and yellow ones alone."

Tony sighed and began to relax. He didn't want to ask what the boys had been doing, but he did anyway.

Theo stopped in the process of reaching for another piece of cheese and peered at him over the top of the lenses. "Not much, just the regular stuff." She giggled. "You know that Jamie can't stand it if Chris ignores him and will just pick and pick at him until he gets a reaction."

Tony laughed. That behavior was definitely the regular one. All of the family knew how it worked. Only Jamie didn't realize that Chris ignored him on purpose to stir up trouble. Thinking about the boys, he said, "Are the quilters bowling tonight?"

"Yes." Her curls bounced as she nodded several times for emphasis. "Since you're going out, do I need to get a babysitter or will you be back soon?"

"I shouldn't be very long. If they go to the shop with you, I'll pick them up after I talk with a few people." He could tell that she wanted to ask him for details but his expression kept her silent. "Your little group is always full of information. Maybe you can find out what they know about the Mize family and about the Church of Divine Revelation."

That caught Theo's attention and she lifted her eyebrows, silently inviting him to tell her more.

CHAPTER EIGHT

As he pulled into the parking lot, Tony noticed that the worn, drab, motel office/church took on a welcoming glow after dark. A string of multicolored Christmas lights connected the building to an illuminated rollout sign. On a brilliant yellow background, bold black letters pronounced "Be Saved—Meeting Now." There were about ten or twelve vehicles parked in the lot. Most of them were older model sedans and full-size pickup trucks. A single motorcycle stood next to a small, black, four-wheel-drive truck. Like Quentin's, the truck had flames painted on the sides. Unlike Quentin's, it sported a rack of roof lights that Tony thought rivaled those on his official vehicle. He parked next to it.

After much deliberation, Tony had changed from his chocolate brown and khaki uniform into a pair of jeans, a lightweight gray sweater and a thigh-length black leather coat. With the coat unbuttoned, the shoulder holster with the big Glock didn't make too much of a bulge.

There didn't seem to be any sense in arriving at this little gathering in full uniform. He didn't want to run them off. He needed information and knew that sometimes his badge and uniform shut as many doors as it opened. The congregation might fear legal action because, as far as he knew, there might still be one state that didn't have laws against using snakes in religious meetings. That state was not Tennessee.

For a full minute, he stood outside, watching the little

congregation through the glass. It seemed like business as usual, making him think that either news of the snake preacher's death had not spread, or he was not the only draw. At one side of the room, a pair of musicians arranged three chairs in an open space. Tony recognized both of the men and knew that they were both excellent guitar players. As least he would enjoy the music at this service.

The average age of the members of the congregation looked to be about fifty-five or sixty. The youngest were a pair of little girls. They might have been eight. On the opposite side of the room, an overweight teenaged boy slouched on a folding chair, gripping his elbows. He paid no attention to the activity around him but stared at the floor. No one spoke to him.

The men looked like they had stepped out of a time capsule. Almost like a uniform, they wore polyester pants and short-sleeved dress shirts. Tony thought that he could see enough hair cream holding back the men's hair to lubricate every vehicle in the county. Not having any hair himself, he had not realized that the greasy stuff was still available.

The women looked as if they had stepped from an even older capsule. Most of them had long gray hair that they pulled back into tight buns. On their tired faces, the style did not give them the finely honed appearance of ballerinas but cruelly exposed the lines of time. The vicious pins holding their hair up looked as if they stabbed into the scalps. Their uniform seemed to be dark cotton print dresses that his grandmother would have called "wash dresses." Tony had to wonder what store still carried that style. None of them wore a trace of makeup. Nothing seemed to soften their lives, but they were smiling and chatting with each other.

The notable exception to the dress code was Pinkie Millsaps. She stood in the center of the room, still dressed in her motorcycle leathers, but she had added a long-sleeved white shirt under the leather vest. The shirt covered all of her tattoos but one pink rose on the back of her left hand.

Wondering why she hadn't seemed to recognize the Mize vehicle that morning, Tony was about to go inside when a familiar voice spoke to his left shoulder blade. "Hey there, Sheriff."

Tony's smile widened as he turned and saw the short but thick-waisted man who stood behind him. "Hey there, Pops."

Owan "Pops" Ogle worked as the county clerk. He was also a world-class mandolin player whose musical talents had been showcased on several bluegrass albums. Music was his first love. Being county clerk merely paid the bills. "Are you a member of this congregation?" said Tony.

"Helped start it up." Pops proudly lifted his narrow chest and adjusted the belt around his lumpy midsection before opening the door for both of them.

As he waited for Pops to enter first, it occurred to Tony that Pops wasn't really fat. At a second glance, his chest appeared to have melted like wax and formed a puddle around his belt buckle. For such a small man, he had amazingly long fingers, which seemed to be constantly in motion. The knuckles were swollen and they looked painful but they didn't slow him down when it came to making music.

"I've been to every church and gathering in the area and just about all of them stray too far afield from the Good Book for me."

Once inside, Tony steered the man to the far side of the room, hoping for more privacy. "How did you come to be using this place? I understand that it belongs to my mom and my aunt." He did not mention how he came by the information.

"I'm glad they finally told you about it. I don't generally hold with womenfolk keeping secrets like that, but I guess it is really none of my business." He paused to adjust his belt again. "I have to confess that I forgot all about this building until they came in to file the papers. When our congregation decided to move to a larger place, I called your aunt and she said we could use it for the time being—you know, as long as we pay for the power and water and keep it clean." His lips lifted into a smile, forming deep creases in his cheeks.

"Tell me about John Mize." Pops didn't look like a man who had just lost his pastor, and Tony couldn't decide how to work up to breaking the news of his being dead.

"Lordy, but that man has the gift. Luckily, he is on the side of good, 'cause he could sell water to a drowning man." His eyes searched the room. "He isn't here yet, but I expect him to arrive at any time. He doesn't like to arrive too early 'cause it stresses the snakes." Pops words slowed to a stop and a worried expression replaced his jolly smile. "I guess you are here about the snakes? We knew that it was only a matter of time before that weasel Stan turned us in."

"In a matter of speaking." Tony's voice dropped. This was the opening that he had been hoping for. "This morning, we found the body of John Mize, or at least we are presuming for now that it is him. There were several snakes in the vehicle with him." He didn't volunteer information about the condition of the body or the fact that the snakes were loose.

"No! What happened?" Pops eyes filled with tears. He swayed, and Tony had to grab his elbow and help him to a chair. "He was just fine last night. Was he in some car accident?"

"We are really not quite sure what happened." That was the truth but Tony hedged, avoiding any other questions. "It would help if you could tell me what time it was when you last saw him."

"We finished our meeting about eight thirty. As usual, him and me were the last to leave." Pops sniffled. His eyes left Tony's face and swept over the congregation. Watching them preparing for the meeting that would not take place, his eyes filled with tears. "After the others left last night, he went out and started his car and let it run for a while to warm up. The snakes don't like bein' cold, you know, and they are always real tired after a service. You got to take care of 'em."

Tony nodded but didn't mention that in his mind, one of the best things about cold weather was that snakes didn't like it. "Did you both drive away at the same time? Did he mention if he planned to stop someplace on his way home?"

"No. Well, not that I know of. When I locked up and got in my car, I'd guess it was just about nine. He was already in his car and the headlights were on. I assumed that he pulled out right behind me." Pops more or less collapsed, clutching his head with both hands. He started making a terrible moaning sound.

"I never met the man," said Tony placing a comforting hand on the older man's shoulder. He let Pops gather himself for a moment. "How did the two of you meet and start up this church?" Can you tell me anything about him? You know, like where he came from and if he has relatives other than Quentin." He glanced around the drab room, watching the congregation. "When I talked to Quentin, I didn't learn much. I might have been talking about a stranger. You'd think a cousin would know a bit about the family, wouldn't you?"

Pops sat up straight. If they hadn't been in a place of worship, the older man looked like he would have spat on the floor. "Quentin is a wastrel and always has been. If he has any redeeming characteristics I don't know what they are. Have you ever known him to work a day in his life for an honest wage?"

Tony couldn't say that he had and shook his head. Quentin's income was suspect but largely unproven. It seemed to be a cross between welfare and larceny, but Quentin was not the immediate problem. "So, what can you tell me about your

Barbara Graham

introduction to Mr. Mize?"

"I met him at another church meeting, oh, maybe two or three months ago." Pops fingers began moving as if they were playing an instrument and he swayed to some music only he could hear. "After the service, we was just standing around and talking, several of us, about this and that and John mentioned that he had taken up serpents and asked us if we ever had." His eyes moved as he watched the rest of the congregation. "A couple of us said we hadn't ever been present at a service like that and that we were curious but not sure whether we wanted to try it or not."

"Did he show you his snakes?"

"No." Pops shook his head. "Then he said that he had some snakes at his place and if we found a place where we could have a meeting, he'd enjoy preaching a bit again."

"I gather you tried it and liked it." Tony didn't think his faith would extend to handling poisonous reptiles, but he felt a grudging admiration for those who did. "Weren't you scared?"

"Nossir, I wasn't and that surprised me more than about anything on this earth." He coughed a couple of times and then looked up and grinned. "To be perfectly honest, I don't much care for snakes."

"What else did he tell you about himself?"

"He confessed that he did some time in a prison, but I don't know where it was or what he was in for. Didn't seem to matter. He told me time and again that prison changed his life forever and for the good. Jesus saved him." Pops wiped a tear from his cheek. "I swear, he must have memorized the whole of the Good Book. If you gave him a verse, he could tell you where it came from. I never did see anyone who knew it that well." Pops fell silent, apparently lost in thought. "Now that you bring it up, it seems like he did say that he was Quentin's cousin and that he stayed up there. He gave me a phone number for his

82

portable phone."

"I'd like to have that number, if you don't mind." Tony wondered what had happened to the man's cellular telephone. It hadn't been in the car with him. Obtaining the phone records might help them track down the next of kin. "He didn't grow up around here, did he?"

"Nope. He said his family was not able to be with him just yet, that he came to prepare the way. I have no idea where they might be. I know that they must have supported him financially because our little group barely gathers enough funds to pay our minimal costs." His eyes remained open even as tears overflowed his lower eyelids. "Now that you mention it, though, it seems like he did say that his wife lived in a nursing home. I got the impression that she had some kind of wasting disease but I couldn't tell you more than that." He pulled a handkerchief from his pocket and wiped the tears that were increasing. "How he must have suffered. Away from his family like that." Pops blew his nose. "Now they must suffer too, losing him while he tended to our poor flock."

The idea that John Mize's wife might be gravely ill and had no idea what had happened to her husband disturbed Tony. As much as he hated the idea of having to break the news to her, the idea that he might not be able to locate her seemed worse.

Pops must have had the same idea and began moaning. His eyes met Tony's and he said, "Don't you know that someone there must be worried about him? Will you be able to find his family? Imagine them not knowing." Continuing to wipe his streaming eyes with one hand, he reached into his hip pocket. Extracting a piece of paper from his worn wallet, he handed it to Tony.

Written in Pops's meticulous handwriting was a telephone number. Tony didn't recognize the area code. "We will find them, with or without Quentin's help." Tony promised as he added the number to his notes. "You have been a big help, Pops. I'll let you know what I learn about his family and his death. There is bound to be a funeral somewhere." He glanced around at the small congregation. The members were settling on the folding chairs, glancing back toward the door. Pinkie sat on the front row, facing a folding table. A few of the men were consulting their watches. "Do you want me to tell the others?"

"What?" Pops seemed surprised that there were others present and then shook it off. "Oh my, I almost forgot all about the service." His hands fluttered faster as he rose to his feet, automatically reaching for his beloved mandolin. "I don't know how I'll be able to do this, but I'll do the telling. I guess we'll pray here for a bit this evening but, without John, I expect that we won't be meeting again. Thank your aunt and mother for me."

Tony watched as he moved to the front of the room and thought that Pops looked like he had aged ten years in ten minutes. Something that Pops said puzzled him. It had to do with the wife. Tony didn't remember seeing a wedding ring on the corpse. If Quentin's cousin had a girlfriend in the area, Pops didn't know anything about her. If Tony knew anything about Pops, it was that a philandering preacher would not receive any praise. Maybe Quentin invented a social life for his cousin, but maybe not. Who would know besides the deceased and the woman herself? Where did they meet?

The group of twelve quilters that Theo referred to as her "bowling group" met every other Thursday night in the back room at Theo's shop. By the time they began to arrive, Theo had Chris and Jamie building a fort.

The boys loved to stack bolts of fabric into walls. After the fort reached the desired height, a battle would begin. Theo couldn't decide whether they battled aliens attacking from Mars or reenacted the siege of the Alamo. It didn't matter to her. The boys entertained themselves, didn't break anything, and at the end of the evening helped put the bolts back on the racks.

Sometimes the members of the group worked on projects together, making charity quilts or friendship quilts. Usually though, they brought their own projects and passed the evening, laughing, sometimes crying, and almost always getting a lot of work done. Their lives and their quilts were intertwined with friendship. Opinions about both were never in short supply.

The members, in addition to Theo and Jane, were Tony's Aunt Martha, their next door neighbor, Edith, a couple of younger women who were fairly new to the area, Susan and Amy, and an older woman named Caro. Caro's sister Betty came for socializing, but her arthritis kept her from holding a needle. Ruby and Ruth Ann had only recently taken the beginning quilting class and so were new members. Gretchen Blackburn was in her late thirties like Theo and Nina Crisp, Theo's best friend since childhood.

Nina and Jane were the only absentees this evening. Jane was off on her date with Red and Nina was confined to her couch, nursing a broken foot.

Theo's little group first became known as the bowlers because of Caro. When her husband had entered the early stages of dementia, over a year ago, his personality changed. Instead of supporting her, he began to bitterly protest her leaving him in the evenings to do something that he thought she could do perfectly well at home. One evening she arrived late and in tears and managed to tell them what he'd said. It took an entire box of tissues to hear the whole story and to come up with a plan.

The group decided that it was unthinkable that she would become a virtual prisoner in her own home. In her defense, they had dubbed the group the "Thursday Night Bowling League." To cheer her up, they presented her with a baby blue bowling ball bag, which she always used to transport her current project from home to the shop. Her husband never did protest again, nor did it seem odd to him that she had suddenly become such an avid bowler when there wasn't even a bowling alley in town.

Theo looked around the room, satisfied with everything she saw. At this hour, the cream and beige striped curtains were closed, making the large space seem cozier. At the far end of the room, the quilt frame supported a red, white and blue sampler quilt. Quilters from all over the area had each pieced a different star block and all of the blocks had been sewn together to make the top. When they finished quilting it, one of the bowlers would sew a binding on the edges and it would be raffled off. They planned to divide the proceeds between the Red Cross and the closest shelter for battered women.

Martha and Susan and Amy were already seated at the frame, quilting, when Caro charged through the doorway, bowling bag in hand.

For the past month, Caro frequently arrived late because her husband had deteriorated to the point that she couldn't leave until their son came by to relieve her.

"Did y'all hear?" Caro's dark eyes sparkled with excitement. Tiny and quick, she darted about the room like a finch let out of its cage. Hovering for a second while she examined each woman's project in turn. "I heard that the little Mexican girl Quentin brought back from out west somewhere shot his cousin and they stashed the body in the parking lot behind Ruby's. Is it true?"

Ruby, Ruth Ann, and Theo looked at each other and then back at Caro. They all looked baffled. Theo thought that each one of them probably held a different piece of the puzzle but clearly none of them had heard anything close to this rendition.

Martha scooted her chair over to make room for Caro at the

frame. "What little Mexican girl?"

Caro's normally pale face flushed with excitement, making her look years younger. "Well, some time ago, I heard from Nellie Pearl Prigmore that Quentin had brought this little girl home with him from Arizona or something." She paused and looked into each face in the group. "You know that Nellie Pearl's house is practically on the road up to his place."

Theo noticed that Caro didn't bother to mention Nellie Pearl's high-powered binoculars and the telescope that the older woman used to watch her neighbors. As that little habit of Nellie Pearl's was a frequent topic of discussion, it hardly seemed necessary. Nellie Pearl had the distinction of being the nosiest in a community of the nosy.

"When you say 'little girl . . .' " Edith's middle-aged face reflected her dismay. ". . . do you mean a child?"

"Oh, no." Caro perched on the edge of her chair and reached for the spool of thread. "I only saw her the one time, but I think she looked about twenty-five or so. It's so hard to tell. I was visiting Nellie Pearl one afternoon and saw Quentin and the girl driving toward town. She stared right at me. I thought she was a homely little thing." Her face reflected her disappointment as she tilted her head to one side and blinked several times. "I guess I expected to see someone that looked more like Jennifer Lopez, even though I know she isn't Mexican."

"Can't you just see Jennifer Lopez shacked up with Quentin Mize?" Martha started laughing. Soon the giggles overtook her and she slid from the chair to the floor. "Not even if she was blind drunk." She howled with merriment. "How could she stand to get that close to him? Have you smelled him?"

"I won't let him in the café." Ruby wrinkled her nose. "He didn't use to smell that bad, but the last time he came in, I thought a skunk had gotten in somehow. My customers started complaining about the stench, and I had to close the place and scrub everything with bleach."

"My husband says that Quentin's skin problems are due to whatever drug he is currently using." Amy reached down to help Martha off the floor but almost immediately the giggles attacked her and she unable to do anything but laugh.

"How would he know that?" Edith's eyes widened. "I mean, well, you know, without taking drugs himself?"

"He's a chemist." Susan answered for her best friend, who sat gasping for breath between bouts of hysteria. "He's probably studied it all in school."

"Actually, that's not true." Amy managed a whisper. "Well, it is true that he is a chemist and that he thinks he knows it all." The women all laughed at that. "In this case, though, he has a friend who works with addicts of various substances who told him that. I have no idea if it is true or not."

"Tell me more about this girl shooting Quentin's cousin." Theo pushed her hair behind her ears to keep it out of her face and gave her attention to threading a stubby little quilting needle. "Tony never tells me anything." After a lie like that, her nose should have grown like Pinocchio's. "How did you hear about it?"

"Let's see." A thoughtful look crossed Caro's face as she slipped her thimble on her third finger and put a few stitches in the quilt. "Oh yes, of course, Nellie Pearl told me." The collective groan coming from her audience made her pause. "I know, I know. I wouldn't usually believe anything she says either, but she seemed so positive when she told me that I believed her. She said she saw Quentin and the girl burying a gun up in those woods between their places very early this morning. There's a patch of rhododendron there and they were hunkered down next to it."

"What?" Ruth Ann and Theo spoke in unison. "Did she call and report it?"

"Are you kidding?" Caro flapped her arms, forgetting that she held a needle. Around her, the women dodged her wayward hands. "After the last time she called 911, she swore to me that she wouldn't call the cops again even if she saw an axe murderer hacking up a body on her front lawn."

"Why not?" Amy asked. She looked from Caro to Theo to Ruth Ann.

"It happened before you moved here. She even wrote a letter to the editor complaining about the sheriff's department." Ruth Ann grinned and answered. "The way I heard it, she called in the middle of the night to report someone peeking in her windows, looking at her. She wanted the sheriff to come over right away and arrest the pervert before he had his way with her."

"Now that is a desperate man." Martha's eyes were twinkling.

"And dedicated." Ruby laughed. "Last time I saw Nellie Pearl, she had on about six layers of oversized men's clothes. The outer layer was the rattiest flannel shirt I ever did see. Not only that, I don't know how she could see anything, even with her binoculars, with that rat's nest of stringy gray hair hanging in her face." She wrinkled her nose. "So what happened?"

"I don't think it is any secret because she told everyone who would listen about it." Ruth Ann hesitated before continuing, looking at Theo.

Theo didn't see any reason why Ruth Ann shouldn't tell the story and nodded her head.

"The sheriff sent Joe Kyle George out to investigate," said Ruth Ann. "He checked all the doors and windows. Then he went on to tell her that with the way the house was situated and the thickness of the curtains she had hanging on every window in every room the only way anyone could peep was to drive uphill and then if they used a powerful telescope, they might be able to look into her kitchen." She paused to take a few stitches.

When she looked up again, her dark eyes twinkled at her audience. "He suggested, and none too tactfully, I'm sure, that she quit spying on her neighbors. He also suggested that only a guilty conscience would make her think anyone would be interested in looking her windows."

Caro jumped into the story. "She told me that she called the sheriff at home after Joe Kyle left and threatened to sue him, the department and the whole county. She wanted him to fire Deputy George but instead, he hung up on her." She fanned her face with her hand. "The language she used, my goodness, I never even heard of half of those words, but no lawyer would take the case, not even Jasper Snodgrass, and you know he'd sue his own mother for her last dime. Then and there, she swore that she would never call them again, no matter what."

"So how could she see Quentin burying a gun?" said Susan. She was the quieter of the two friends. "I mean, why would he bury it where she could watch him?"

"That's a good question." Caro looked shaken. "I guess she's done it again. Told me a whole big story and I believed it."

"I wouldn't be sure that she didn't see something, you know, the way she spies on everyone. I just wouldn't swear that she knew what she saw." Martha handed her the spool of thread. "I'll tell you what she reminds me of. I watched a television show once where the nosy neighbor kept a journal of the comings and goings and did a bit of blackmail. I wouldn't be surprised if she didn't have a list somewhere herself."

Mollified, Caro went back to her stitches. She hadn't taken more than five when she focused on Ruby. "Sweet girl, when are you going to marry that nice deputy?"

Ruby simply smiled and shook her head.

Martha jumped into the conversation. "Speaking of getting married, though, I heard that Prudence Sligar and Deputy Darren Holt are engaged."

"We should make them a quilt."

CHAPTER NINE

At ten o'clock on Friday morning, Wade arrived at the station to report to Tony. "Doc Nash got the results from the toxicology tests and finished the autopsy." The wide smile on his face proved his resilience, but he still looked a bit green around the edges. "You want to read it or do you want me to give the you highlights?"

Tony, who hadn't gotten much sleep the night before, thought that he really wanted a long nap followed by a large cup of coffee. Instead, he sat at his desk reading the log of calls taken by the night shift. Thankfully, the night had been a fairly quiet one. When the influx of tourists visiting the national park began, the number of calls would increase. For now, the local crimes consisted of a report that vandals had either stolen or maimed some yard ornaments, a domestic violence call and a complaint filed against a driver who left a station without paying for his gas. Tony shook his head. The fool would probably lose his license for that.

Since he'd heard about it from Theo, Tony's mind kept returning to Caro's account of how Nellie Pearl claimed to have seen Quentin burying a gun. Someone needed to pump Nellie Pearl for information, but he knew that she would never talk to him. Maybe he could get Theo to do a little more unpaid police work.

He finally answered Wade's question. "Just give me the bottom line."

"The guy did die from snakebite, just like Doc thought." Wade waggled his left thumb and pointed to the soft tissue between his thumb and forefinger. "One bite was right there in that boneless area. Don't you know that had to hurt?" He shook his hand as if the very thought caused him pain. Then he touched his right forearm. "There was another bite about here and based on the distance between puncture wounds, Doc thinks it was the copperhead that bit him there. He is sending tissue samples off to the lab just to be certain."

"Can he guess at the timeline? Did the bites occur before or after the handcuffs were closed?"

"From the way the hand and arm swelled, Doc says that the handcuffs were probably on when the snake bit his hand or were fastened immediately after." Reaching into his shirt pocket, he produced a small plastic bag containing a gold wedding ring. "He had this on but we couldn't see it yesterday because the hand was so badly swollen and messed up."

"Pops Ogle thinks that the wife is in a nursing home but didn't know more than that. He couldn't even guess what state she is in." Tony took the bag and held it up to the light. Nothing unique. Just an ordinary gold band with only the manufacturer's name engraved inside. He put it with the rest of the man's belongings.

Lacing his fingers together, he rested them on the file and faced Wade directly. "So what do you think? Accident or homicide?" Tony knew what he would call it but waited for Wade to make his conclusion.

"I think that we can rule out suicide and accident, don't you?" Wade examined a pair of his own handcuffs. "After all, you are not going to accidentally attach yourself to a steering wheel in a dark parking lot and then slap a snake in the nose or whatever it takes to make a tired snake bite you. Not even if you are an idiot, and by all accounts, this guy knew his snakes."

"If someone wanted to make it look like an accident, it sure wouldn't make any sense to leave the handcuffs behind. I'd say that it is pretty obviously homicide, but why do it like that?" Tony said. "The guy handles snakes all the time, so how could you be sure the snakes would bite him or that the bite would be fatal? Wouldn't you assume that he would have some immunity to bites? I would, but maybe it doesn't happen." He leafed through some papers that he had printed off the Internet. "It says here that most snakebites are not fatal."

"Maybe it wasn't intended to kill the guy. Maybe it was just supposed to scare him or keep him there until someone else came along and found him. The bites could be incidental."

"Or maybe keep him there until the person came back to let him go." Tony rubbed his stomach with the side of his hand. "Maybe they played a game of sorts." He cocked one eyebrow at his deputy. "Not a game that I would play, but maybe it's a form of Russian roulette or just plain old 'chicken.' You know, like who can stay in there the longest? If so, his playmate probably ran away when he realized the guy died."

Ruth Ann knocked on the doorframe. "John Mize is dead." A wide smile decorated her face as she waved a paper at the men. Waiting for their reaction, she gently blew on the new coating of baby blue polish on her fingernails. Her eyes twinkled with amusement.

Now that they had worked together for several years, Tony had enough experience to recognize her expression. He forced himself not to flinch.

Wade straightened and said, "We already know that, Ruth Ann."

She flashed him a saucy grin. Baiting the younger man always seemed to entertain her. "Yes, but do you know when he died? Exactly?"

Wade scooted forward on his seat and started to explain.

"Even Doc doesn't know exactly when, but it was definitely the night before last, between ten and four in the morning."

Even as he spoke, Ruth Ann's head started shaking. "Unfortunately, that's not quite true." She looked past the deputy and her eyes met Tony's. "You were right, Sheriff, there was something 'off' about the driver's license. It is a genuine Tennessee license and it did belong to Quentin's cousin, John. This same John lived in Maryville until he died in an accident about a year ago."

Handing Tony the paper, she grinned at the deputy. "Oh, Wade, I almost forgot to tell you that Stan's here with those snake boxes you wanted. I had him put them on your desk. Is that okay? Should I ask him if he removed the contents?"

She blew Wade a kiss and went back to her desk.

Tony didn't bother to look at the paper she'd handed him. He knew that Ruth Ann had given them the heart of the story. Instead, he focused on his deputy. "You see what you can do about identifying him by his fingerprints, and I guess I'll have another little chat with Quentin. I'm not sure how, but I think he is in this up to his spotted nose, but first, I want to talk to the Maryville Police." He reached for the telephone.

"There is one more thing." Wade didn't stand. "Doc found something else when he cleaned up the dead guy. It seems that our dead preacher had prison tattoos on both hands and on his arms and chest. He had to have been inside for quite a while to get that many. Doc cleaned him up pretty well and then I took some photos of them. We might be able to use them for identification."

"Prison tattoos and a false ID? We knew he'd served time but not where or why." Tony smiled his encouragement and started dialing. "That's good work. Tell Sheila to pick up Quentin's girlfriend and bring her in here. Maybe she can tell us something about the man. After all, he did stay there for a couple of months. She must have learned something."

He wondered how he would explore the tidbit that Theo had brought home about Nellie Pearl and a buried gun.

"Stan," said Tony. Thinking about Ruth Ann's message, he was speaking to himself. "Is he still here?" His hand stopped dialing and reached for the disconnect button on the phone. Something teased his brain. What had Theo told him? Something about Stan disliking Winifred. No. That wasn't it. He remembered Pops complaining about Stan. "Bring him in here. I want to talk to him."

"I'll get him." Wade covered the space between the desk and the door in two long strides.

Stan trotted into the office, his belly bouncing under a blue and yellow striped golf shirt. "I'm taking real good care of those snakes, Sheriff."

"That's good." Tony motioned to Wade and the deputy pulled a chair closer to the desk for the chubby man. "That's not why I wanted to talk to you."

"It's not?" Stan's genial smile widened. His expression was open, pleasant. He looked as if Wade had just offered him a plate of Christmas cookies instead of an uncomfortable chair.

"Nope." Tony leaned back in his chair and fiddled with his pen. "I want you to tell me about the altercation that you had with our snakebite victim."

"I don't believe I know what you mean." Stan's eyes narrowed. His rear end stopped just short of the vinyl seat.

"I heard that you got into an argument with the man at the grocery store. Do you remember him now? He's the very same man that you pretended not to know. Maybe you two argued again out at the old motel?" The sudden change in Stan's countenance told Tony that his guess hit the target.

The corners of Stan's mouth drooped and he collapsed onto the chair. "I told him that he ought not treat those snakes like that." Stan began wringing his hands. "I didn't want to mention it because I know it sounds bad. I didn't do anything to him. I swear I didn't, but now that I think about it, I might have threatened him. I guess someone heard me."

Tony neither confirmed nor denied his statement. "When was this?"

"Oh, I dunno. It happened maybe a couple of days after your mom and aunt told me that they were renting out the office." His fingers dug into the chair arms like he needed to hang on for dear life. "I went out there, you know, just to see what was what and I saw them messing with the snakes."

Tony drew a series of circles in his notebook. "Were they having their service?"

"Yessir." Stan's head bobbed. "They didn't have curtains on the windows so I watched. Those poor snakes." Tears welled in his eyes. "Afterwards, I confronted that preacher out in the parking lot."

"And? What did he say?"

"Said it wasn't any of my damned business but that he doesn't use the same snakes all the time. On alternating nights, he lets them rest."

Tony frowned. "Was that all?"

"Yes," said Stan.

Tony didn't believe him but decided to let it go for the moment. He really wanted to find out the true identity of their victim before he went further into his investigation. After all, Stan wasn't going to leave town.

Moments after Stan left, his intercom buzzed. Quietly, Ruth Ann announced that Sheila had arrived with Quentin's girl-friend.

"Send them to the greenhouse."

CHAPTER TEN

The only window in the greenhouse barely qualified as one. All formal interrogations took place in there. State of the art cameras and recording equipment monitored the room. Simple and stark, the floor to ceiling beige tile and gray vinyl flooring could be hosed down with bleach and hot water. A drain in the floor made it simple. A steel table, steel chairs and steel door set with a tiny Plexiglas window. In the greenhouse, the outside world ceased to exist.

Tony joined Sheila and Angelina Lopez. Thirty seconds later, Tony wanted Quentin's girlfriend out of the state. Sitting in front of him was a walking illustration of what illegal drug use could produce. Miss Lopez had, at least in Tony's opinion, done enough drugs in her twenty-five or so years that she could tolerate being in an enclosed space with Quentin. To be fair, she wouldn't win first prize either. Tony knew little about her other than her name and that she had come home with Quentin from a trip to Arizona. Her use of the English language seemed no worse than Quentin's.

She carried no form of identification at all.

Short and squat, she sat across from him, her legs splayed. The thin, black nylon pants clung to every crease and ripple like body paint. The crimson crop top revealed more than it covered. Cut low across her breasts and riding high above the roll of flesh that was the widest part of her body, the sleazy fabric looked as if it was about ready to come apart. A matted, filthy, fake leopard jacket covered her arms and hung down her back like a shawl.

"How long have you lived here, Miss Lopez?"

The best guess in the sheriff's office put Quentin's Arizona trip at about the time of the Super Bowl football game in January. Since then, Quentin had gone downhill fast.

Tony repeated his question.

"About a year." She dug into the mess of hair and stabbed something with a broken fingernail. After glancing at it, she popped it into her mouth.

It wasn't even a good lie.

Tony fought the impulse to hide behind Sheila when the gross woman began touching herself in front of him. The prostitutes that Tony had arrested in Chicago looked like nuns in comparison. Keeping his eyes glued to hers, he hurried through the questions. The pupils and irises were the same shade of black. Acne covered her dirty, coarse skin and her black hair looked like it had been caught in something and then cut free with a dull knife.

Tony forced himself to focus on her eyes. "Do you remember where Quentin spent Wednesday night?"

"Wednesday?" Angelina returned to her digging and looked up. "With me."

She said it with such certainty that Tony knew she lied again. He doubted that she remembered Wednesday. He tried a different approach. "What do you know about Quentin's cousin?"

"Nothing."

"How long has he lived at your place?"

A shrug.

Tony's gaze dropped to her mouth and he shuddered. Her teeth were broken and brown and there was a vicious sore on her lip. She smiled and ran her tongue over it. Tony reached for the bottle of antacids. "Do you know his whole name?"

"John." She shrugged. "Just John. He's okay. He gives me money." She leaned forward and Tony could see all the way down her top to the roll of fat at her waist.

He focused on her eyes.

"You are a handsome *hombre* even with no hairs." She patted her head. "You wouldn't have to pay me no thing." Her eyes were glued to his crotch and her tongue traced the outline of her mouth.

Her assessment didn't flatter him, and her unspoken offer held no temptation. Tony looked at Sheila. "Take her home. Please." If he looked at her one more second he might lose his professional cool and throw her into the parking lot.

Seconds after the women departed from the interrogation room, Ruth Ann arrived with a spray bottle of disinfectant and a wad of paper towels clutched in a glove-encased fist. If he didn't know better, he'd think she almost looked sympathetic.

"That didn't take long." Ruth Ann sprayed the table, chair and surrounding floor.

"I don't think she knows anything, even when she is not high. I just couldn't stomach being in a closed space with her and had Sheila take her home." He moved the chair that he occupied closer to the open door. "It's too bad there is no window in this room." The room had been designed to keep prisoners from escaping, but it also kept fresh air outside.

Ruth Ann's nose twitched. "What *is* that stench, anyway? It is positively vile. It smells worse than old-fashioned dirt and sweat."

"Chemicals." Tony flipped through his notebook. "Quentin smelled like that yesterday, but at least we were outside then." He watched the efficiency of her movements. "It's certainly not part of your job, but I really appreciate you coming in here and cleaning up but I'm afraid your efforts will be wasted. I sent Darren after Quentin. They should arrive any time."

Clearly dismayed, Ruth Ann straightened. "Oh, well, it is a head start anyway." Holding the dirty paper towels away from her face, she headed for the door and paused, looking at him over one shoulder. "Did your mother enjoy her date?" Her dark eyes sparkled with mischief.

For a second, Tony's thoughts were so consumed by comparing her lively black eyes with Angelina's empty ones that he didn't comprehend her question. When her words hit him, he reeled. "My mom had a date? With whom? Nobody tells me anything. Did Theo know?"

Ruth Ann nodded. "Jane and Red went to Knoxville to a play. I wouldn't have known, but I saw them coming home last night together and she filled me in this morning. Gave me all the details." Her smile widened.

"Did she have a good time?" Tony had wondered if his mother would ever actually go out with another man. He'd have to ask Theo why she didn't tell him. "What did they do after the play?"

Pretending she had not heard his question, she said. "The play was excellent." Ruth Ann extended her little finger as she began to count off the points. "She enjoyed the dessert after the play, but they both prefer the pies that Blossom bakes." She added another finger. "Red behaved like a perfect gentleman." She added her third finger and fourth fingers. "He kissed her goodnight but it was only a kiss on the cheek."

The opening notes of the "William Tell Overture" shrilled in Tony's pocket. As he opened the little cellular phone, Ruth Ann left the room, closing the door behind her. Caller ID informed him that the Chief of Police in Maryville returned his call.

"Hey, Chief, I see you got my message." Tony leaned back in his chair, tipping the front legs off the floor. "What can you tell me about the death of your John Mize?"

"Well, we know from his blood alcohol level that he had to have been blind drunk when he crashed his car into a new vehicle out at a dealership near the airport. It wasn't the first time he's over imbibed, either. My mama would call him shiftless." He coughed. "What a way to go, though. He wasn't wearing a seat belt and went through two windshields, his own and the other vehicle's as well. Died at the scene in a brand new car."

"I remember hearing about that. How fast was he going?"

The chief cleared his throat. "Well over a hundred."

"Ouch. Is there much family left?" In Tony's experience, the Mize clan stuck together whenever possible. Quentin just happened to be the only member left from his branch.

"Yep, but they are all accounted for. Most of them live in town and are generally pretty law-abiding. A few of them live a little ways out of town, and I sent a couple of officers out there to check up on them. A couple of the cousins did mention that some relative from out of state had been visiting a while back. The best description that we got put him in the medium height and weight category and he looked a lot like someone named Uncle Jesse. But—" he paused to clear his throat. "I can tell you that he preached around here for a short time. Although the relatives said that he did have snakes with him, it looks like he didn't use any of them in his services though. Still, it sounds a lot like your man, doesn't it?"

"It sure does." Tony sat forward, slamming the chair legs onto the floor. He grabbed a pen. "That's got to be him. Any idea what name he used there? They would know that he wasn't John."

"Cousin Hub." There was more rustling of papers. "No one seems too sure what that stands for and no one had any idea he was using John's license. They think he took it from a box of John's belongings and, for what it's worth, I believe them. They may not be a bunch of Harvard grads, but they are an honest lot. They took him in because he was kin and didn't miss him when he left."

"Hub? Maybe that's short for Hubbard. I wonder if that's his first or last name." Tony was thinking out loud. "Now why do you suppose a God-fearing preacher turned up here using a dead man's identification?" He didn't mention the stolen license plate.

"You got me, Tony." Amusement threaded the Chief's voice. "I only met one snake handler and he was so law abiding that he probably used turn signals when walking down the sidewalk. His world only held good and evil, black and white with no shades of gray."

"He probably didn't consider that using his snakes in a service here is against the law," said Tony.

"Most likely he didn't feel that the laws created by men matched those of his religion. Still, I never would peg one for carrying false identification."

"Yeah, I agree. Thanks for all your help and let me know if you learn anything else about this man. He's sure got me puzzled." Tony stared unseeing at his notes, mentally shuffling the information he had. John Mize—or whatever his name might be—was not a familiar sight around Silersville. In an area where many of the residents worked a couple of jobs to make ends meet, how had he supported himself?

A vision of the thick wallet rose in his mind's eye. He doubted that more than a quarter of the county population had ever seen a hundred-dollar bill much less owned twenty of them.

He wondered if the man had a bank account.

The questions were piling up faster than the answers.

THE SECOND BODY OF CLUES

On the wrong side of the fabric, mark one diagonal line from corner to corner of each 2 1/2 inch square of fabrics (B) and (D) and 48 of the squares of fabric (C).

UNIT 1—

Stack the 48 rectangles of fabric (E) right side up. Next to it stack the 48 squares of fabric (B) right side down. The marked diagonal should run upper left to lower right. Place a square (B) on the right end of the rectangle and stitch on the drawn line. Repeat until all 48 are sewn. Fold the corner of the square up to make a triangle. Press. Trim back layers leaving 1/4"? seam allowance. You now have 48 rectangles EB which are unit 1's. Set aside.

UNIT 2—

Repeat the process with 2 1/2"? by 4 1/2"? rectangles of fabric (A) and squares of fabric (D). After trimming, stack these rectangles right side up with corner of D in upper right.

Set squares of (C) with right side down and diagonal line running from lower left to upper right onto left corner of the rectangle. Sew on drawn line. Continue until all 48 are sewn. Fold the corner of the square up to make a triangle. When sewn there should be a large arrow point of (A) facing corners of (C) and (D). (Flying geese) Trim back layers, leaving 1/4" seam allowance. Continue until you have 48 geese ACD. These are unit 2's. Set aside.

CHAPTER ELEVEN

Excited that her van worked again, Theo headed for Nina's house. It had been a rotten winter for her best friend. After fifteen years of marriage, her scum-bucket husband decided to "pursue his destiny" in a city, living with a much younger woman. Without warning, and only three days before Christmas, he had moved to Charlotte to live with an Internet sweetie. There hadn't been much money in the bank when he had been home, and he had taken most of that with him. Too spineless to tell Nina what he planned to do, he left a note on the kitchen counter.

Two days later, while Nina visited her attorney in Knoxville, a hit and run driver sideswiped her car and it needed extensive bodywork. Merry Christmas! The insurance company wanted to total it because it would cost more to repair than it was worth, but she had no money to replace it. By New Year's Day, the two kids had chicken pox. The final straw hit last week when she slipped on a toy car that belonged to her eight-year-old son Tommy. She and the toy fell down the back steps at her own house. Nina broke her left ankle.

Nina needed some good news.

"Hey, kid." Theo let herself into the spacious, modern house and found her friend in the den. "Luckily, you broke your left ankle." Ignoring Nina's glare, Theo smiled warmly as she dropped a transparent plastic box with a blue lid onto the coffee table. A grocery sack dangled from her left elbow and she balanced a couple of mysterious items on top of the box. "You might have gotten depressed if you'd broken your right foot."

"Because I wouldn't be able to drive? I did think of that." Nina adjusted the pillow under her foot. She lay on the couch, still in robe and nightgown. Her auburn hair needed washing. Half of it escaped the ponytail holder. The royal blue robe contrasted nicely with the lime green cast that protected her ankle.

Theo shook her head. "Because of your sewing machine. I have lots of work for you to do, and have you ever tried to use the other foot when you are sewing?" Her laugh filled the room when she spied Nina's toes. Her toenails were painted with hot pink polish. Little flecks of glitter caught the light. "No way. Did Ruth Ann come by and paint your toenails? You don't even own any polish."

Nina's laughter joined hers. She wiggled her toes, admiring the sparkle. "Amy did it. She got a big box of preteen goodies for Christmas. Glitter filled everything. My mother always gives her the absolute best presents." She grinned as she pointed to the pile of packages that Theo balanced in her arms. "Speaking of presents, what did you bring me?"

"No presents, just work. Lots of work." Theo paid Nina to piece sample quilt tops for the shop and to test Theo's patterns for accuracy.

"Good." Nina pushed herself upright. "I'm going nuts here. The kids are at school and Doc says I have to stay off my ankle for a week and then he'll okay me to go back to work." A spark of desperation glowed in her leaf green eyes. "The substitute they stuck in my classroom knows zero French. She's called me eighty times in the past two days. God only knows how she will survive."

"What have you been doing?" Theo glanced around and saw magazines and the television remote. "You could appliqué or hand quilt. Pretend you're at quilt camp."

"I know, I know." Nina lifted a pair of binoculars from her lap. "I could do something but I'm depressed. I've been propped up here like Jimmy Stewart watching the birds and the comings and goings of my neighbors. I must say that they are a dull lot." She lifted an eyebrow. "No one has buried a body in the garden in the two days I've been watching. I don't know how Nellie Pearl stands that much spying, but maybe her neighbors are more interesting than mine." Setting the binoculars on the floor she adjusted her position on the couch and studied Theo's face. The corners of her mouth pulled down. "Enough about me. You look a bit unraveled. Is everything okay?"

Theo sighed. Talking to Nina always helped her sort out her chaotic life. "I'm fine." She blew a wayward strand of hair out of her face as she shuffled her armload. She managed to drop a package of cookies onto Nina's lap. "But, as usual, I am running around like a chicken looking for its head. The book deadline is coming up fast and I seem to have somehow misplaced several weeks from my calendar. I am totally unprepared to deal with going to Paducah next month." She set the plastic box on the floor and slipped the grocery bag off her arm and held it high. "First things first. Your dinner is in here. Just heat and eat." She vanished into the kitchen with it.

"Aren't you going to tell me what it is?" Nina opened the package of cookies and held one in her teeth even as she tightened the band around her auburn ponytail.

"No. The good news is that I didn't cook it. I picked it up at Ruby's."

Nina's relief was reflected in her smile." You know it's cruel to tease people with broken ankles. Just for that, I'm not going to feel sorry for you when you go to Paducah to teach and to see one of your quilts hanging in the show of shows."

Theo grinned and shrugged as she dropped onto the rocking

chair next to the couch. The thrill of having one of her quilts accepted into the American Quilter's Society annual competition and show in Paducah hadn't diminished. In her eyes, it was the World Series of quilting. Pulling the plastic box closer to her feet, she opened it with all the flair of a magician producing the rabbit from a hat and handed Nina a sheet of paper.

"Something for *you*. The next clue to the mystery quilt."

Nina abandoned her cookies and grabbed the paper and scanned it eagerly. "I still don't know what this is going to be. What else do you have in your magic box?"

"Work. Lot's of work." Theo handed her a sheaf of papers, patterns and instructions, before she produced a stack of jewel-toned fabrics and another of neutrals. Each fabric had a note pinned to it. "I'll leave the arrangement of color to you. I want the effect of an Oriental rug." She handed Nina a rough sketch and dived back into the box. This time, she emerged with a stack of reproduction fabrics that looked just like the fabrics used in the 1860s. "Use the same layout but with these fabrics. That should be enough to show a contrast in styles, don't you think?"

"Is that all?" Nina sat caressing the fabrics.

"For today." Theo pulled a brown sack from the bottom of the box and dropped a bag of M&M candies next to Nina's feet. "This should keep you going for a little while." With a calculated smile she mumbled, "Has Jane told you about her date with Red?"

Nina was lifting another cookie to her lips when she stopped. "Did you just imply that Jane, our Jane, went on a date with Red?"

Theo nodded. "You really shouldn't miss bowling night if you want to keep up with things. And put away those damned binoculars before you do turn in another Nellie Pearl." Theo snatched a couple of cookies from the package. "Actually, the bowlers don't know about the date. I just told them she couldn't come." She opened the cookie and licked the center. "Jane went to a play with Red and I haven't heard anything since."

"That's why he got home so late last night. He is usually home by five and he stays home a lot. Sometimes I see him walk over to the Tomlinsons. I think they play checkers or something." Her eyes widened. "I *am* turning into Nellie Pearl, aren't I?"

Theo nodded. "Red's a nice man and I'm glad to see Jane get out a bit."

"Yeah, ten years is long enough to wait before dating." She chuckled. "Remember Old Man Ferguson? He started dating Olive Peters between the time his wife died and the funeral."

Theo frowned. "I think he wanted someone else to cook and clean for him. He probably couldn't put sugar in his own tea."

"That's the truth." Nina closed the cookie package and lay back against the pillows. "I feel so isolated on this couch. Tell me what else is happening in town?"

Theo told Nina the basics of the dead man in Ruby's parking lot. Not knowing either the man or the circumstances, they concentrated on the horrifying idea of being in a car with loose snakes.

As if unable to bear the idea of the snakes, Nina changed the subject. "Did you know that Prudence is pregnant again? Who do you suppose is the father of this one?"

For a change, Theo thought she did know, but she wasn't sure. She wouldn't speculate, not even to Nina, but Deputy Darren Holt had her vote.

Prudence Sligar remained a community mystery. Born and raised in the hills around Silersville, she loved the area, and except for the time she attended beauty school, had always lived there. Her grandmother had been a seer, a wise woman, who lived life on her own terms. Maybe that had encouraged Prudence's own independence. Never married, Prudence had produced a brood of fatherless children. Local gossips had been thwarted at every turn. No one knew who any of the fathers might be. Just as she had defied them when she painted the exterior of her beauty shop, the Klip 'n' Kurl, pink and purple, she felt no compunction to satisfy the curiosity of the citizens.

"She is engaged to Darren. Maybe he knows, but he sure isn't the father of that brood." She smiled. "Do you think even the children know? Do they visit their fathers? Does she get child support?"

"Well if they do, they are ahead of my children right now." Nina adjusted her position again. "That honey he met on the Internet is bound to be disappointed. I just know that he told her he has money and a fabulous body." Her caustic grin suggested that he had neither.

"Don't you assume they were both telling lies?" Theo snorted. "Not that I want one, but I could claim that I had a forty-inch bosom."

Nina laughed as she stared at her friend's flat chest. "Closer to an IQ of forty."

Theo tossed a pillow in Nina's face.

Tony was puzzling over the information about the real, but dead, John Mize and his mysterious cousin when Wade burst through the doorway.

He carried an extra large evidence envelope wrapped in both arms, held closely to his chest like the game winning football. The threshold of Tony's office was the goal line. A sudden smile pulled the skin taut over the high, sharp cheekbones his Cherokee grandmother had contributed, giving him a savage appearance. A hint of wolf glowed in his eyes.

"You know those snake boxes that Stan thought were so odd? Well guess what?" Wade didn't wait for Tony to form a reply.

"They have false bottoms. I found a wad of cash and a boatload of pills inside them."

"What kind of pills? Are they identifiable?" Tony guessed from Wade's expression that the answer would not make him happy. Drugs were the bane of law enforcement. The problem existed everywhere. No community was immune. Even worse, in his mind, was the ocean of problems that drugs compounded.

"Oh, yeah." Wade's smile grew even wider. "Our dead guy was hauling Hillbilly Heroin. Lot's of it. All twenties and forties. He had full jars of a hundred tablets and some of those little bubble packs stashed in the bottom of those boxes. If he needed that kind of medication, he had to suffer a lot of pain." The expression on his face declared that he didn't believe pain had anything to do with the reason for such a large supply.

"Hell and damnation!" Tony stared at the envelope. "That's all we need. Someone bringing bootleg OxyContin into our area. Let's hope he only transported it and hadn't started distributing it." Tony smoothed his scalp, wishing he had hair so he could pull it out.

It never failed to amaze him what people would willingly do to their bodies. They would take every prescription medication produced and see what else they could do with it. If they saw a new plant, they would try smoking it or chewing it or steeping it like tea. The things people would do to score drugs baffled him. They would steal, prostitute themselves, and even kill. Most of the crime he had seen as a Chicago cop related directly to someone wanting a fix of something. The night a junkie shot Tony in the stomach, he was off duty and the guy was too strung out to know the name of the planet.

"We have a big enough drug problem around here already." Unaware of his actions, he rubbed his stomach before he slipped a few antacids into his mouth. "I haven't heard anything about more drugs than usual, have you?"

Wade shook his head. "Maybe he just suffered from a lot of pain and they were prescribed for him." Even as he spoke, he didn't look as if he believed that story for a second. If prescribed, all of those pills would have been either in a prescription bottle or labeled with a doctor's name and instructions. "My uncle took them when he had cancer. He claimed OxyContin was a miracle drug and would have traded his car for them if he had to. I've heard that people have killed themselves when they haven't been able to get it."

"It is powerful stuff, all right, but I'll bet your uncle didn't get very many of them at a time and didn't keep them in a box with poisonous snakes. I also bet he took it the way the doctor prescribed it." It confounded him how people could see what illegal drugs did to others and still try them. "I don't suppose the ones you found in the snake boxes were conveniently labeled with the name of a pharmacy or distributor?"

"No, but we'll be able to track them by the serial numbers on the jars. They are factory packages. Did you know that they are delivered in an armored truck in some places?" Wade frowned as he passed the envelope to Tony. "There were only smudges of fingerprints on the jars. Nothing I would be able to identify with any accuracy."

"How much cash?" Tony inspected the notations Wade had made on the envelope before handing it back to him. "How many milligrams are we talking about here?" He knew that the going rate for illegally obtained OxyContin continued to rise.

"I found fifty thousand in cash." Wade checked his notes. "I make out twenty thousand milligrams in forties and four thousand in twenties in the jars. The bubble packs add another thousand or so milligrams, so a minimum value of thirty thousand." He handed Tony a paper. "Here's a list of the serial numbers."

A low whistle passed through Tony's lips. "I guess I'd better put in a call to the district drug task force. I'm sure they will be delighted to hear about this. Nothing makes their day brighter than hearing about some new angle." He paused, considering the conflicting information about their drug-running, prison-tattooed, snake-handling preacher.

The facts didn't add up. The possibility existed, although it was slim, that the man had reformed in prison and had no idea what he carried in those boxes. On the other hand, Quentin had to be involved in this whole drug scenario, didn't he? But how? The man was simply not smart enough to engineer a plan to obtain that many prescription pills. Tony thought of Quentin as more of the do-it-yourself, grow-your-own kind of degenerate. That thought triggered a memory of something he had seen up at Quentin's place.

Wade stood in front of his desk, watching him. After a minute or so of silence and inaction on Tony's part, he cleared his throat. "Do you want me to call them? I need to lock this stuff in the evidence locker first, but then I could make the call."

"No. That's okay. I was just thinking." Absently, he smoothed his bald scalp. "I'll give them the serial numbers, and I just thought of another question that I need to ask them."

Tony could hear Darren and Quentin in the hallway. "What I really need you to do is to get back to your fingerprint project. We need to get those prints out for identification. We know our body is in the system." Tony's eyes returned to the photograph of the tattoos. "For the county to get its money's worth from all that expensive fingerprint training that you got from the FBI in Quantico, you need to get on it."

Nodding, Wade left the office and Tony buzzed Ruth Ann. "Tell Darren to put Quentin in the greenhouse. He can either wait inside with him or stand outside and guard the door, but he is not to leave. I want him to stay for the interview."

The crisp response from Ruth Ann informed him that Darren and Quentin had stopped into the interrogation room for a moment and then moved on to the drunk tank. Furthermore, she thought they should have gone there as soon as they entered the building and not bothered to pass near her desk. Quentin was obviously so high on whatever drug that he had been taking that it would be a long time before his orbit would bring him near the earth again.

Tony's stomach rumbled. Popping three more antacids into his mouth, he dialed the number for the drug task force. He had no idea how long this conversation might last. He would probably have to talk to the DEA as well. He had to let them know about the OxyContin, but more urgently, at least in his mind, he had to find out if Quentin was cooking methamphetamine up at his place. If so, someone trained by the DEA would have to come and deal with that. Dismantling a meth lab was extremely dangerous and specialized work that his tiny county couldn't begin to handle.

He doubted that Angelina would help with the process. He needed her out of Quentin's house. Maybe he could still catch Sheila and have her bring the woman back into town.

He reached for the telephone.

CHAPTER TWELVE

No one had to tell Tony that Blossom Flowers had a crush on him.

Theo once suggested that Blossom would love anyone who treated her like a real person and not like a slave. The beleaguered woman had lived at home for her entire thirty years, with all of the other Flowers issuing directives to her. Theo also said that Blossom worked as much for the freedom of being out of the house as she did for the money.

Tony agreed. Being nice to her paid off on this day when Blossom arrived at the Law Enforcement Center carrying a whole pie, freshly baked, just for him.

"What's the occasion, Blossom?" Tony had to step back so the large woman could squeeze through the doorway. Her scalp showed under the little flame-orange tufts of hair. He sympathized with her because, like him, she had almost no hair.

His mouth started watering the instant that he spied the crumb-coated pie. The scents of warm apples and cinnamon teased his nose and his stomach growled in response.

"I wanted to thank you." Blossom started to set the pie on his desk but paused when she couldn't find a clear space on the whole surface.

"For what?" Why was she thanking him? Relieved that it didn't appear to be a bribe, Tony set a stack of folders on the floor, making room for the pie. He really wanted a piece of that fabulous pie. A big piece of it. After she left, he would take it to the lunchroom and share the rest. Maybe.

"For talking to Ruby." Her protruding eyes filled with tears. "I really like that job and would hate to lose it."

"There was never any problem with your job, Blossom. Ruby's only concern was for your safety. You should give yourself more credit." Tony almost groaned when he saw her lower herself into one of the steel and vinyl chairs that faced his desk. She seemed to be settling in for a visit. "Do you get along with the others down there?"

"Oh, yeah, Miss Ruby is real nice to work for and Red always has a funny story to tell me. Even the waitresses are always saying that they get extra good tips from anyone who eats a bite of my pies or cakes." A happy smile lifted the corners of her mouth, giving her plain face a pleasant glow.

Tony had talked to Red on several occasions and he had seemed like a nice enough man. Now that he knew his mother had gone on a date with him, Tony's curiosity grew. What separated Red from the other eligible men in town? "Tell me about Red."

"Well, I guess his hair used to be red and that's how he got his name, but it looks all white to me." At Tony's encouraging nod, she continued. "He's a foreigner, of course, and always sad, even when he's telling me a joke."

Tony knew that Blossom's family considered anyone whose grandparents hadn't been born in Park County to be a foreigner. Tony knew about being a foreigner. His family hadn't moved to Tennessee until he was eight and his classmates had treated him, for a time, like he had arrived from another planet. Theo, a direct descendant of Amoes Siler, was not a foreigner. "Why do you think that Red is always sad?"

"It hasn't been too long since his wife died of the cancer, you know, and before that his daughter died. That's one of the reasons they moved up here, you know, getting away from the sadness." She pawed around in her tote bag and finally located a box of Junior Mints. Pouring a mound onto her palm, she shoved the whole pile into her mouth. "He was retired, but now he's the morning cook. I don't quite know how you can be retired and still have to be at work, do you?"

Tony didn't want to discuss the philosophy of retirement. "Do you know what business he was in before he retired?" Tony had to fight to keep his eyes away from the pie. The aroma pulled him like a magnet.

Blossom shook her head, then stopped. "Wait." A chocolate-flecked smile creased her face. "Yeah, he did say once that he was a bookkeeper or banker, something with letters."

"CPA?" In Tony's eyes, the worn little man with the droopy, bloodshot eyes looked like an accountant. Whenever Tony saw him, everything about him seemed very tidy and precise. Only the grease smears on his old-fashioned bifocal glasses eluded his penchant for cleanliness.

"That's it." Blossom cheered, half-rising from her seat.

The way she lifted up made Tony think of a game show contestant with the winning answer. Maybe she practiced cheering with the television. If Wade hadn't poked his head into the office, Blossom might have stayed the rest of the afternoon.

Until Tony saw Wade and Blossom side by side, in such close quarters, he hadn't really noticed before but the young deputy had the thickest black hair Tony had ever seen. He kept it cut close to the scalp, but instead of showing skin, it looked like a fur cap. It wasn't fair. Viewed next to Blossom's, her hair looked even sparser. As for himself, Tony could feel the movement of air on his scalp.

"Hey there, Blossom." Wade gave her a big smile. "I hate to interrupt but I need to talk to you, Sheriff." He waved a sheet of paper.

Blossom heaved herself to her feet and headed for the door.

"When you finish the pie, just drop the pie plate at Ruby's. She knows I brought it over here."

"Thanks again, Blossom, for the pie. In the future though, I want you to remember that I was just doing my job. Ruby never intended to fire you." Lifting the pie from the desk, Tony followed her through the doorway and waited until she reached the end of the hall. Beckoning with his head, he signaled his deputy. "Come with me, Wade. You can tell me what you've got and have a slice of pie at the same time. Your expression tells me that I am going to enjoy both things."

Wade passed him and walked backwards toward the lunchroom. "We've got a positive ID for the prints that were on that sardine can from the motel cabin." Wade's dark blue eyes crinkled at the corners. "That same guy left a few of his fingerprints on the car, and they are similar to some partials on the drug containers."

"Wonderful." Tony pulled a couple of dinner plates from the cabinet and loaded them up with enormous slices of pie.

Wade didn't waste any time. The moment that he settled on a chair, he shoveled a huge bite of pie into his mouth. A moan of pleasure accompanied the aroma of apples. "That's so good."

For a moment, work was forgotten as they both enjoyed the first pleasures of the dessert. "Okay, I can think now." Tony grinned. "I thought I'd never get to taste it. Let's see who that fancy fingerprint education has turned up."

Tony pulled the paper from underneath Wade's elbow and began to read it out loud. "Peter 'Sammy' Samson." He studied the photographs. Sammy did not look like a handsome man. "My, my, looking at the length of this, I'm can see that Sammy has not been a good boy. Let's see what he has been doing in other states." As he read, he ate slowly, savoring each delicious morsel.

Wade cleared his throat. "Care to share?"

"Didn't you read all this?" Tony watched Wade wielding his fork.

"Not all of it, just enough to see that it wasn't Quentin." The skin at the corners of Wade's eyes creased with his smile. "I was so excited that I got a positive hit, I had to come and brag on myself."

"Good job. I see that he has enjoyed room and board in both Texas and Georgia. Most of the charges seem to be related to burglary and drug possession." As he chewed, Tony examined the photographs, full front and profile. Sammy's left eye looked normal but the right one appeared to be slightly crossed as it peered through a mop of tangled dark hair. A scruffy mustache covered his lips. "Not exactly a beauty, is he? Do you remember seeing him around town?"

"Nope, and I've already made copies of this for everyone. I said to be on the lookout for him." Wade swallowed his last bite of pie and eyed the slices left in the pie pan. "Read on down to where it describes his tattoos. I did study that. Those 'Hate' and 'Kill' tattoos on his knuckles have to be prison tattoos. I'll bet you a dollar he and our mysterious Mr. Mize were in the same prison."

"Could be," Tony shrugged. "But those are not uncommon prison sentiments. The drug possession charges interest me a lot though. I am very curious about the current whereabouts of our new boy. When I talked to Kenneth with the drug task force, he said that those serial numbers on the Oxy match up with some bottles missing from a shipment in Kentucky."

"So do you think this is a case of a falling out between business partners?"

"I have no clue. He's on parole, so contact Georgia and see what they know about his last knowns. They are not going to like hearing where we found his fingerprints." Tony wanted to lick the plate but settled for scraping the last tiny bits with the side of his fork. "I don't suppose you have any more on Mize, Hub or whatever?"

"Not yet, but it takes longer if they are partials."

The lunchroom shared dishes and appliances with the jail kitchen. Daffodil Flowers Smith, Blossom's oldest sister, cooked for the jail and ran a tight ship. She considered this her domain, her kitchen. Anyone who left a mess would hear about it and then be barred from the area. Respecting her rules both men put their plates and forks in the dishwasher. Then they checked that they hadn't made a mess on the table before they headed back to Tony's office.

"If I could have gotten a clear set from all five fingers on one hand, we would be done." Obviously thinking about the process, Wade shivered and his face lost some of its color. Working with the distorted fingers was a singularly unpleasant duty.

The expression on his face made Tony grin. "Really enjoyed that, did you?" Wade's expression promised retribution, but before he could say a word, Tony's desk phone started ringing. His intercom and the cellular phone in his pocket joined in almost simultaneously. "What in the . . . ?" Tony pushed the intercom button as he reached for the tiny phone.

Wade lifted the receiver.

Ruth Ann's voice came through the intercom. "Theo's found a body."

Theo's voice came through the cell phone. "I found a body."

The receiver pressed to his head, Wade said, "We just heard. Theo's found a body."

CHAPTER THIRTEEN

When Theo left Nina's house, she felt better. Her friend's spirits had revived in spite of the problems she suffered. Daniel's defection hurt, but Theo suspected that Nina didn't really miss him.

From Theo's standpoint, having Nina's help with the new patterns lifted a weight from her shoulders. She knew the quilt tops would be sewn soon and that they would be constructed perfectly. Nina's workmanship was superb. If Theo's pattern had an error in it, Nina would find the flaw and tell her all about it.

Theo inhaled, enjoying the hint of wood smoke coming from one of the other houses. Nina lived in one of the new homes built along the stream that flowed from the Great Smoky Mountain National Park. Only a few years earlier, the land had been part of the McMahan family farm, a farm that produced more brambles than it did anything else but children.

Seeing the vision of prosperity and determining that it exceeded the merits of tradition, Nina's father subdivided the farm into two- and three-acre lots. Individuals built large single-family homes within the first year. Old man McMahan kept the best lot for himself and gave the second best to his only daughter, Nina. In point of fact, the land and house still belonged to him.

What had chafed Daniel Crisp turned out to be a blessing for his wife. Nina's husband could not sell the house, nor could he make any kind of claim on the property. Even if she had no money, she would have a home.

Old man McMahan wanted to preserve as much of the natural beauty of the area as he could and still make a killing in the real estate market. To that end, he made plans for wilderness areas. He protected the plots by deeding them to the county. One of those formed a small, forested park in the very center of the little subdivision.

The redbud trees were just getting ready to start blooming. Drawn by their beauty, Theo wandered in and smiled to see the first magenta blossom unfurling. Everything pointed to this being an early spring. Checking for further signs, she looked under the trees for any early blooming flowers. Delighted when she spied a few early yellow violets, the blossoms just peeping through a layer of dead leaves, she knelt down. Brushing away a few of the damp leaves that clung to the petals so that she could admire the dainty yellow faces, it took her a few seconds to identify the human hand only inches away from her own. In contrast to her small, pale hand, the skin on the other looked like it had been freeze-dried.

With a gasp, Theo jerked upright and immediately started digging in her purse. "Thank goodness for cell phones." She mumbled to herself as she found her phone in the bottom of her purse. She pushed the button that automatically dialed 911.

Rex Satterfield's nasal voice asking her the nature of her emergency jarred her into more coherent thoughts. "Hey, Rex, this is Theo. Now that you ask, I guess I really don't have an emergency. I've found a body or part of a body, but even I can tell that it has been dead for quite awhile." When she realized she was babbling, she pulled herself together and gave Rex a brief description of her discovery and location. She disconnected and dialed Tony's number. When he answered, she breathed a sigh of relief. "Tony, guess what?"

"I know, I know. You found a body." His words crackled

through the phone followed by another sound.

Recognizing his laughter, Theo frowned. "It's not funny."

Tony stood with his arms crossed over his chest, his eyes trained on Theo's face. Only a hint of freckles gave it any color. She hadn't found a body after all. It turned out to be only part of a body, just a hand and forearm, but it was human. She had a right to be unnerved.

Doc Nash had been consulted by telephone and he had flatly refused to come to the scene. He claimed that he needed more than one body part to determine if someone was deceased. Growing testier by the second, the man finally shouted that the loss of one arm was not enough. A head, yes; an arm, no.

Tony thought the doctor sounded even more out of sorts than usual.

Theo leaned against the blooming redbud, all but surrounded by her husband. "I know you'd prefer I call you before I call 911, Tony, but I swear it was almost like someone else was doing it and all I was doing was watching." Theo peeked around his shoulder and eyed the deputies as they marked off the area with yellow tape. "The moment I heard Rex's voice, it dawned on me what I had done, and now everyone with a scanner or everyone who knows someone with a scanner is going to come this way."

Knowing that his wife was right only made Tony's frown deepen. He tried to cheer up both of them. "Maybe no one heard it."

The line of onlookers forming near the road squashed that idea. Drawn out by the activity in their park, the residents of the area clustered together near Nina's yard. Nina herself stood braced with a pair of crutches, watching everything through binoculars.

Tony waved.

Park County was too small and too poor to have many of the resources available in the larger counties. One thing they could not afford was a trained canine officer. Like the fire department, the search and rescue team consisted of a small cluster of trained and dedicated volunteers. Balanced on the line between professional and volunteer were Deputy Mike Ott and his bloodhound, Dammit.

Mike didn't look like a cop. Most of the time, he didn't even look like an adult, even though he was about thirty-two. He was the average man. Average height, slightly less than average weight, his features were neither unattractive nor handsome. Born to do undercover work, Mike starred in every school play from kindergarten through high school and had even been a drama major at UT. Now he dedicated himself to law enforcement and had become so good at undercover work that other agencies wanted to borrow him. Tony didn't know what he would do without him.

Dammit, the bloodhound, was his baby. The huge, russet and black dog, with acres of skin hanging from its face, adored Mike. They first met when Claude Marmot, the area's professional trash hauler, called to report a case of animal cruelty.

Marmot-the-Varmint, as most people referred to him, spent a fair amount of time digging through the trash he carried to the dump. One day, he spotted a man beating a big puppy with a tire iron. When he refused to stop, Claude picked up a length of pipe and proceeded to give the man a taste of his own medicine.

The dog's owner had vanished by the time that Mike arrived to investigate. Mike fell in love at first sight. After the veterinarian checked the puppy for injuries, Mike took him to his home. He named the puppy Sam, but the name didn't stick. He spent more time calling it Dammit than Sam. The dog grew to be stubborn, headstrong, irritating, opinionated and bigger than his car. Mike claimed he was perfect and took him everywhere.

Over the past couple of years, Mike worked hard to train the dog to track, and it had paid off. One time Dammit had found a couple of lost campers and another time an old woman with Alzheimer's disease who had slipped away from her caregiver. Now Mike and Dammit were preparing to comb this area.

Tony couldn't imagine how they could do a decent search of this area without a dog. The terrain in the McMahan subdivision was rough and heavily wooded. There was only one small stand of evergreen trees. The other trees in the park had been shedding leaves for hundreds of years. It would be impossible to sweep them all aside to look for the rest of their new body. With any luck, Dammit would be able to locate it. After all, if he could track the scent of someone moving down the road in a car, finding something like this should be a snap.

"What do you think?" Theo asked as she watched man and dog working together.

"I don't want to think about it." Tony lifted a curl away from her face and bent over to look directly into her eyes. Behind her lenses, her hazel gold eyes looked huge and innocent. "If that's part of Nina's husband, I have only two suspects."

"Really?" Theo's eyes searched his face. "Who are they?"

"Let's just say that if it's him, you're only number two on my list." The way Theo's mouth opened into a silent O amused him. He wasn't really concerned. He knew that if the hand was part of Daniel Crisp and Theo knew anything about it, she would have left it alone or, more likely, buried it.

Tony walked Theo to her minivan in silence. As she reached to close the door, the afternoon sunlight glinted on her wedding band. It reminded him that he still hadn't talked to Quentin about his cousin's wife. Hadn't he claimed that the man wasn't married while his congregation said the opposite? He needed to find that answer. Leaving Mike in charge, he headed back to town. If Quentin had sobered enough, Tony would take him over to the morgue and let him identify the body.

Tony entered the county communications office.

From his chair, dispatcher Rex Satterfield could keep an eye on the padded cell and on the holding cell at the other side of the room. The jail itself was behind another set of security doors. At the moment, Rex was talking to the deputies on duty. As part of his job, he monitored their activities and locations. He glanced up at Tony.

"Mike has found a few more body parts." Rex might have been describing lost library books for all of the emotion he expressed. "That dog of his is really something, isn't he?" He didn't even pause to see if Tony had a response. "Sheila is on her way back without Quentin's girlfriend. Evidently Sheila couldn't find her up at the house, and now Sheila's on her way to help Mike. Darren is at lunch with his intended, and Wade is in his cubicle." Rex had earned his reputation for being completely unflappable. "No one has reported seeing the fugitive Mr. Samson."

"Thanks, Rex, how's our visitor?" Tony inclined his head in the direction of the padded cell. "Do you think Quentin is coherent?"

The dispatcher burst out laughing. It sounded like a donkey braying. "Oh, man, not even close. He's in there talking to his regular visitors."

"Visitors?" Since visitors were never allowed in this area, Tony found Rex's comment intriguing. He craned his neck to see the entire area around the cell. It was empty.

"Yeah, his regular visitors are bats. A whole group of invisible bats, or is it a herd?" Rex paused to wipe his streaming eyes. "Animal-type bats, not baseball. The last time he spent some time in here, he told me all about them."

Tony strolled over to the cell and studied Quentin. He quickly surmised that the bats were frequent visitors in Quentin's personal universe because he apparently knew all of them by name. They seemed to be hanging from the ceiling in one corner of the padded cell but, of course, Tony couldn't tell that for sure. Eavesdropping on the conversation, he did learn that one of the bats was named Elvis. Quentin seemed to be pleading with Elvis for permission to sing along, promising to only sing harmony and backup. Evidently his plea succeeded and Elvis agreed, because Quentin began warming up his voice with a series of commercial jingles.

Quentin's singing voice was a pleasant baritone that surprised Tony. Standing in the corner of the cell, Quentin began to croon, "In the Ghetto." Shaking his head, Tony backed away from the door and met Rex's amused gaze. "Nope. He's not even close to our planet." It would probably be hours before his orbit brought him near earth again. Tony couldn't wait that long.

Wade saved the day. Carrying a handful of papers, he found Tony watching Quentin. "I know who our corpse is. We don't have to wait for Quentin to land." He paused to listen when Quentin, and presumably Elvis, launched into a heartfelt version of "Love Me Tender."

Rex grinned. "That one's my personal favorite. They do a real nice job with that one." He turned back to his screen.

"Which corpse?" Tony just loved to pull Wade's chain. The younger man made it almost too easy.

"The first one." To all appearances, unperturbed, Wade held up his printout. "Harold Usher Brown, but he goes by Hub. He has a record of multiple offenses. His last known address was Lee State Prison in Georgia."

"Paroled?"

"Nope. He served his time and got out eight years ago. He's been off the Georgia radar ever since."

"Harold Brown. I know that name, but why? What had the late Mr. Brown been doing to earn his room and board?" Tony massaged his scalp and the back of his neck.

Wade ran his finger down the list. "Just about everything. Mostly small time, until he killed a man in a bar fight and had to do real time. Let's see. Grand theft auto, larceny, domestic violence, assault." Wade shook his head. "That's a long way from being a preacher."

Tony nodded and started pacing. "Why is that name so familiar?" A tiny blob of apple pie filling clinging to Wade's tie caught his eye. He stopped abruptly. "Ruby."

"Ruby?" Clearly confused, Wade looked over the paper he held, reading the information again. "What's she got to do with this?"

"I'm not sure." Tony headed for the Blazer. "Maybe everything. You're about to find out."

CHAPTER FOURTEEN

"How long have you been Ruby?" Tony took a sip of coffee and watched a range of emotions chase across her face. He knew part of the story because she came to him and told him about herself shortly after he won the election. That had been two and a half years ago.

Ruby glanced at Wade before returning her gaze to Tony. An untouched stoneware coffee mug rested on the table in front of her. "Five years now." A smile of pure delight illuminated her face "Old Ruby even sent me a pink flamingo key chain for an anniversary present."

Before joining the two lawmen on the café deck, Ruby had removed her apron and donned a short jacket of soft, red fleece woven with a pattern of black horses. She stroked the sleeve with one finger and grinned at him. "I talked to Old Ruby just last week and she said that living in an RV in Florida is almost heaven. It is what she was born to do and she will never miss being cold."

Tony had to laugh. Even in the heat of summer, Old Ruby had worn a sweater under her apron. She had not been the first Ruby, but she was the one who had held the title for the longest. Old Ruby was the most recent one. Ruby didn't have to be a woman. For a while Ruby had been a beefy man with a penchant for bar fights. The name simply went with the business. Little Ruby's birth certificate and driver's license listed her as Maria Costello. Her marriage certificate listed her as the wife of Harold Usher Brown.

On the back deck of Ruby's Café, the sun streamed through the lattice and warmed the air, but it stayed cool enough that they were comfortable in their jackets. From where they sat they had a good view of the Smokies. The almost constant haze that had given them their name had lessened and they appeared closer than usual.

The parking spot where the Focus station wagon had been was in Tony's line of sight but not Ruby's. For a little privacy, Tony had suggested they might enjoy sitting outside while he asked Little Ruby a few questions. Once there, he hesitated while he decided what approach to take.

"Why are you asking this today?" Ruby's voice was soft and her expression of confusion mirrored that of the deputy. "Does this have something to do with the car Blossom found in the parking lot?"

"Yes, it does." That was the opening Tony needed. "I'm afraid I have some bad news for you." He cleared his throat. He hated delivering bad news and watched as Ruby released her mug and gripped the edge of the table with her fingertips. The bones gleamed under her skin. Clearly, she needed to physically brace herself against coming pain.

"What happened?"

"It appears that your husband is dead." Tony watched her process the information. First he saw relief that the news wasn't what she expected. The relief was quickly replaced by an expression of seething anger mixed with outright fear. Fascinating.

"No, he can't be! That's not right!" Ruby shouted. "Not yet. I have to talk to him first."

"Husband?" Wade looked as if he had come into a movie in the middle. His head swiveled as he looked from face to face. "Whose husband?"

Tony took Ruby's hands and held them tightly. Even though

she had just released her warm coffee cup, they felt like ice. "The man in the car." He cleared his throat as he tipped his head in the direction of the parking lot. "The driver's license he carried identified him as John Mize, but his fingerprints identified him as Harold Usher Brown."

As the words sank in, Ruby's big brown eyes widened, swallowing her face as they filled with tears. "Was he alone?" Although she spoke softly, she became frantic, struggling against his restraining hands. The blood drained from her face, making her look like she had been carved from wax.

"Yes. No one else was in the car." Tony released her hands and reached into his pocket for his handkerchief. He doubted if she realized that tears were streaming down her face. He meant the glance that he gave Wade to keep the young deputy silent. It worked.

"There were snakes and boxes for the snakes, but nothing that would indicate anyone else has been traveling with him."

"Snakes? Why would he have the snakes with him?" A series of violent shudders racked her whole body, and then she exhaled in a great gust of air. "He had to be just passing through. Wasn't he? Maybe he left her at the motel where he was staying. Have you checked them all?"

Seeing signs of hope appear on her face, Tony shook his head, cutting off her words. "No, Ruby. He's been staying with relatives in the area and has been here for a while. He spent time over in Blount County before coming here. Alone." She flinched with each word as if they caused her physical pain. He felt like a bully delivering one blow after another.

Eyes glassy, Ruby shook her head. "That doesn't make any sense. This is a small town. Why wouldn't we see him? What was he doing here? Wouldn't she have to be with him?" With each word, her voice rose until it turned into a scream. "Where is she? Where's my baby?"

Those words sent Wade surging to his feet. "Baby?"

At his sudden movement, Ruby looked up at the confused young man. One glance quieted her. She inhaled and released the air in a long, unsteady breath.

"I told the sheriff this story a long time ago but asked him to keep it private. You know how things get around in this town?" She waved him back into his chair. "I married Hub just before I turned sixteen." Remembered pain twisted her face. "To be honest, my mother arranged for me to marry him. She threatened to drag me to the altar and beat me with a stick until I agreed to the marriage."

Wade looked shocked. "Why did she want you to marry him? He had to be much older than you were, because Doc Nash thinks he was in his mid-forties." He didn't give her a chance to answer before he said, "Why didn't she marry him herself?"

That comment did bring a smile to her face. "He wouldn't have her. He liked girls, not middle-aged women."

"Did she know about his prison record? Did you know that he had killed a man in a bar fight?" Wade shook his head. "The man deals in drugs and pornography."

"Oh, yes, she knew all about him and loved him for it." Ruby's face became pinched and she played with her empty coffee mug. "He confessed his sins to his congregation at least four times a week. It was his thing, you know, about how he had changed his life in prison, memorized the Bible, and was spreading the word."

Tony leaned forward. "He truly memorized the Bible? Pops Ogle said that too, but it sounded so . . . so amazing."

"Most of it, I'd say. He had an almost photographic memory, so he could pull out the passage that he wanted and quote chapter and verse, but he twisted it to suit himself." It took both hands, but Ruby managed to lift the cup to her lips. "He thought he was God's equal. With his silver tongue and evil ways, he preached for the power it gave him and not for any other reason. I always thought he was the devil incarnate."

Her eyes lifted to the mountains, and Tony thought she might have been praying.

"Unlike me, my mother thought that he was God and all the angels rolled into one. So, you can imagine that when he mentioned he wanted to marry me, she was honored by his offer. I didn't want to have any part of him and tried to run away. Mama caught me climbing out the window." Her breathing became shallow. "So, I married him. He broke my arm on our wedding night. Married life went downhill from there."

Although the story was not new to him, hearing it again made Tony feel as savage as if all of the layers of civilization were just a veneer. He wasn't sure if her mother or her husband had been the more cruel of the pair. A glance at Wade's face showed him the same outrage. Neither said a word. They just let her tell the story.

"You've heard the expression 'barefoot and pregnant'? It wasn't long before that was my life. We moved constantly. He took me to church with him, but I was not allowed to talk to anyone. He made me sit next to him and hold the box of snakes." She shuddered. "I had no telephone, no money, no friends, no shoes and every day I was getting bigger and bigger. Only when I grew big as a whale did he leave me at home." Unconsciously her hand dropped to her flat belly.

"He wanted a son. I had a girl. She was perfect, and I named her Anna." In her anguish, Ruby couldn't continue and her words faltered to a stop.

Tony finished the story. "When they got home from the hospital, he went wild and almost beat Ruby to death. Her injuries were so bad that she had to stay in a hospital in Atlanta for almost a month. By the time she could get around again,

Mr. Brown had vanished and so had the baby. We are still looking for Anna."

No one spoke for several minutes. Lost in thought, Wade
fiddled with the earpiece on his sunglasses. "Did you ever hear
anything about her?"

"No." Ruby answered. "The message he left with my mother
said that I was a bad mother and that he had to protect Anna
from me. For the baby's sake, he wanted to make sure I would
not see her again until I mended my evil ways."

"Then what happened?"

"They both disappeared without a trace."

"And your mother," said Wade. "Did she take your side then?"

"No. She blamed me for everything."

"Did you go to the police?"

"Yes. The Atlanta police were very kind, but what could they
do? They were understaffed and she belonged as much to my
husband as she did to me. For all anyone could say for sure, he
had taken the baby and gone on trip. My mother didn't help
my case and there was no real proof that he had even been the
reason I ended up in the hospital. I could have fallen off a
bridge. Maybe they were just waiting for my health to improve.
I don't know." She traced a stain on the table. "I started going
to a support group for battered women and I got my GED and
then I got a job."

"How did you end up here?" Wade made a gesture that
encompassed the café, the town and the area. "Did you know
someone in the area?"

Ruby shook her head. "One day I realized that no matter
much I wanted Anna, Hub would never bring her back. By
then, two years had passed with no word about them. I hired a
private detective to keep searching for her and then loaded
everything I owned in my car. I decided to let fate determine
where I would live."

Almost as one, they all looked at the rusted-out, ancient Honda that Ruby still drove. "It broke down here and Old Ruby took me in." She did smile then. "And the rest, as they say, is history."

Tony didn't smile. "I know that Mike takes his vacation each year and spends it searching for Anna and Hub."

Ruby froze, suddenly wary. "Yes?"

"Any chance that he found Hub?"

CHAPTER FIFTEEN

That evening, Theo couldn't help but notice that Tony behaved in a most peculiar manner. She was accustomed to Tony's daydreaming, especially when he was thinking about the book he was writing. This felt different. His welcome home kiss and hug had been too much. It wasn't passion. It was more like he was saying goodbye.

After dinner, he became agitated when the boys wanted to play outside after dark. His restlessness increased when they did not seem pleased by his offer to join them. Theo thought that he acted as if he had to spend every second with them because he might never play with them again.

"Leave the boys alone and sit down." Stomach churning, Theo dropped onto the kitchen chair across the table from him and continued to clutch the damp dishtowel with both hands. She blurted out the first thing that popped into her head. "Are you thinking of leaving us?" She couldn't help but wonder if Nina's husband had been like on his last night with his family.

"Heavens, no." Wide-eyed, Tony looked at her like she had zapped him with a bolt of lightning and then had grown two heads. "Why would you think that?" He leaned forward to hear her whispered reply.

"Because you are acting like you are saying goodbye to us, and because the boys and I have no intention of leaving you, I thought mayb—." She stopped and then started again. "Why are you acting so peculiar tonight? You're distant and yet possessive of the boys." With a shrug, she looked down at the dish-towel she had tied into a knot. "I know that if someone had threatened us, you'd have a knife in your teeth and a gun in each hand."

She could feel hot tears welling in her eyes even as he reached for her hands. Turning her head, she hoped he wouldn't see them. She tightened her grip on the towel.

He covered her hands with his. They felt warm and strong and some of the tension eased.

"This thing with Nina really has made you jumpy, hasn't it?" When she nodded, Tony frowned. "You have to believe that I will never leave you. Cross my heart." Freeing his right hand, he made an X over the left side of his chest.

She believed him. Finally, she managed to give him a small smile. He grinned in response. She thought his pirate's grin made him look just like Jamie, only without the mop of blond hair.

"A knife in my teeth, huh? I guess I'll have to get an earring, too." He pulled the dishtowel out of her hands and attempted to tie it around his head.

"Well, then, what *is* going on?" She had to laugh. He looked absolutely silly. A bright yellow lemon decorated the corner of the dishtowel that he'd draped over one eye.

Before he could decide what to tell her, the telephone inter-rupted. Karen Claybough, Wade's sister, had recently started working as the evening dispatcher.

"Uh, Sheriff, I would never bother you at home, and it's, uh, well, not exactly an emergency, but uh, I talked to Wade and he said that if I didn't call you, he would."

"What's up, Karen?" Tony relaxed. If Karen had an emer-gency, she wouldn't be dithering around.

"Lady Godiva is riding through the cemetery and Sheila is

off duty, so Wade said that you should get the call. I'm really sorry."

Tony groaned. Lady Godiva's real name was Lucy Smith. Fifty-something, Lucy had developed a fondness for topless horseback riding. Two or three times a year, her husband would lose her and she would show up in town, usually after dark. As the only female officer, Sheila usually got the call to round her up.

Tony's name followed Sheila's on the call list. For some reason, all of the other deputies seemed to frighten her. Lucy functioned very well in spite of having slightly less than average intelligence. A charming, sweet woman, she gave birth to and raised two perfectly normal children. Lately, though, topless riding seemed to fulfill some primal need. It only became a problem when she rode into town.

"Dammit, Karen, where is her husband? Why can't he keep those damned horses locked in the barn at night?"

"I don't know, sir." Karen sounded confused. "I tried calling him, but he isn't answering the telephone."

"He's probably out looking for her." Resignation laced every word. "Okay, I'll go get her and take her home. You get whoever is handling animal control this week to meet me at the cemetery. I assume Lucy is riding that overweight red roan. That damned animal hates me and it will try to take a chunk out of me if I turn my back on it. I'm sure not responsible for taking it home." When he disconnected the phone, one glance at his wife's amused expression told Tony that he didn't need to explain.

While he got ready, Theo rummaged in the closet, looking for an old shirt for him to give Lucy. He could hear Theo mumbling that this must be the way Lucy got new clothes because she never returned anything.

Tony couldn't disagree.

He stomped down the stairs, "You know, don't you, that the

sheriffs in larger counties are mostly administrators. I'll bet they
don't get called out after dinner to chase Lady Godiva through
a creepy, dark cemetery. They get to stay home and watch
basketball on the television like normal people."

Theo rolled her eyes. She heard this complaint all the time.
"I suppose you'd rather do paperwork and attend meetings all
day?"

"No way." He all but ripped the old T-shirt from her hand
and headed for the door. "When I can cavort in the moonlight
with a half-naked woman? Who needs paperwork?" His description left out the fact the middle-aged woman was not exactly
easy on the eyes.

The sound of Theo's laughter followed him out the door.

Tony awakened to the sound of rain pounding on the roof.
Knowing that the saturated ground could absorb no more water,
he groaned. He wondered what was happening at the crossroad.
At the lowest point in the county, the crossroad of Main Street
and the almost-highway known as Glover Road was always the
first place to flood. He'd drive by there on his way to work and
check on it.

This Saturday would be just another day of work.

By the time he showered and dressed, Theo had coffee ready.
Wandering into the kitchen, he paused to enjoy the moment.
For him the aroma rising from the coffeepot almost surpassed
the taste.

The boys looked content, curled up in front of the television
watching cartoons. A fire crackled in the hearth. Their eyes were
glued the screen. Stretched across their feet, Daisy was cleaning
their cereal bowls with her big, pink tongue.

Tony paused to tickle the boys. Jamie retaliated by scuttling
out of his nest and jumping onto his father's back. He wrapped
his thin arms around Tony's neck and hung on like a barnacle

in Superman pajamas.

"D-ad, cartoons are on." Giggling, Chris pulled a flannel quilt over his head and rolled around on the floor.

With Jamie still clinging to his back, Tony kissed the back of Theo's neck and poured himself a cup of coffee. Although clearly amused by the antics of her family, she seemed distracted.

"What's wrong?"

"Wrong? What could be more fun than a rainy Saturday with two dead bodies to discuss? It will be bedlam at the shop." Theo put frozen pancakes on a plate and popped it in the microwave. She eyed his uniform. "Will you have to work all day?"

"I'm afraid so." He would much prefer to spend his Saturday working on his book or just hanging out with the boys. When he took the job as sheriff, he knew there would be times that his job would dictate his schedule. "Murder has to be considered a priority even if the victim *was* scum."

He wondered if Mike and Dammit had found enough of a body to make an identification possible. What if they had found Daniel Crisp? No one but Nina claimed to have information on where he went. When he'd asked Theo about it, even she hadn't seen the note. On the other hand, no one had expressed any concern about his absence.

Theo looked like she was going to ask him something and then changed her mind. "Maybe I'll see if Karissa can stay with the boys today. They'll go nuts if they are locked inside at the shop."

"Sounds good to me." Tony eyed her pancakes. "Any more of those?"

Tony stopped at the newspaper office on his way to work. He carried with him an old police-booking photograph of Harold Usher Brown. The face, except for the oddly shortened eyelashes, did not much resemble the corpse that had been found in the car.

Winifred was editor, reporter and janitor at the little office.

The newspaper came out twice a week, Monday and Thursday evenings. Most people in the county read it from cover to cover because it contained lots of valuable information, if not news. There were listings of marriages and divorces, along with the listings of tickets written for everything from loose hogs to driving under the influence. Parents read the paper to learn who their children should not be dating.

"To what do I owe the honor of this visit?" Winifred's face pinched into a point.

Tony had not been Winifred's favorite person ever since he had refused to go to the high school prom with her over twenty years ago. Since then, they developed a working relationship, but she had a chip on her shoulder.

He smiled. "I have a photo that the department would like you to publish. Any information we can get about his recent contacts and activities would be appreciated."

Winifred studied the mug shot. "It's not a great photo. It could be my Uncle Elmer."

"I know, but it's the best we have for now. Can you clean it up a bit?"

"Some. I'll put it on the front page of the next edition." Winifred mumbled but did not look up from the photo. "You ought to ask Stan about him."

"Stan?" Tony could only think of one Stan, and he hadn't seemed to know the dead man. "Stan-the-Snakeman?"

"Yep. Stan Livingston and this man were yelling at each other in the parking lot of the Food City. I'd know that yellow truck anywhere, and those weirdo eyelashes aren't too easy to forget either." She thumped the photograph for emphasis. "Not that Stan is my favorite citizen, but this guy gave me the creeps."

"Do you know what they were arguing about? Could you

pick out any words?" Even as he asked, Tony found himself wondering what Winifred had against Stan.

"Nope." Winifred placed the photo gently on the counter. "It didn't look like either of their vehicles got dinged in the parking lot, you know. It looked personal."

The rain worsened.

At the station, Tony found Mike sitting in the hallway, waiting for him. Tony thought that he looked like he had aged about twenty years overnight. Eyes closed, he sat slumped on his spine on the plastic chair set aside for visitors. He still wore his uniform but it looked soggy. He shivered. Next to him, Dammit sprawled on the floor, sleeping, his back pressed against the wall. His long legs twitched with every snore that shook his heavy frame. The loose chestnut skin of his face pooled on the floor along with his ears, making it look as if his head had melted. The heavy towel that Mike had used to dry the dog only added to that impression. The dog used it for a pillow.

Seeing Tony, Mike jumped to attention. He held a sheaf of papers with both shaking hands. "Good morning, Sheriff."

Tony felt sorry for him.

Mike probably hadn't gotten any more sleep the previous night than Tony had. The moonlight had been chased away by cold rain mixed with snow. By the time he got Lucy to her home and then to his own, he'd felt as frosty as an ice cube. Once in bed, it seemed to take forever until he warmed up. Then, visions of the recent events began flashing through his brain like a slide show, keeping him awake.

In spite of his turmoil about Mike searching for Ruby's baby, he knew in his heart that his deputy had not been responsible for her husband's death. At least the man would not have died until Mike had the answer to every one of his questions.

"Might as well come in and sit down." Tony opened his door

and made Mike precede him. He hung his dripping jacket on its hook. "Let's start with your search from yesterday. What did you find out at McMahan's farm?"

Mike remained standing. "According to Doc Nash, Dammit found enough pieces to make an adult male. The skull and pelvis established that much. We put everything we found into one body bag and now it is on the way to the state lab. Someone there will have to decide if all the pieces are from one guy and try to identify him. We didn't find three arms or anything weird like that. Doc didn't see any obvious cause of death like a bullet hole in the skull." He pressed the heels of his hands against his eyes. "He did notice something odd though. It seems that all of the upper teeth are gone and we never found the jawbone, so dental records won't help. Doc couldn't tell if the guy had teeth before his death." Rubbing the stubble on his cheek, Mike seemed surprised that he hadn't shaved. "Must have missed a spot this morning."

"How's Ruby?" Tony leaned back in his chair and fiddled with a pen, releasing the cap and then popping it back into place with his thumb. His eyes never left Mike's face.

"Frantic." Mike strode forward, stopping just short of the desk. "I swear to God, Sheriff, I had no idea that her husband was anywhere in the state." His skin turned gray. "If I had known, you can bet that I would have treated him like a prince."

"At least until you learned what you needed to know." The clicking sound made by the pen cap continued, neither speeding up nor slowing down.

"True."

"Then what?"

"I don't know." Mike shrugged and stared at the wall behind Tony's head for a long moment before looking back into Tony's eyes. "I don't think of myself as a violent man, but maybe it's better that I don't have to find out if I'm capable of doing

143

something like that." A shiver ran through him. "All those poisonous snakes in the car. The thought gives me the willies."

Tony nodded, but his expression did not change. "You don't mind showing me your handcuffs, do you?"

Stone-faced, Mike dropped both pairs that he customarily carried onto Tony's deck. "They are mine. I always have my initials etched on them."

"I know that, but you could have a drawer full of them at home." Tony kept his voice mild, but there was a definite warning in it. He barely glanced at the cuffs before he handed them back to Mike and then rose from his chair and crossed to a small cabinet by the door. He pulled a blanket from the stack inside. "Put those cuffs away, sit down and tell me what you know for sure about Harold Brown. I'd guess that you are our resident expert on the man."

Mike settled onto the chair and Tony tossed him the lightweight blanket. "Thanks, boss," he said as he wrapped it around himself. "I can tell you that he was born and raised in North Carolina, not too far from here. His father bootlegged tobacco, strictly small time, and ran a little still on the side. All I've learned about him makes me think that our Mr. Brown discovered that stealing produced higher profits for even less work than his father did and took to a life of crime like the proverbial duck to water."

Mike yawned. "He didn't finish high school. After he left home, he drifted in and out of every state in the southeast. You've seen his sheet. Arrests for robbery, drug possession, larceny plus innumerable smaller offensives. No convictions for anything major until he killed a man in a bar in Georgia. There wasn't even much of a fight. Witnesses said that the other guy complained about something petty and Hub just pulled out an old revolver and hauled off and shot the man, right between the eyes."

"Sounds like a gem." Closing his eyes, Tony rubbed the side of his nose with the side of his index finger. "So when did he take up serpents and religion, in general?"

"Prison." Mike laced his fingers together. "Information gets a little more vague here, but evidently he had a near photographic memory and he claimed to have memorized the entire Bible. He did memorize at least most of the New Testament. I have to say that impresses me. I've never even read it cover to cover. If he had used his abilities in a positive manner, who knows what he might have accomplished, but he didn't."

The sound of Dammit snoring in the hallway came through the open door. Mike appeared to relax a bit.

"Somewhere along the way, he decided that being a preacher would act like a free pass. His redemption and calling to religion impressed all kinds of people after he was released." Mike shook his head in disbelief. "Since he served his whole sentence, there was no question of him violating parole. He has been involved in some questionable activities."

"Like what?" Tony sat forward. "Anything that might supply motive?"

"Nothing definite. Relatives of an elderly woman in Columbus, Georgia, filed a complaint. They were sure he asked her for money and was the reason that she made some very large cash withdrawals." Mike rubbed his eyes again. "There was no proof of wrongdoing, and she flatly denied it, so it was dropped."

"Anything else?"

"Only whispers. Never any proof. Never any witnesses." Mike frowned. "He moved a lot."

"When you went on vacation last year and searched for him, what did you learn?" From the corner of his eye, Tony watched as Dammit wandered through the doorway and stopped and yawned before resting his enormous head on Mike's knee.

"He left Georgia and his congregation there in the fall. He

told them that he had been called to preach in Mississippi and had them take up a special offering." Mike's eyes dropped away as his hands seemed to disappear into the dog's loose skin. Petting the dog appeared to be his focus, but his eyes were haunted as they returned to meet Tony's. "He never said anything to anyone there about his ever having a wife or a little girl. Not one word."

"That's probably when he headed up this way."

Mike nodded. "I completely lost track of him." A faint smile lifted one corner of his mouth. "It might have helped if I'd known that he was some shirttail cousin of Quentin's."

"True, but maybe not." Tony pointed to the open doorway with his thumb. "Go home. Get some sleep. You and Dammit both look like hell."

As Tony watched the man and dog vanish, he thought that he understood and sympathized with Mike, but he realized that he had no true understanding of Hub's mind. A man who would steal his own child away from her mother, beat any woman, or use his ability with words to fleece a congregation seemed as far from his own personality as anyone could get.

The man deserved killing, no doubt about it, but Tony believed that the deed should have been done by the state, not by a private party, at least not in his county. He could feel the heat of anger surge through his veins. Whoever had done it had better stay away from Tony's family. He groaned. Maybe Theo was right about the knife in his teeth and guns blazing. He certainly felt murderous enough.

Minutes after Mike left, Ruth Ann buzzed him on the intercom. "Sheriff?" Her voice carried through the room, as soft as air and as sweet as honeysuckle. As far as he was concerned, that sound carried more menace than the rattles on a snake. "You have a visitor."

Tony wanted to fling himself under his desk and hide.

CHAPTER SIXTEEN

"Sheriff, Mr. Lundy is out here." Amusement filtered through Ruth Ann's voice. "He says that he has something important that he needs to tell you."

Tony groaned. Eighty if he was a day, Orvan Lundy seemed to have a burning need to confess to any number of crimes as long as they were ones that he hadn't actually committed. Old Orvan was neither a saint nor a particularly nice man. It wouldn't surprise Tony if the man had committed worse crimes than killing Hub.

"Put him in the greenhouse and give him some coffee, would you? I'll be there in just a few minutes." He thought they might as well let the little guy stew for a while.

Tony could already picture the man. He invariably came dressed in clean, but well-worn, overalls. The collar button on his long sleeve plaid shirt would be fastened. It was part of his outfit, no matter how hot the day. Tony was sure that Orvan would have dyed his gray hair with black shoe polish for the occasion.

A glimmer of amusement lifted Tony's spirits as he recalled one summer day when the air conditioning had been out and Orvan had been confessing to something. The oily shoe polish had melted and dripped down the sides of his face. His attempts to wipe it away had resulted in a series of smudges that resembled jungle camouflage. Tony grinned. Maybe he could use a little amusement after all.

When Tony joined them in the sparsely furnished little room, Ruth Ann and Orvan were chatting companionably about her nail polish. From what Tony could gather, Orvan wondered if she thought that it would make a better hair coloring technique than a scrap of cloth and a tin of shoe polish.

Ruth Ann looked like she might encourage him to try it.

As soon as they spotted him, Orvan jumped to his feet and saluted. His liver-spotted hand hit him square in the right eye and he emitted a squeak.

"Sit down, Orvan. You don't have to salute me. This is not the military for heaven's sake." As the man complied, Tony could see that today his choice of shoe polish had changed from black to more of a reddish-brown. "New hair color?"

"Yes, sir." He lifted his hand almost touching the polish before he lowered it slightly. "Do you like it?"

Tony watched as Orvan smoothed his sideburns, using only the tip of one finger. As usual, he had tinted only the hair on the very top of his head, leaving his sideburns the same soft gray as mouse fur.

"Says oxblood on the tin." Orvan preened.

"Quite nice." Tony settled onto one of the steel chairs that flanked the steel table. Bolts attached the table to the floor. "Ruth Ann said that you have something important to tell me." With a tip of his head he made a pretense of encouraging her to sit down and take notes. In reality, he knew that it would take a stick of dynamite in her manicure drawer to convince her to leave during one of Orvan's confessions.

"She's a real jewel, ain't she?" Orvan cast her a smile of pure adoration, exposing more gaps than teeth. "Generous, too. She give me a cup of coffee." A gentle burp through his uncovered mouth spread the aromas of coffee and whiskey around the table.

"Have you been drinking this morning?" Tony crossed his

arms over his chest and tipped the chair onto the back legs. "You need to be sober to confess."

"Oh, I'm sober. You got to believe that. Just had one little nip to give me the courage. It ain't easy telling you the horrible thing I done, you know. I killed that man." Tears filled his red-rimmed eyes.

Tony thought they looked cloudier than usual. The old man's cataracts were getting worse.

"What man is that?" said Tony.

"You got more than one corpse?" Orvan's expression jumped from desolation to delight. If he had won big money gambling over in Cherokee, he couldn't have looked any happier. "That's really something, ain't it?"

"Who is *your* deceased?" Tony wouldn't have been surprised if somewhere along the way, Orvan had actually killed someone. The old man's life had certainly not been spotless. Someone had suggested once that guilt compelled him to confess, but he still didn't want to go so far as to give the real facts.

"Deceased?" He paused a second to process the question. "Oh, it's that there feller you found in the car. Don't suppose you could tell me about the other one?" Seeing the shake of Tony's head, he looked crestfallen but not surprised. He adjusted the buckle on his overalls. "I put him in the car after I done the deed."

"Really? Why did you do that?"

"Well, I couldn't just leave him laying in the open, could I? Not with the others of his kind around." His expression couldn't have been more horrified if Tony had suggested that he should drink cranberry juice instead of whiskey.

"What do you mean?" The chair legs thumped as they hit the floor and Tony leaned forward, his attention completely focused on the little man. "Others of his kind? What kind is that?"

Orvan laced his fingers and placed them in his lap and stuck out his lower lip. He looked liked a sulky child, albeit an old, old child. "You want to hear this or not?"

Tony had plenty to keep him busy, and the idea of Orvan leaving had a real appeal, but he took a deep breath and nodded.

"I seen him sliding down the wall over at the bank. I recognized him right off and I followed him. I knew that he must be one of those big bats, you know, the poisonous ones, not like them little fellers that eat bugs in the park." His hands twitched and he laced his fingers more tightly. "No sir, he were a genuine one like, oh what's his name?"

"Dracula?" It surprised Tony that Orvan knew enough about what really happened on planet Earth to know about the little brown bats. The previous summer, small wooden houses and tiny bats had been put in the city park to help keep the insect population under control.

"Who?" Orvan looked like he had never heard the name before.

"Dracula?"

"No, I don't believe I've heard that name before." He reached for his coffee, clutching the heavy stoneware mug with both trembling hands. Gnarled and mottled with age spots, his fingers looked a lot like they belonged on the hand Theo had found. "Well, it don't matter about the name. I knew that I had to make an arrow from a white oak branch."

"Why white oak?" said Ruth Ann.

Tony saw her hands start to shake. He knew that Ruth Ann couldn't resist questioning the man, egging him on. He could tell that it wouldn't take much to make her laugh out loud, and it looked like she would have to laugh soon or explode.

Dead serious, Orvan gave her a look of absolute shock. "It has to be a white oak or they come back after three nights and carry away the soul of their killer. I'm surprised that you asked 'cause everybody knows that."

"I've never heard that before, but that's okay. Go on. What happened after you made the arrow?" Tony propped his chin on his fists, his elbows braced on the table. The fiction writer in him had to admire the imagination of this old man. He forced himself not to look at Ruth Ann. He glanced up and saw that Wade had arrived and stood in the doorway, his arms crossed over his chest.

Tony ignored his expression of amused interest.

Orvan moved to the edge of his chair and flapped his arms like wings. "Just then, the thing started to fly and lucky for me, it seemed kinda slow gettin' off the ground. That did give me time to take good aim, and I shot it right in the heart. The moment it fell to the ground it turned back into a man. I carried him to the first car I seen and put him in the back seat." With a flourish like he'd slammed a car door, he sat back and grinned, showing them every tooth and space in his mouth. "That's how you come to find him there. Do I get a reward?"

Deadpan, Tony looked at Wade. "You did check to see if Orvan's fingerprints were on that car door, didn't you?"

"Yes sir, I did. In fact, I thought of him right away, but I'm afraid that they didn't match."

Tony admired his ability to keep a straight face as Wade stepped aside to allow Ruth Ann room to bolt. She left, dashing through the doorway as if pursued by a giant poisonous bat.

Orvan looked crushed. Holding out his palsied hands to the deputy, he pleaded with the young man. "Will you try again? Maybe they changed?"

Before Wade could formulate an answer, something bumped him from behind and he whirled to face into the hall.

Seeing Wade's movement, Tony looked out and saw Blossom's yellow slicker headed for his office. As the slicker brushed against the walls, it created a swishing sound, not unlike the one made by windshield wipers. This time she wore the matching hat and left a trail of water in her wake. Her hands were empty. No pie this trip.

It struck Tony that anyone could reach his office. He needed to increase security or, at the least, enforce what little they had in place. To reach this area, Blossom had to walk by Rex's window, then pass through a door that should have been locked.

Tony's cell phone rang. He pressed the green button. "Sheriff."

At almost the same moment, Tony heard what sounded like every other telephone and pager in the building ring. From the corner of his eye, he saw Wade grab his own phone.

Orvan dived under the table, wrapping his arms around his head. He didn't seem to care that his shoe polish would migrate from his hair to his sleeves.

Blossom trotted past, traveling the other direction. Her little feet moved more quickly, increasing the tempo of the swishes.

Ignoring her, Tony gave his full attention to Rex's phone report.

CHAPTER SEVENTEEN

Rex didn't waste time with preambles. "The road is under water over at the crossroads. Deputy Holt says that two cars are stalled already."

"When?" Tony could visualize the dispatch desk. Rex had control of contacting all emergency services, including the sheriff's department, the fire department and search and rescue.

"The first report of flooding came in five minutes ago, so I sent Holt over to check on it."

"Did you get an estimated depth?" Phone pressed to his ear, Tony almost reached his office before he remembered that he needed do something about Orvan. Looking over his shoulder, he thought that the old man looked tired and sad. "Better go home for now, Orvan, the water's rising."

Head bobbing, Orvan adjusted his overalls and shuffled down the hallway.

"Hang on." Rex put him on hold for a second. "The water crossing the road at the lowest point is currently eight inches deep and rising. You ought to know that Ziggy's on his way in."

"Okay." Tony disconnected. From his window, he could see the first group of volunteer firemen arriving and heading for the trucks. Search and rescue workers were entering the building by another door. The two groups could work together, but the rivalry between them verged on feud status. They could not share the same door.

Tony watched as Ziggy Blackburn, the county disaster

coordinator, strolled through the front door of the city building and headed for his small basement office. Of medium height and slightly more than medium weight, Ziggy exuded a degree of calmness that made the unflappable Rex look hysterical.

Ziggy's real name was Sigmund. The product of a German war bride and a dour Scot, he'd trained from his earliest days to exercise self-control and composure. When not in charge of disaster planning, Ziggy managed the local Wendy's and refereed high school basketball games. According to witnesses, the only time he looked even slightly ruffled was the night his wife, Gretchen, gave birth to twins. Her labor had begun before the game, which she attended, of course, but the babies weren't inclined to wait until the game was over.

She broke the news to him at half time. When the game restarted, Ziggy lost control and began running back and forth across the court, blowing his whistle and flapping his long arms like the stork himself. Luckily for all involved, a volunteer referee trotted onto the court and ripped the whistle out of the man's mouth and the game went on. Without Ziggy.

Tony was still talking to Rex when the dispatcher decided Sheila needed emergency backup.

Tony charged out of his office and climbed into the Blazer. Lights flashing, he tore out of the parking lot. He managed to buckle his seat belt as he drove.

Because the Blazer stood taller than the patrol cars and had four-wheel drive, he would be able to ease through areas closed to all other traffic. Sheila might be in serious trouble. That extra height could make a critical difference.

The last time she radioed in, her report put her just past Nellie Pearl's house, in the small settlement at the base of the road to Quentin's place. Due to a mudslide and fallen branches, the dirt road up the mountain had become impassable. Sheila reported seeing a man that matched the description of Hub's former cellmate, Sammy Samson. She was on her way to check it out.

After ten minutes passed without hearing from her, Rex demanded reinforcements.

Sheila always kept in touch.

The rain had moved into what Tony classified as the deluge stage. Even with the windshield wipers working as fast as they could, visibility had deteriorated from poor to none. Everything became the same shade of pearl gray. The falling water looked exactly like the water splashing up to meet it. Ahead of him, the sky overflowed with black clouds painted on the charcoal background of the mountains. Here the sky became darker than the ground. Only an idiot or someone with official business would be out on the roads now, but there seemed to be no shortage of idiots in Park County.

Tony hoped his flashing lights would be effective. He didn't want to use the siren, but he drove fast enough for everyone to need to see him and get out of his way. In his rearview mirror, he watched another set of flashing lights. Wade was coming up behind him, his patrol car throwing up a showy plume of mud and water.

When they arrived at their destination, they could see Sheila's patrol car parked, not at Nellie Pearl's house, but slightly off the road near the woods. Was that where the old woman claimed she saw Quentin burying something? The patrol car sat empty, the driver's side door slightly ajar. Around it, the grass and weeds appeared trampled, but all they could see was mud and water.

Wade pointed uphill. "There's a light."

Tony's eyes followed Wade's finger. Sure enough, up the hill and just inside the darkness of the sheltering trees, a light beckoned them. The light jerked, illuminating first a branch and then danced across their faces to point somewhere else. It had to be a flashlight.

It could be Sheila or even children playing.

An ominous tickle at the base of his spine sent a surge of adrenaline though his system. Tony radioed Rex and released the rifle from its lock inside the Blazer. If they needed to shoot, it had better range than the pistols.

Wade trotted next to him, shotgun in hand.

They made their way up the slope as quickly as they could. Footing was treacherous; Wade fell once. Tony fell a couple of times. As he climbed from his knees back onto his feet, he couldn't decide whether the mud or the rain-slicked vegetation caused more of a problem. Even dressed in their rain gear, they were soaked to the skin before they ran twenty feet.

Cautious, they followed the light, staying low and hidden behind the trees and brush.

Sheila was alive.

She lay on the ground, curled in a fetal position, slowly moving the flashlight from side to side. It rested on a small branch, and instead of holding it in her hand, she rolled it back and forth with her palm.

The normally immaculate young woman looked as if she had been mauled by a bear and dragged over the mountain. Her blond hair hung free of its normal braid, and the ends swirled in a puddle, collecting twigs. In the mud at her feet they found two bodies. Blood slowly seeped from a cut on Nellie Pearl's forehead. Unconscious, the old woman lay as still as death. Laying on his side next to her was Sammy Samson. One pair of handcuffs held his wrists together behind his back. A second pair of handcuffs connected him to a mountain laurel.

He was swearing a blue streak.

Sammy looked even muddier than Sheila did. The way he continued to flop around like a fish in the muck wasn't going to improve his looks.

At the sight of her smashed radio, the pieces scattered about the area, Tony quickly notified Rex that Sheila was alive. Even through the poor reception, Tony heard Rex's sigh of relief.

Ashen and shivering, Sheila gradually worked her way to her feet. "Thanks for coming. We had a bit of a scuffle when I tried to get the cuffs on him. He resisted arrest."

Tony thought that she had a gift for masterful understatement. Her breathing seemed shallow. The glassy expression in her eyes warned him that she was hurt, but he didn't see more than superficial scratches.

"Criminy fire, Sheila," said Wade. He knelt by the old woman's still body, checking her pulse. Blood seeped from a terrible gash on her left temple only to be washed away by the rain. "What's been going on here?"

Tony asked Rex to send the ambulance. He lifted an inquiring brow in Sheila's direction.

"I'm fine." Sheila answered the unspoken question. "I'm not sure what happened to her. She's been unconscious since I arrived, but breathing on her own. That's been . . ." she scraped mud from the face of her watch. It took her three tries before she could see the numbers. "M-maybe fifteen minutes. How can that be?" Sheila looked at her trembling fingers like they belonged to someone else. "I woke up on the ground. Could I have been unconscious?"

She pushed her tangled hair away from her face, leaving a smudge of mud on her cheek. The movement made her wince. Looking down, she seemed to notice a frayed hole in her chocolate-brown uniform shirt just below her badge. She started to examine it with her index finger when her face lost the last vestiges of color and she swayed. She seemed unable to pull her gaze from the dark hole.

"That ought to have killed you, you bitch." The enraged, but stupid, drug dealer watched her examine the hole as he struggled to his knees. He spat a mouthful of mud in her direction. He missed.

The realization that she had been shot hit Tony and Wade at the same time. Tony leaped to Sheila's side.

Wade apparently misjudged the distance and accidentally tripped over Sammy, knocking the man face down into the mud. He reached down and pulled Sammy up to his knees before accidentally tripping over him again. Several times.

"Let me see." Tony pushed Sheila's hands out of the way and gently unbuttoned her shirt, checking for injuries. There was no blood, but the hole went almost all the way through the protective vest. The bullet rested on the plate over her heart. "Thank goodness you have this on." He thumped the vest. "Can I loosen it?" At her nod, he worked the straps that held it close to her body.

Wade went back to Nellie Pearl's side and draped first his jacket and then Tony's over her. She didn't move. He ran down the hill and came back with a pair of blankets from the trunk of his patrol car.

"How is she?" Sheila craned her neck to see around Tony.

"The bleeding's about stopped, but she doesn't seem to be conscious at all." Wade stood and looked toward town. "The ambulance is almost here. I can see the lights." With his flashlight, he signaled the paramedics and ran back down the hill to help them with their equipment. He slipped and swore the whole way.

Watching Wade, Sheila started to laugh, but the sound turned into a strangled sob. "Are you sure the bullet didn't go through?" She wrapped her arms across her chest and dug her fingers into her upper arms. Tears seeped from under her closed eyelids, washing narrow tracks through the mud. "I never hurt so bad."

Tony picked Sheila up and moved her away from Nellie Pearl. He propped her against a young oak tree and forced her to sit. The paramedics were going to need a lot more space to work on the old woman.

Tony worried about Sheila. A glance revealed that her pistol was in its holster. Sheila seemed to be having trouble breathing, and the color still had not returned to her face. Tony thought that the force of the bullet hitting her at close range had to have at least bruised her ribs, if not broken one.

The paramedics needed to check her out, but for the moment they were both concentrating on the old woman. Following their instructions, Wade stood behind them, providing temporary shelter with a blanket.

Tony could see no sign of a gun or drugs. "What did he shoot you with?"

"He dropped it." Sheila gasped and tipped her head indicating uphill. "In that hole, along with whatever he had stashed there."

Following her directions, Tony walked up and then down. "I don't see a hole. How far up?" The ground had been churned into a quagmire of mud, twigs and leaves. Any footprints or a trail had been obliterated.

Squinting through the rain, Sheila looked confused. "It shouldn't be that far. Maybe take a step to your right. There. You should be right in front of it."

Tony looked down. A rivulet of liquid mud slipped past his feet and eddied in an indentation before sliding on down the hill, acquiring more leaves and twigs as it went along.

"Do you suppose this puddle was a hole a few minutes ago?" He didn't wait for an answer but poked a stick into the water, measuring its depth. "It's definitely a hole." Rolling up his sleeves first, he pulled on a pair of gloves. The only way to reach the bottom of the hole was to kneel in the muck and stick his hand in. Within seconds, every part of him but his back was coated with mud. It was impossible to get any wetter. He turned his head and grinned at Sheila. "Theo's going to have a fit."

Sheila started to laugh but pain stopped her and she gasped and pressed her hand to her chest. "Because of the muddy laundry or the shooting? I've always wondered if you have to wear your vest in the shower?"

Tony knew that it was not exactly a secret to anyone in the department that Theo was paranoid about officers being shot. His insistence that his officers wear their vests had nothing to do with his wife. It was just the smart thing to do.

"Oh, hell, I forgot about the shooting. I might as well not go home tonight. Theo is bound to be on a rampage." His eyes met hers. Seeing her eyes twinkle and some color return to her cheeks, he relaxed. "You think your mama would let me sleep on her couch? Mine won't. She's even worse than Theo."

"Oh, God, no! Don't tell my mother." Sheila whispered as much to the paramedic who had left Nellie Pearl's side and begun examining her as to Tony. She tried to smile. "Maybe we could both stay with Wade."

Tony thought that the expression on his deputy's face was not encouraging. Wade didn't appear to have any sense of humor left. In fact, he looked as if he would strangle both of them if he wasn't so busy. He kept checking the paramedics who were hard at work on Nellie Pearl and Sheila, but he concentrated his attention on Sammy. Every time Sammy lifted his sorry head, Wade shoved his face back down.

Kneeling in the mud, Tony's search paid off. He pulled a Smith and Wesson .38 Special from the hole. The next treasure he examined looked like a kid's lunch box. The old-fashioned kind. It was a red plastic rectangle with a simple latch. The picture was too faded to identify. The last thing he pulled out was the remainder of a thick brown envelope. Waterlogged, the flap dangled uselessly. He stacked all of the items together.

"Wade, take that piece of garbage down and put him in the Blazer. When you come back, bring me a cardboard box. I want to get this stuff out of the rain." Tony pulled a soggy roll of antacids from his pocket and chewed on the driest ones. As soon as Wade was on his way, leading their prisoner down the hill, Tony kept Sammy's back squarely in the rifle sights. He watched until Wade locked Sammy in the Blazer without incident, before turning back to Sheila. "How are you feeling now?"

"I'm fine, Sheriff. I feel like a mule kicked me in the chest but I can still do my job." She started smoothing her hair into a braid and stopped when she noticed that her hands were filled with mud and twigs. At least she had stopped shaking. "Before I go back to work, I would like a shower, though, a very long, very hot shower."

"Not so fast." He frowned. "After you see the doctor, you can have your shower. After your shower I need a fully detailed, written report on everything that happened up here. After that, you clean every speck of mud out of your handgun." Taking her elbow, he led her down to the cars, almost carrying her. He doubted that she realized the extent of her injuries. "Have Rex get you a new radio."

Sheila glanced back at the broken pieces of her radio, scattered on the ground. When she looked up at Tony again, she seemed resigned.

"But before you come in to work, you bring me a note from Doc Nash saying that you are fit, mentally and physically, or I'll put you behind a desk until you retire."

CHAPTER EIGHTEEN

Even with the women packed together like sardines, Theo's shop couldn't hold everyone.

The deluge prevented some of the women from going home. Others arrived, drawn to the shop any time the weather turned bad. Women fought for workspace around the charity quilt. The ones who weren't quilting sat around socializing. A few were even buying fabric.

Jane told Theo that she'd lost count of the number of times she started another pot of coffee.

The crowd became so overwhelming that Theo abandoned her design project to help behind the counter. A mountain of bolts needed to be returned to the shelves. Theo grabbed three off the top. As she prepared to put them away, Prudence Sligar arrived. Theo couldn't believe her eyes. The stately hair stylist who dabbled in fortune telling was not a quilter. Normally a confident woman, the champion arm wrestler, owner of a small business and soon-to-be the bride of Deputy Darren Holt, she looked exceptionally ill at ease.

"Are you taking up quilting, Prudence?" Theo stopped directly in front of her.

Prudence's gaze bounced away from Theo and traveled over the multitude of fabrics and colors in the room. Almost involuntarily, one hand reached to caress the fabrics. "I would like to. I went over to the quilt show in Pigeon Forge and thought they were all so lovely." Her hand released the fabric and moved to her belly. The bulge of her latest pregnancy was noticeable. "Maybe I could make a quilt for the baby, but that's not why I wanted to talk to you." Placing her hands on the cutting table, she leaned closer to Theo, giving them a semblance of privacy.

"What's wrong, Prudence? Did you 'see' something?" Theo knew that sometimes the fortuneteller hit the mark. Prudence's grandmother had been a "wise woman," and she hoped to carry on the tradition.

"No. Darren called to tell me that Sheila got shot today. Luckily, she had on her vest. I guess it saved her life." She didn't seem to notice Theo's expression. "I was wondering how you deal with that fear, because I'm here to tell you that it about made me pass out cold when he told me about it."

The bubble of air that Theo sucked into her lungs threatened to choke her. She could feel the blood leaving her head. "Sheila was shot? When?"

Prudence's shoulders lifted and lowered. "It must have been early, 'cause when Darren called to tell me that he couldn't meet me for lunch, it was already all over with. He spent the morning tied up with the flooding down at the crossroads and didn't have too many details. Didn't your husband tell you about it?"

"Not yet." Clearly, Sheila was fine so Theo forced herself to breathe. "I'm sure that I'll get the details from him tonight."

Prudence twisted her engagement ring around and around on her finger. "Maybe it would be better if we didn't get married. Is the fear just too much?" Tears filled Prudence's too-green-to-be-natural eyes.

"Sometimes, but not usually." Theo placed the bolt of fabric back on the counter. "The memory of the day Tony got shot comes back to me sometimes and almost takes me down. You have to remember, though, that I would worry about him no matter what his job was. I'm a worrier and I'm really good at it. Carpenters get hurt too, you know." Talking about this to Prudence seemed to be clarifying it in her own mind. "The other half of the truth is that Tony is a lawman. It truly is such a part of his nature that he would be a different man without it." She patted the taller woman's shoulder. "If you don't marry Darren, will you stop worrying about him?"

"No." Prudence answered immediately.

"Then, there's your answer." A burst of laughter from the back room drew her attention. A couple of the women teased Jane about her new hair color and social life. "I think that new hair color you gave Jane is quite becoming."

Prudence smiled. "Is she seeing very much of Red?"

"I think that they are just friends, nothing serious." Theo didn't like the expression on Prudence's face. Jane was not only her mother-in-law, but Theo loved her like the mother she had never known. "Why? Is there a problem with that?"

Prudence lowered her voice so that only Theo could hear. "You know that I am not fond of gossip, but I think that you should know that he drinks, maybe a lot." She examined the papers that Theo had been holding. "Mystery Quilt, Clue Three. What's that mean?"

After a quick glance in Jane's direction, Theo asked. "Why do you think he drinks? Is he intoxicated when he gets his hair cut?"

"No, although sometimes I'm not too sure. We were in Knoxville a few weeks back and stopped at the liquor store out near the mall." Her voice lowered more. "It looked like he loaded at least a case of vodka into his car. He might have bought more than that. I don't think that he saw us."

"Well, you were there and we stop there just about every time we go to Knoxville. Their selection of wine is good and the prices are fair." Theo shrugged. "As long as the sale of alcohol in this county is limited to beer and wine, I think you'll continue to see everyone you know up there. As far as Red is concerned, Jane says that he is nice but that he has his own set of problems. Maybe she already knows about the drinking, but thank you for the warning." Just then, seeing her mother-in-law's approach, she changed the subject.

"You asked how to make a mystery quilt. It's quite simple as long as you follow the instructions in order." Theo handed Prudence a copy of clue one. "See, it tells you how much of what colors you need. The subsequent clues give you cutting and sewing information."

"But what will it look like when it's all sewn together? There's no picture." She turned the paper over to look at the back. Nothing.

Theo grinned. "That's the mystery."

"Oh, I see. That sounds like fun. Do you have to be real experienced? I haven't done any sewing for years." One hand reached out to touch the fabric behind her, petting it like a dog.

"No." Jane shimmied in between the women. "I would suggest that you get a rotary cutter, ruler and protective mat. It will make cutting your strips and squares more accurate and a lot faster than using scissors." She pushed Theo out of the way. "Just remember that the blade is incredibly sharp. You can't let your children play with it."

"Will you help me?" Prudence's concerns had been replaced by curiosity and she clutched a bolt of beautiful fabric printed with honeysuckle flowers. Her beautiful, bottle-green eyes glowed with lust.

"I'd be happy to teach you how to use them and give you a couple of safety tips," said Jane. "I know the perfect pink for you to use with that fabric.

Theo had to laugh. Jane knew a convert when she saw one and she was a great saleswoman. It wouldn't be long before

Prudence would be hooked for life. Not for the first time, Theo wondered if there was some addictive component in fabric sizing.

Tony got home at ten that night but it felt even later than that. Before going inside, his used his flashlight and made a quick check of conditions around the house. The creek along the side of the house was running higher and faster, but here, at least, it stayed well inside its banks.

Thankfully, the rain stopped by mid-afternoon, or the flooding would have been much worse. As the day played out, his department had been so incredibly busy that Tony had never had time to put on a clean uniform. He spent most of his time helping people out of the mud and stacking sandbags. Half of the water he'd been working in came from melting snow. The other half was just damned cold. Exhausted now, he felt frozen and miserable and hungry enough to eat the front door.

The latest hospital report listed Nellie Pearl as critical, still unconscious. She'd been airlifted to Knoxville, and the doctors there had no idea when, or even if, she would awaken. According to them, she had lost a lot of blood. Other injuries included a fractured cheekbone and severe concussion.

Tony speculated that Nellie Pearl had been watching from her window and had followed Samson up the hill. That spirited old lady must have thrown common sense aside and confronted the devil himself.

Even if Samson turned out to be innocent of some of the things he was suspected of doing, which was doubtful, he had attempted to kill a cop. His confession in front of three witnesses would nail his sorry butt.

With the blessing of his Knoxville attorney, Kate Wyatt, they arranged to jail Samson in Sevier County. Tony didn't want the creep getting so much as a hangnail in the Park County facility.

Miss Wyatt might be young, but she was smart as a whip, and she would be the first one to cry foul if Sammy was treated with anything but kid gloves.

Tony eased the front door open, listening. The old house welcomed him. The moment he stepped inside, Daisy ran to greet him. As he rubbed her ears and chest, her long plumed tail swished hard enough to wag the whole dog. The boys would be in bed already. Tony hated missing their evening routine of bath and stories, but sometimes it just couldn't be helped. He locked his gun in the safe. Following the faint sound of the television, he found Theo in the kitchen, sitting in her favorite chair, a quilt in progress draped over her lap. A fire crackled in the fireplace. The room smelled of wood smoke and cookies.

She looked up and smiled at him.

He loved coming home. On a night like this one it felt like going to heaven. The old house always needed work but they loved it, and this room was its very heart. Although it had been modernized several times, it remained hopelessly out of date. Decorated with a mixture of styles and periods, it looked a little ratty but it fit their family. Long ago, the raised fireplace had been used to prepare meals, but now it only supplied heat and comfort.

Theo sometimes told them stories about growing up in this house as a child, orphaned and living with her grandparents. She would gloss over the isolating, lonely years. The Silers had been good, kind and exceedingly old. They didn't believe in electricity. Using a kerosene lantern for light, Theo had done her homework at the scarred old table. She and her grandfather had baked cookies and bread in an old woodstove.

Theo wasn't crying. Tony could tell that she knew about Sheila, but her serene smile welcomed him home. She had come to terms with her fears. Relieved, he pulled off his hat and bent over to kiss her.

She shivered. "Your lips feel like ice, and I don't think that they are supposed to be that shade of blue." Although she smiled as she touched his cheek, tears filled her eyes. "You are absolutely frozen. Have you eaten anything?"

In response, his stomach rumbled and he shook his head. Too tired to speak, he simply stood absorbing the heat from the fire and the peace of being home.

"Go take a hot shower and I'll heat some stew for you." She climbed out of her cocoon and stretched. Under a short robe she wore pink flannel pajamas decorated with little white lambs. She looked cute as a bug. "You'd better leave those clothes here and I'll put them in the mud room."

He unbuckled the heavy duty-belt and put it on the table. He added his badge and emptied his pockets. Numb fingers made unbuttoning his shirt difficult. Theo took pity on him and helped. Soon he was stripped to his shorts. As he headed into the bathroom, he silently thanked the former family member responsible for installing a bathroom down here. He wasn't sure that he would have had the strength to climb the stairs. They had recently fitted the old-fashioned claw foot tub with a shower nozzle and an oval, chrome shower curtain rod. Encased in the billowing, cream-colored shower curtain, he let the hot water pound over him until Theo came to tell him that the stew was hot. Bless her thoughtful heart, she had even brought him a sweatshirt, sweat pants and wool socks.

Halfway through the second bowl of stew, he started to feel warm again. "I suppose you want to know about Sheila?" Her nod gave him the answer he expected. Cocking an eyebrow at her, he grinned even though it felt like it would make his face crack. "Just for my information, how did you find out?"

"Prudence." Theo answered.

"How in the—? Never mind. I think I can guess." He stole the flannel lap quilt from Theo. "Tea leaves or Darren?"

"Darren, of course. She came to me because she is worried about marrying a cop." Grabbing a corner of the quilt, she pulled but lost her grip.

"And did you break their engagement?" Once he had the whole quilt, he reached for her and dragged her onto his lap, resting his chin on her shoulder. "Did you tell her scary stories and beg her to marry a farmer?"

Wide-eyed, she shook her head. "I told her the truth."

"Which is?" Serious now, he waited for her answer. The firelight reflecting on her glasses hid their expression.

"Nobody's safe." She smoothed the eyebrow over his left eye. "I told her that I would worry about you no matter how you earned a living."

"What if I lived on welfare?" Some of the tension left him and he toyed with the curls in her hair, pulling them away from her face and releasing them, smiling when they bounced back like springs.

"Stop playing with my hair." A devilish grin lit her face. "You could be sitting in front of the television, drinking a can of beer and eating nachos when a car crashes through the picture window and flattens you and the recliner."

"Damned lucky then, I guess, that we don't have a picture window." He sighed heavily and pasted a mournful expression on his face. "I suppose that was a fresh plate of nachos. Were they extra cheesy?"

"You bet. Lots of cheese and easy on the jalapenos so Daisy would be able to clean them up for you." At her name, the golden retriever lifted her head momentarily and then went back to her nap, rolling onto her back.

"Now tell me what happened to Sheila."

CHAPTER NINETEEN

"You've heard most of it," said Tony. "At least the part where Nellie Pearl spied on Quentin, thinking he was burying things in the woods."

Theo nodded.

"Sheila was patrolling near Nellie Pearl's when she thought she saw a man named Samson, but he was too far away to identify." Theo shivered and he pulled the quilt up around her shoulders. "Samson is a suspect in Hub's death. She radioed in but followed him up the hill, away from Nellie Pearl's house." He paused for a mouthful of hot chocolate. "Sheila worked her way up behind him and got close enough to watch when she saw Nellie Pearl unconscious on the ground. Samson was either putting something into or taking it out of a hole."

He held Theo close and steadied his breathing.

"Samson saw her, pulled his gun and shot her, just like that. The impact of the bullet hitting her vest knocked her to the ground. You can't imagine how much that hurts. She blacked out." Tony swallowed against the lump in his throat. "While she was down he destroyed her radio. She's damned lucky he didn't shoot her again."

"Oh, Tony."

Theo's expression of dismay stopped him.

"It's true." He stared for a moment at the glowing embers. "When Sheila came to, they got into a knock down, drag out fight. With the rain and the mud, I guess it turned into a real brawl. By the time we got there she had handcuffs on him and it looked like she was wearing half of the mountain on her uniform and in her hair. Compared to her, I looked clean when I got home."

"Is she all right?"

"Doc says that the bruise on her chest is a humdinger and that one of her ribs is cracked. She is going to be sore all over tomorrow but as much from the hand-to-hand as the shooting. In short, she gets a desk for a while." Pressing his face against Theo's shoulder, he yawned wide enough to make his jaw crack. In the quiet room, the sound seemed to boom. "She was always the scrapper in that family. Her brothers were more afraid of her than of anyone else around." He moaned. "I just know that she is not going to like the desk."

"Are you afraid of her?"

"You bet." Tony yawned again and let his eyes close. Heaven was right here. He was warm and fed and Theo wasn't mad at him.

"I think you can handle it after a good night's sleep." Theo unwrapped herself from the layers of Tony's arms and the quilt and appraised him as she stood up. "Go to bed."

"I'm okay here."

"No. You look like death warmed over." Tugging his hands to get him to his feet, she commanded him, "Go to bed."

Without the energy to argue, he went. He gripped the banister and used it to pull himself up the last few steps. He barely made it onto the bed before he passed out.

At a very early hour of the morning, he awakened and climbed out onto the veranda. The wood beneath his bare feet felt cold and damp, sending a sharp chill through his toasty warm body. In the deep silence that comes only at night, he could hear the familiar sounds of water rushing over rocks. The lights in the park were bright enough to show him that the creek had not risen any higher.

Peeking into the room shared by the boys, he saw Chris rolled into his covers, like Cleopatra in a rug, only his hair and feet exposed to the night air. In the next bed, Jamie looked like a mattress ad. He slept on his back with his hands crossed over his chest and his blankets as smooth as they had been when he went to bed.

Daisy's bed, a big round nest upholstered with dog bone fabric, occupied the center of the room. It was empty. Daisy lay stretched across Jamie's pillow. The boy's pale blond hair blended perfectly with hers as he used her for his pillow. She lifted her head and stared at Tony until he stepped back. Tony wondered why they had ever invested in the dog bed. He wasn't sure if Daisy had ever been on it. The oversized animal alternated between being Jamie's pillow and being stretched out between Chris and the wall.

He went downstairs and toward the kitchen. Theo had moved his things from the table onto a bench in the mudroom and spread them out to dry. His body armor was dry. Dried mud clung to the belt and empty holster. He needed to clean the weapon again, even though he'd cleaned it twice the day before. Retrieving his Glock from the gun safe in the front closet, he set it on the table. Before sitting down, he collected a handful of chocolate chip cookies and a tall glass of milk. He placed those next to his gun cleaning equipment. He cleaned for quite a while, until he was convinced that no mud remained. It was a big job that required a second trip to the cookie jar. Satisfied, at last, he locked the Glock up and went back to bed.

Theo rolled over when he climbed in. She sniffed the aromas that Tony carried with him, gun oil and chocolate, and with a satisfied smile snuggled up against his back.

In the morning, Tony sat in his office, going over the events of the past day and night. Deputy J. B. Lewis stopped by on his way home to tell him about Roscoe's antics.

In Tony's opinion, Roscoe Morris was not the sharpest tack in the box. In fact, people often noted that he was about as sharp as a bowling ball. Someone suggested that his county record for the most years spent in middle school might even be the highest in the state. It was a record that he was proud of. Whatever his lack of intelligence, he did possess a certain animal cunning and, best of all, Roscoe was a genuinely nice man.

A lover of baseball like Tony, Roscoe attended every game in the community and always cheered for both sides. The little boys liked it when they could spend time with Roscoe. He would entertain them with a piece of string and nimble fingers, weaving simple designs like Jacob's ladder.

According to Deputy J.B. Lewis, Roscoe had a busy night. J.B. settled in to give his report within earshot of Sheila and Ruth Ann. J.B. loved to tell stories, so his oral reports were long and detailed, while his written reports supplied minimal information.

Tony knew that J.B. liked working nights. His patrol encompassed the town, although he was not restricted to it and because the only law enforcement agency in Park County was the sheriff's department, there was never a squabble over jurisdiction. He went where he felt like going.

"I arrived at the four way stop just in time to see Roscoe pass through it, towing a vending machine, headed out of town." J.B. lifted a thermal coffee mug to his lips.

"A vending machine," said Tony. "Why?"

"I'll get to that in a minute, but I swear, Sheriff, I thought I was hallucinating. 'Cause there he was, in that old paintless pickup of his, trucking on down the road. Sparks were flying from the bottom of that candy machine." J.B. laughed so hard he had to stop and take in great gasps of air. "I sure didn't need the tracking skills of Daniel Boone or Davy Crockett to follow his trail. Between the flying sparks and that godawful scraping noise, my great-aunt Tillie couldn't have lost him, and she's been blind and deaf for a century. Roscoe had to stop twice along the way and reattach the chain." Clutching his sides, he finally managed to blurt out, "Roscoe's in love with that machine."

"Not really," said Ruth Ann.

"That's what he said." J.B. went on with his story. The flood had encouraged Roscoe to do a certain amount of impromptu thinking, ill advised as it was. Roscoe had been down at the crossroads, helping stack sandbags, when he saw a vision of loveliness across the road. The vending machine usually sat in the covered walkway of the Riverview Motel and Cabins. It had been moved to the higher ground of the parking lot. When a stream of sunlight leaked through the bleary sky and reflected from the chrome buttons, he fell in love.

Roscoe told J.B. that for a long time the machine had been one of his favorite restaurants. Now it seemed to be available for the taking, just waiting for him. Romeo had met his Juliet. One of the last to leave the area, he was relieved see that no one had moved his love. His old pickup truck was not pretty, but it was strong. Backing up slowly, Roscoe positioned the truck only inches away from the object of his affections.

At first, he attempted to lift the vending machine, but it was too much for him to handle alone. Then he tried to push it into the bed of the truck, hoping it would topple into place. That didn't work. He couldn't leave it. Almost frantic, he tried everything he could think of to get it into his truck. In desperation, because he couldn't leave it behind, he wrapped a length of chain around it and attached it to the trailer hitch on the back of his truck and drove back to his residence at the Oak Lawn Trailer Court.

"If there had been less water on the ground, the sparks dancing from the steel rubbing on the pavement would have ignited countless grass and forest fires." J.B. rubbed his eyes.

"Please, stop." Sheila raised a hand to stop him. She moved like an arthritic turtle, tender in every muscle, bone, nook and cranny. "You are killing me." Every breath taken was an obvious insult to her bruised ribs, and J.B.'s story reduced her to tears.

"Sorry, Sheila, I didn't stop to think. I know you're sore." J.B. reached over and gave her a fatherly pat on the hand. "We'll finish this report someplace else."

"Over my dead body." Sheila spoke so forcefully that she winced again. Reducing her voice, she gave him her best glare, "Don't you dare not tell me."

J.B. just stared at her. His expression showed that he didn't know what he was supposed to do.

Ruth Ann solved his dilemma. "Tell the story, J.B., but slow enough so she can breathe from time to time." She glanced at her fingernails. The cerise polish that she had been applying when J.B. started the story stuck to the tissue that she used to wipe her overflowing eyes. She shrugged and reached for the polish remover. "Was Roscoe surprised to see you?"

"I guess you could say that. He made it to his place maybe thirty seconds ahead of me. Even with all the water, I wanted to make sure that he didn't start a fire with that thing."

"Why didn't you just pull him over?" Tony stretched, feeling the knotted muscles in his back loosen a bit. With his thumbs hooked into his belt, he leaned against the doorframe of his office. "That would have taken care of it."

"I couldn't. I had to see where he took the thing. Have you ever watched anyone sleepwalk?"

Tony nodded.

"It's kind of the same feeling. You don't want to wake them up, and at the same time, you sure are curious to see what they'll do." J.B. swallowed a big mouthful of coffee. "Anyway, when I pulled up behind him at his trailer, he was standing next to the thing, kissing it and caressing the buttons."

"So he didn't steal it to take the coins?" said Sheila.

J.B. shook his head. "He swore that the money had nothing to do with it and I believe him. He wants to keep her. I'm telling you that he is in love with her. He'd probably marry the damned thing if she would say yes."

"Where is it now?" Tony tried to maintain a modicum of dignity and professionalism but failed miserably. The mental image of skinny little Roscoe with his stringy hair and over-crowded teeth kissing a vending machine was too much for him and he burst out laughing. "Does it have a name?"

"She, not it." J.B. waited until Sheila and Tony could suck a little air in before answering. He nodded and that caught their attention. "Dora." He continued after a brief pause. "I had the Thomas brothers come out and load her on a flatbed and lock her up for the night."

Ruth Ann reacted first. "Dora?" Tears streamed unchecked down her face. All pretense of working on her fingernails was over. "Why Dora?"

"I asked him that myself." J.B. paused.

"And?" said Sheila.

J.B.'s lips twitched. "He said that he called *her* Dora because that's *her* name and so what else would he call *her?* I must say that he seemed rather indignant."

"Had he been drinking?" Sheila's eyes were wide. "The last time I talked to Roscoe, he didn't seem likely to fall in love with a vending machine. A truck maybe, you know, or something else with tires."

"Naw. There was no alcohol on his breath and he passed all of the field sobriety tests. I don't think he had any drugs or alcohol in him at all. He'd been working down at the creek all evening. Just Roscoe being Roscoe, you know." A rumble of laughter worked its way through his whole system. "That man never has more than three wheels on the road on a good day."

Tony nodded. He had seen Roscoe earlier in the day. The skinny little man had worked like a demon, stacking sandbags. Tony hated to punish Roscoe after all his hard work. He started reading through J.B.'s reports. They were incomplete and he gave up. "Did you arrest him?"

"Oh, yeah, you haven't heard it all." J.B. yawned and drank more coffee.

"There's more?" As one, his audience leaned closer.

"I had to arrest him for the license plate scam that he was running." He glanced at their faces to make sure that they were all paying close attention. "You see, I've been hard at work while you were all snoring in the dark."

Tony thought that J.B. should be on a stage. He was the Will Rogers of the area.

J.B. teased them by making a big production of finishing his coffee and then cracking his knuckles. Satisfied that he had their full attention, he went on with his report. "Roscoe supplied the snake handler with Queen Doreen's license plate."

"No way." Tony straightened.

"Yep. It turns out that Roscoe has quite a collection of license plates for sale. Most of his stock, he stole from tourists passing through. He normally takes just the front plate of cars and trucks from states that require two plates. Roscoe's favorite seems to be Ohio. Half of that state must have had the front plate ripped off by Roscoe, and the other half has never visited the area."

"If he has a collection, why take the plate from her majesty, the mayor's wife?" said Ruth Ann.

From her words and expression, Tony assumed that Ruth Ann's relationship with the mayor's family had not improved.

"That was a special order. Our preacher requested a Park County plate. Right after that, Roscoe happened to be passing through a parking lot and he took the first license plate that he came to."

"How did the preacher know to contact Roscoe?" Sheila's question mirrored Tony's thought.

"That one's easy. Quentin recommended him." J.B. shook his head. "Before you ask, I don't have any idea how Quentin knew about Roscoe's business venture or why they didn't steal the plate themselves instead of paying Roscoe a hundred dollars for a 'finders fee.' "

"You didn't have a warrant." Tony didn't ask.

"Didn't need one." J.B. raised his right hand like he was being sworn in. "I read him his rights about six times, but Roscoe begged me to take the license plates. He said that maybe the judge would let him keep the candy machine in exchange for them. I told him that it doesn't work that way but he insisted."

Tony stepped into his office and retrieved several antacids from the jar on his desk. Realizing that there were only two left in it, he wrote himself a message on a sticky note and stuck it on his door before he returned to the impromptu meeting. "I guess we'd better let Archie know. He'll know how many laws Roscoe broke. The license plate thing is not going to just go away."

Ruth Ann's phone rang. Picking up the receiver, she held it to her ear for only a couple of seconds. Her eyes twinkled as she met Tony's eyes. "Rex called with a message."

"What?" From her expression, he assumed that no one had found another body.

"Tell the sheriff that Elvis has left the building and Quentin is ready to talk."

CHAPTER TWENTY

Tony was thankful that Quentin seemed grounded enough that Carl Lee Cashdollar, his attorney, would allow him to be interviewed. Freshly showered and dressed in the fashionable orange and white striped jumpsuit supplied by the county jail, Quentin still looked like hell. His body aroma was much improved but still not completely pleasant. The chemicals that he ingested had taken a toll.

"So, Quentin," Tony waved the man into a chair next to Carl Lee. "How are you feeling today? Your lawyer thinks that you are up to answering a few questions."

Quentin shrugged but remained silent. He stared at Sheila, who sat at the desk almost directly opposite the greenhouse door.

"Well, let's just go over a few things while you consider it." Tony, like Quentin, watched as Sheila made her careful way to the door and handed him several sheets of paper. The moment she left, Wade entered the room and closed the door. "We found your fingerprints on the door handle of the car driven by, but evidently not owned by, Harold Usher Brown."

Brow furrowed, Quentin looked baffled. "Who is that?" He addressed his question to his attorney but Carl Lee shook his head, looking as confused as his client.

"We know that your dear cousin John Mize has been deceased for a while and that Mr. Brown assumed his identity. Would you care to tell us why?" Tony shuffled the papers he held but didn't look at them.

"Brown? Is that Hub's name? I had no idea. I thought it was Mize." Quentin relaxed on his chair. "He's my cousin on my mama's side." He jerked forward, then slapped himself hard on the side of his head. "He did say somethin' like that. My mama weren't a Mize until she married my pa. I guess she used to be a Brown at that. She and Pa's uncle, Jesse I think, was relations."

When it looked like Quentin was ready to start giving a detailed account of his entire family tree, Tony raised his hand to stop the man. "Just tell me why he wanted to use John's identity and what he was doing here."

"That's pretty easy." Quentin picked at his skin. "He showed up with them snakes one day and introduced himself. I knew he was a true cousin just by the way he looked. My mama had those same kinda spooky eyes but she never cut her eyelashes like that. He uses these itty-bitty little scissors and cuts them one at a time. Freaked me out to watch him."

"Cut his eyelashes?" Tony remembered that Quentin's mother had eyes that protruded and there was white visible all around the irises. It made her look wild and scary and most of the children who saw her believed she was a witch. Her personality had done nothing to dispel the idea.

Tony opened the file. A close-up photograph of the victim's face lay on top. Sure enough, the stubby eyelashes were cut so short they almost disappeared. He hadn't noticed that they were cut before, just that they were unusually short. He passed the photograph to Wade who took one glance and shuddered.

"Why would he do that?" said Tony.

"That's just plain creepy looking," said Wade.

Carl Lee studied the photograph and shook his head.

"Hub told me it was so people could see his eyes better and that the better people could see them, the more they trusted him." Quentin's head bobbed several times. "Trust is a big deal when you are in the preacher business. That's why he started calling himself Mize. He said that using a local name gave him connections 'cause people don't much take to strangers.' "

"What can you tell me about the things he kept in those large boxes in his car?" Tony hoped Quentin would tell him about the drugs or money.

Quentin made a series of strange snorting sounds as he sat up straight. Tony wondered if he was laughing or having an asthma attack.

"Things?" Quentin pounded on his leg with his open hand. "He didn't keep *things* in those boxes. He kept snakes in them, lots of snakes and brought them in the house. Sometimes, he would set them boxes all together so the snakes could watch the television." He shuddered. "I didn't care for them but old John, er Hub that is, he loved them ugly creatures. I even seen him kiss one. The way he talked to them it was like how guys talk when they want some female to put out for them. You know, all that honey baby, you've got great legs, I'll buy you a beer and you can scratch my itch, kinda thing."

Smooth talker. Tony wondered if that eloquent line had attracted Angelina. "That's all there was in the boxes?" Quentin's expression of total bewilderment was enough of an answer. "Okay then, what can you tell me about where he got the license plates on his car?"

"I know that." Quentin chortled and slapped the side of his leg. "I told him to put Roscoe on it. Figured if anyone had what he needed, it'd be him."

Carl Lee's hand twitched. It looked as if he was ready to use it to silence his client.

"It says here that the car was stolen in Atlanta." Tony's fingers toyed with the papers in the file but he did not look away from Quentin.

"Now hold on there." Quentin put up his hands as if to shield himself from the words. "I don't know nothin' about no stolen car. He showed up here driving that little sissy car and all I know's that he wanted to get a local plate."

"You didn't think it strange that a preacher would want a stolen license plate?" said Wade.

"He said that preachers don't make much money and most of that's got to go to charity and so God don't mind a few shortcuts like used license plates." Quentin scratched his arms while he looked into Tony's face. "I'd think you'd know all about that, what with your late daddy bein' in the same line of work."

That rendered Tony speechless. His father had been a Methodist minister. While Tony admitted he had not paid as much attention to his father's words as maybe he should have, he felt sure he would have remembered hearing a theory like that.

Wade jumped in. "What about drugs? Did he have any connection with any kind of illegal substance?"

"Drugs?" Wide-eyed, Quentin's head moved from side to side.

Tony believed his confusion couldn't have been feigned. Quentin couldn't possibly be that good an actor. Cousin Hub had not included Quentin in his business arrangements.

"Hub didn't do no drugs. He said that they were the devil's own invention but Lordy, he sure could drink." He chuckled. "Some nights he drank store-bought and some nights he drank shine but, nossir, not drugs."

"We noticed that he wears a wedding ring." Tony saw no reason to tell Quentin about the OxyContin. "We need to notify his wife and family about his passing. His using your Cousin John's identity has clouded that important issue for us. Do you know where they are? Does he have children?"

Quentin's face said it all. He had no idea. For all he knew about this cousin, he might have been a stranger who had arrived at his door. If Hub hadn't had the same odd eyes that his mother did, Quentin might not have even accepted him as a relative.

"Okay, try this question then." Frustrated beyond belief, Tony massaged his neck, hoping that relieving some of the tension would make him more patient. "Why were your fingerprints on the driver's side door on that little car of your cousin's? Did you ever drive it?"

Quentin shook his head. "Never touched it."

That was a lie and everyone in the room knew it. No one said a word. They all just stared at him. His attorney jabbed him in the ribs with the pen he gripped. "I mean, leastways, I never drove it anywhere. I might have touched it, you know, as I walked by and all."

"Under the handle?" Tony flipped his papers again. Then he studied a report clipped into the folder. His eyes lifted and he stared at Quentin. "Exactly when did you say it was that you last saw your cousin?"

"When he was alive or after he died?" Quentin looked pleased with his saucy question.

Tony felt pleased with it too. In fact, he felt as pleased as an unsupervised puppy discovering an open trashcan. "I wasn't aware that you ever had a chance to see him after he was deceased. Would you like to tell me when you would have done that?"

No one said a word.

Only the sound of Carl Lee cracking the knuckles of his big hands interrupted the silence of the little room. He took his time and cracked each knuckle with careful precision. With each crack, the expression on his face became more forbidding.

Built a lot like his uncle the mayor, attorney Carl Lee Cashdollar had the long-boned build of a basketball player. In spite of the fact that there was very little meat on him, he was known to be strong and fast and could easily palm a basketball.

Quentin's mouth opened and closed as he looked at his unhappy lawyer. Then he paled and slid down on his chair until he was almost on the floor. He seemed fascinated by the ceiling.

"Assuming for a moment, that my client might have seen his cousin after his untimely demise," said Carl Lee, leaning forward and meeting Tony's eyes. "Is that necessarily a problem?"

"That might depend on a number of factors." Tony stared at Quentin. "I presume that the last time our killer saw Hub, he was dead. So I would guess that the killer was the last person to see him alive and the first to see him dead."

"Assuming his cousin was already dead, is there any reason to hold my client?" Carl Lee's hands twitched.

Quentin's eyes filled with tears but he sat up straighter. Hope bloomed on his homely face.

"Not necessarily." Tony scribbled something in his notes before looking first at Carl Lee and then at Quentin. "I would be interested in exactly what time this assumption occurred. It could help establish the time of death."

"You don't know when he died?" The words seemed to leap from Quentin's mouth.

Tony shifted on his chair. "We have a range of time but wouldn't mind narrowing it down a bit." He watched as Carl Lee wrapped one big hand completely around one of Quentin's upper arms and squeezed—and not too gently at that.

"Tell them everything you know about that night or I'll let them arrest you." Carl Lee's voice sounded low and dead serious. "In fact, I'll help them arrest you."

"You mean I haven't been arrested?" said Quentin. "Then why am I wearing this outfit?" He tugged on the left sleeve of the jumpsuit. "Is someone taking care of my dogs? Angelina won't feed them right. Even her own dog don't like her."

"You haven't been arrested for the death of your cousin. That's all we are talking about, for now," said Carl Lee. "Tell them about finding your cousin."

Quentin stuck his lower lip out as if he was a three-year-old denied a treat and shook his head.

Carl Lee cracked one of his knuckles again and Quentin started talking.

"Like I told you before, Hub went to town to do his preaching. I came to town a bit later for a little fun at the Okay." He didn't need to use the full name of the bar. "It was pretty late when I left there, but I don't know the real time. I went by Ruby's 'cause Hub owed me money. He wasn't in the car." He coughed. "Then I parked over near the trailer park and fell asleep in my truck for a while." He rubbed his eyes with his knuckles like he just awakened.

"I just remembered." Quentin sat up straighter. "When I went by Hub's car again, it was running, but the lights was off, so I pulled up and looked in. That had to be a bit before four. I couldn't make him out real clear so I opened the door just a crack. One of them damn snakes was just a-sittin' on his lap like they was goin' for a joyride." He shivered. "I slammed that door and left. I swear to God, Sheriff, he was dead as they get."

"The back lot at Ruby's seems like an odd place to just drive by and see a parked car. You can't see it from the road. You can hardly see it from the café." Tony's eyes narrowed. "How did you know he would be there instead of at your place, and why would you bother even looking for this cousin you barely knew?"

Clearly uncomfortable with these questions, Quentin looked as if he had swallowed a porcupine. "He liked to park there. Don't ask me why. I asked him once, and he about bit my head off." There was no answer to the question of why.

"Did you see anyone else back there, either time?"

Quentin started to shake his head and stopped. "Just that Pinkie woman on her Harley."

Tony examined his notes. That fit with Pinkie's story.

"Do you know a Sammy Samson?" Tony watched as Wade shifted his chair back a little from the aroma that seemed to be increasing as they sat there. The benefits of Quentin's soap seemed to be wearing off. "We think that maybe he was a friend of Hub's."

"What's he look like?" Quentin started chasing imaginary insects again. "I ain't too good with names sometimes."

Tony placed a photograph on the table. "Is this man why you were looking for your cousin?"

"I seen him around." Head bobbing like a cork in a heavy sea, Quentin looked under the table and then under his chair. "What did he do?" He threw a glance over his shoulder.

"Besides shoot one of my deputies?" Tony slammed his fist on the metal table. The sound of it echoed around them. He couldn't disguise his anger. It felt like electricity pouring from his body. He noticed that everyone in the room sat up straight as he struggled to conquer his rage.

"We think he also hit Miss Nellie Pearl Prigmore in the head hard enough to do more than knock her out. She had to be airlifted to Knoxville, and she is still in a coma." He flipped the file closed and laced his fingers together, staring at Quentin. "If she dies, the charges against him will include murder."

Quentin looked lost.

Carl Lee looked concerned.

"About now, I suppose you are wondering why I am telling you this. Would you like to know where we found him?" He waited for the answering nod. "They were up near her place, in the woods. When we caught up with him, he had drugs in an old lunch box and a gun and an envelope containing a tidy little sum of money stashed in a hole in the ground." Leaning forward, Tony smiled. "Would you like to guess whose finger-prints we found inside that lunch box and all over some plastic sandwich bags filled with meth?"

Shaking his head in denial, Quentin looked ready to burst into tears. His chin quivered and his teeth were buried so deeply in his lower lip that it was starting to bleed.

"Yes, that's right, they are yours. A positive match." Tony relaxed in his chair and watched. The next move was Quentin's. Tony was prepared to wait him out.

Carl Lee kept his firm grip on his client's skinny arm. His long fingers met and appeared to be squeezing, hard, as he whispered something in Quentin's ear. Quentin was shaking his head at every word. It didn't take much thought to realize that the young lawyer was not happy with his client. In fact, it looked as if Carl Lee was ready to throw Quentin to the wolves.

"It was my stuff." Quentin's almost colorless gray eyes moved to Tony, and Carl Lee released his arm. "Sammy's got no right to mess with it." He squirmed on his chair. "It's for . . . what do you say? Personal use."

Wade pulled the file over to his side of the table. He flipped through the pages until he found what he was searching for. It was an inventory of the contents of the lunch box.

"If you *personally* use that much meth, Quentin, why bury it so far away from your house. Isn't it kind of a pain to have to walk or drive a mile, dig up the box, rebury it and then go back? Why not just keep it under your bed?"

Quentin gnawed on his torn lip. A glance in his lawyer's direction made him chew faster. "I put it there so my girlfriend won't use it all, and—" His lips kept moving, but silence reigned.

"And?" The three men leaned closer to catch his words, but after taking a breath thought better of it and sat back.

He gave his lawyer a last desperate glance. "If I didn't have what I'd promised to have when the man came to pick it up, I don't know what would have happened to me." He released a long and sorrowful sigh. "Angelina don't care nothing about me as long as she gets all the stuff she wants. She says that since it's her recipe, she should get the most."

"What man?" Tony intended to get back to the subject of Angelina Lopez and her recipe.

"You know, the one you was askin' about. Sammy." Quentin's twitching picked up speed. "Hub said that he was one mean bastard, and I guess he should know 'cause they met in prison. Sammy was his cellmate. The two of them was always goin' off somewhere together and that was fine with me." The twitching had turned into shivering. The vibrations were so intense now that his chair began to move around on the linoleum flooring.

Tony couldn't quite decide if Quentin was having a bad reaction to the drugs in his system or if he was just flat-out scared. Either way, he was not in any shape to tell them anything more for a while.

Tony tipped his head to pull Carl Lee away. They went into the hallway.

"Are you planning to arrest my client?" Carl Lee frowned. His Adam's apple bobbed above his shirt collar. "Do you have evidence that he's guilty of anything more than possession?"

"Not at this time. You tell me what to do because I don't know." Tony headed for his office with Carl Lee trotting along next to him. "He's having some major drug problems that just locking him up won't help. Yesterday afternoon, his driveway was totally impassable, so he won't be able to go home until some serious clearing is done."

Tony opened the fresh jar of antacids. Not bothering to use his hands, he shook some tablets directly into his mouth and crunched on them. "I don't think he killed his cousin but I don't know that for sure. His fingerprints were on the car, but that is not enough cause to arrest him. His girlfriend is cooking some serious stuff up there, and he is involved in that little project up to his bloodshot eyeballs. If that's not bad enough, we have his connection to Samson and Nellie Pearl."

He offered the young lawyer his jar of antacids.

Carl Lee took four. "Can you keep him here a couple of days, you know, for his own good?" Carl Lee looked as if his own words had taken him by surprise.

"We are not running a hotel and we sure are not running a detox center." Tony looked at the clock. It was already almost noon. He started easing his way to the door, anxious to leave. "If he isn't under arrest, we have to let him go. It's up to you and Archie to argue the charges. We picked him up because it is against the law to be cruising around intoxicated. He is as sober now as he ever gets, and he is all yours."

"Can I make a couple of calls?"

"Go for it."

"What about Samson? Where is he?" After consulting his PDA, Carl Lee started punching the buttons on his cell phone. "I don't want him coming after Quentin."

"He is not going anywhere. Sevier County has him locked up tight, and the judge over there has refused to even hear bail requests until Monday afternoon. If you're concerned about Samson coming after Quentin for something, I think you can relax. I don't expect that he will be granted bail for the attempted murder of a police officer."

"Does he have any ties to this area?" Carl Lee looked as if he doubted it would make any difference in this case, but sometimes a relative who was willing to vouch for the accused would sway the judge determining bail. "Personal? Business?"

Tony shook his head. "Only illegal business." Tony could tell that Carl Lee knew something about Quentin and Samson that he wasn't sharing with the Sheriff's Office. "What's going on, Carl Lee?"

Carl Lee shook his head and held up a finger like a pause sign. "Give me a minute." He moved away from Tony and started talking into his tiny phone.

A moment later Tony's own phone began to ring. The state attorney's office asked that Quentin be housed in Park County. They needed him as a material witness in a case. Rather than risk losing him, he was to be given room and board. The county would be reimbursed. Given no choice, Tony agreed.

Curiosity threatened to eat him alive but Carl Lee's lips were sealed.

When they returned to the greenhouse, a few words whispered into Quentin's ear, obtained cooperation and even a bit of gratitude.

Tony watched Quentin all but skip back to his cell.

"Soon, Tony, soon," said Carl Lee. "All will become clear."

CHAPTER TWENTY-ONE

Sunday morning, instead of going to church, Tony sat at his desk, trying to make sense of the past few days. It wasn't working. His eyes moved from his notes to his watch. He couldn't be late. He had important plans with his sons.

Tony possessed a deep and enduring love for the game of baseball. His favorite team was the Chicago Cubs. Spring training was in full swing and today the Cubs would play the White Sox.

Due to the magic of satellites and cable television, Tony would be able to watch the game in his own home. He dreamed of vacationing in Arizona during spring training. He longed to lounge in the sunshine and soak up the sounds and smells that went along with the game. Football didn't have them and basketball didn't either. Something about the smell of grass, the heat and the crack of the wooden bat filled some primal need in him. Seeing baseball on television was better than nothing. A semi-rabid Cubs fan since early childhood, he freely admitted that the reason he eventually moved to Chicago after he left Silersville and the Navy was to be nearer his beloved team.

He wanted to be home in time for the first pitch. He and the boys made big plans to watch the game together and eat popcorn and hot dogs.

Keys in hand, he checked his watch once more as he headed to the parking lot. He'd meet his family for Sunday dinner at the Riverview, then take the afternoon off. No identification had been made on the bones.

Hub's killer could be anyone.

Ziggy intercepted him before he reached the Blazer. The expression on the emergency coordinator's face made Tony's stomach clench. The usually unflappable man looked almost panicky.

"I've got an important date with my sons, Zig. Can whatever this is about wait until tomorrow?"

"I'll let you decide after I fill you in." Ziggy rubbed his bloodshot eyes and focused on Tony's left shoulder. He wasn't tall enough to be eye-to-eye with the sheriff and refused to look up to meet his gaze.

Tony sidled closer to his vehicle.

Ziggy stayed right with him. "Yesterday's little flood could have been a lot worse, you know. Nobody's house flooded and no cars washed off the road. It will still be a good while before all of the trash is cleaned up." He didn't wait for a response but went on with his informal report. "If we had one more inch of rain or if it lasted one more hour, we'd have a really serious situation."

"I'm aware of this." Tony released his breath and opened the Blazer door. His impatience was multiplying by the second. "Is that all you have to say?"

"Not exactly." Ziggy's manner turned hesitant. That was out of character. The man liked to call a spade a spade.

"Then, what exactly?" Tony knew they were both running on coffee and willpower, and there was no offense meant or taken with the curt response.

"You know Possum Calhoun?" Ziggy stepped back and met Tony's eyes then, clearly watching for a reaction.

"Of course." Tony frowned. "There's nothing slimier than that kind of trash, is there?" In his mind, Possum was the foul-smelling scum that grew in warm dark places. The man was the prototype for the Hollywood version of a hillbilly. Tony hated that designation and he hated Possum Calhoun. Only part of the reason was because Possum liked to beat his wife, Sally. If they had reproduced, he would have beaten the children as well. One of Tony's greatest frustrations was that no matter how many times Possum was arrested, Sally always welcomed him home. She never pressed charges. All attempts by the local advocates to help her fell on deaf ears.

Sally loved Possum. Sally feared Possum.

Possum made Quentin look nice and ambitious. Clean, too. His yard, if that was the correct name for it, was a stinking pile of refuse. He and Sally inhabited a former shack. Tony didn't know what else to call a poorly constructed shack after it disintegrated from years of neglect and harsh weather.

"His wife believes he is missing and probably dead. Sally thinks that Possum must of drowned and been washed away."

Eyebrows raised, Tony faced Ziggy. "First I've heard of it. Why did she call you instead of my office?"

"She didn't." Ziggy shifted his weight back and forth. "She talked to my brother, Pete. I'm sure you know that he sells insurance, and I'll bet that he has contacted everyone in the county at some time trying to sell another life insurance policy. It seems that Sally wanted to know if Possum had any insurance." Ziggy's expression indicated that he would never believe Possum would do anything so decent and responsible. "You know as well as I do that if there was a policy, it would be on Sally and he would be looking to collect. Anyway, Pete called and told me about it and I thought that I'd just check and see if you had heard anything about Possum. If he drowned, I need to put it in my reports and try to understand how it happened because the water never got very deep."

"I'll send someone out to check on it when I get a chance." Tony sat in the car. "I can't say that it would exactly break my heart if Possum died. That is, of course, assuming there was no foul play involved." Tony guessed it would be a real challenge to investigate the suspicious demise of someone whom he had considered killing himself.

Theo knew that she and the mayor's wife were never going to be good friends. She had determined that long ago. The fact that Theo was at this moment considering killing the woman only emphasized her decision. Clenching her teeth, Theo thought she would snap if she heard one more diatribe about the importance of her sainted husband, the mayor, herself or her business. Doreen Cashdollar had developed into a real pain in the community's backside.

Just this morning, Doreen backed Theo into a corner, literally trapping her between the ladies room wall, the sink and her well-groomed, size-four body. What she lacked in physical bulk, she made up for with determination and sheer gall. Her hair color and style changed almost weekly. She spent so many hours at the Klip 'n' Kurl that Prudence had to consider Doreen something along the lines of the goose that laid golden eggs, but one whose constant honking made earning them a trial.

As far as Theo was concerned, one of the worst things the woman did was import shoddy quilts made by virtual slave labor in the poorest of the poor third-world countries and sell them for a pittance in her gift shop. She advertised, "Smoky Mountain Hand-quilted treasures $29.95, all sizes."

Customers who came into Theo's shop to purchase quilts and not fabric would frequently exclaim about her high prices. These same customers did not notice, or if they noticed, care that the quilting stitches were long and far apart or that the fabric was so sleazy it was practically cheesecloth. People would carry these imported quilts home, souvenirs of the Smoky Mountains, made overseas. Some of the consignment quilts

Theo had for sale were not much better quality, but at least they were local products.

Doreen's Gift Shoppe was the new name over the door into her store, but everyone in Silersville knew that it was still just the front side of the Cashdollar Funeral Home and Gift Shoppe. A new sign would not make any real changes in the business itself. Doreen filled the large room, packing it with greeting cards, wind chimes, relishes and honey, scented candles and soap, and many other assorted items. Some of it was exquisite and some of it was just plain trash. She did a thriving business with both tourists and locals and to be fair, Theo had to admit that most of the crafts and all of the preserves were produced locally.

Doreen's morning attack at church was to try to convince Theo to keep her shop open on Sundays all year around. Theo kept it open on Sundays during the busiest tourist season of the year but didn't like doing it. It went against her personal beliefs about what Sunday meant. Any quilter who had a desperate need for needles, thread or fabric on Sunday would call and get Jane or Theo to come down and open up for them anyway.

Chris and Jamie ate dessert while Martha and Jane were commiserating with Theo over Sunday dinner at the Riverview Motel and Café when Tony arrived.

Seeing the two little boys diligently scraping every molecule of hot fudge from the bottom of their tulip-shaped sundae dishes, made Tony grin. "Ladies, boys." He noticed that his aunt Martha, a more svelte version, and his mom were working on enormous chef salads while Theo struggled with an oversized platter of chicken fried steak and mashed potatoes. The Riverview served mammoth portions. His little wife could eat for a week and never finish that pile of food. Without saying a word, she pushed the plate over to him and reached for her glass of iced tea.

Clenching the fork in his hand, Tony didn't start eating right away, but stared at his mother and her sister. "So, which one of you would like to explain about the old motel?"

Jane didn't look up from her salad to greet her youngest child. If the way she continued to stuff lettuce into her mouth was any indication, it must have been weeks since her last meal. She seemed dedicated.

Martha looked him in the face but she had the deer-in-the-headlights expression. She blinked and refocused on her salad. "Motel?" She managed to mumble around a chunk of tomato, sending a couple of seeds flying into her glass of iced tea. "What are you talking about, Marc Antony?"

The use of his full name didn't win her any points. "I think you know the one."

The older women concentrated on eating, unable to tear their eyes away from their lunches. Theo's eyebrows rose above her glasses, but her mouth stayed shut.

"No? How odd." The fork he held began to bend. "Think back a couple of months to a purchase you ladies made together. It is an old, dilapidated motel on the highway to Townsend." Tony had to work hard to keep his voice low. "As far as I can tell, it needs a little work to bring it up to the exacting standards of the town dump."

The women froze.

He shoveled a fork full of meat and potatoes into his mouth and stared at them as he chewed. He swallowed. "Should I send Marmot-the-Varmint out to give you pointers on running a landfill?"

That snapped their heads up.

Jane fluffed her newly blond hair and opened her mouth but paused. Martha jumped in and started talking before her sister made a sound. "Don't take that tone with me. We had Caesar Augustus check it out, and he did a most thorough job. I must remember to commend him on his diligence."

Tony leaned forward. He raised a palm to stop her before his aunt had a chance to propose Gus for sainthood. "And my big brother said it was a good building? A fine investment?" He could feel an expression of doubt settling on his face, tightening his muscles. His throat closed and when he spoke again, his words were oddly rasping. "I can't believe Gus has gone completely off his rocker. He uses two-by-sixes to frame a doghouse. A little doghouse."

His mother gulped the bait. And the hook. "Gus said it was a total waste of money." Jane found her voice at last, but it squeaked and cracked. "And he also said that if we bought it, the whole mess would need to be hauled away." She stopped suddenly as she realized she had said more than she had intended.

The way her lips slammed together, Tony thought that she didn't look as if she ever planned to talk again. "So, upon hearing such a glowing recommendation, you just had to have it." He couldn't seem to swallow his potatoes or their story. "Please explain." He was met with stony silence. His mother and aunt sat and stared at the mounds of lettuce.

A glance at his wife's face assured him that she had no idea what they had done. That made him feel better. Across the table, the boys abandoned their spoons and now surreptitiously tried licking the chocolate syrup out of the bottom of the tulip-shaped glasses. It wouldn't work.

Jamie wore a look that made him appear much more mature than his six years. Tony knew that his ears operated like a radar system. That little boy could eavesdrop from across town. If you wanted the freshest gossip or news, he was the best source. Tony's eyes met Theo's. She nodded.

"Why don't you boys go out and play for a couple of minutes?" Theo waved the boys toward the door.

"We're almost done here and the game starts in just a little bit." Tony handed Chris a fresh napkin. "I don't intend to miss a single play."

Chris wiped the chocolate sauce from the end of his nose. His eyes widened behind the lenses of his glasses. He had Theo's eyes, huge, hazel gold and nearsighted. "Are you gonna arrest Grandma?"

"I'm not planning to." He waited until Jamie and Chris were safely outside before glaring at the pair of women. "Game's over. You have a drug dealer's fingerprints in one cabin and the preacher of the congregation that met in your office building has been murdered. Talk."

"We didn't know anything about that." Jane lost her defiant expression. "Pops asked if they could rent the office and we said okay. I've known him for years, and there didn't seem any harm in renting to a group like that. You know, not quite a church but more of an old-timey gathering is how Pops described them. He said they didn't have any money but they were willing to clean up the place in exchange for using it a few evenings and Sundays. It seemed like a good deal, and it was just going to be for a little while."

"They never told us about the snakes." Martha jumped in. "We didn't rent the cabin. Whoever left fingerprints didn't have our permission to stay there. We only agreed for them to use the office." She gave up dealing with her oversized salad and handed it to a passing waitress. "We wanted to wait until we had our plans laid out, and then we were going to tell you all about it."

"We had to tell Gus but we didn't tell anyone else." Jane patted his arm. "It's so exciting. We're going to turn it into a folk art museum and a sort of camp for learning the old crafts. We originally thought the old motel rooms would work okay for classrooms and that eventually we could build a dormitory building. Gus said we will have to tear all those cabins down and start over." Once she began her description, she rattled on for a couple of minutes without coming up for breath, until she blurted, "Please don't tell anyone until we are ready to make our announcement."

Whatever he had guessed, he had never come close to their plan. It left him speechless. Thank goodness, Theo wasn't. She leaned forward and pumped the older women for details. "You mean like the museum over in Norris with the old buildings and the garden and all that other great stuff?"

"Sort of." Martha beamed. "We don't expect to have buildings like that, but there is a lot of good old stuff piled in local barns and attics. A lot of treasures are just rotting in rickety old sheds. We just want to borrow them and put them on display." Folding her hands together, she gave Theo a tentative smile. "We weren't going to bring it up for a while, but we thought that maybe you could teach people how to make quilts in the old way. You know, hand piecing, and using scissors instead of a rotary cutter."

Tony recognized the ploy as a diversionary gambit and didn't give his wife a chance to respond, but continued his questions. "Did you ever go out and check on your property after you gave Pops the go-ahead?" Tony almost asked where they had come up with the money, but was pretty sure he wouldn't like the answer.

"Once." Jane looked to Martha for confirmation. "Only a week or so ago, we drove out there and we were pleased by the way it looked. The office looked spotless and the ground around the buildings had been just raked. You could see the rake marks in the dirt. The man working out there seemed quite nice."

"He wasn't working when we talked to him." Martha corrected her sister. "Remember, we weren't even sure he had been doing the raking because he was sitting on the stoop, eating potato chips."

"That's right." Jane's head began bobbing. "Didn't you think he was pleasant though?" She waited for her sister's nod of agreement then looked back to Tony. "We chatted for quite a while and I remember thinking that he acted sort of vague, mentally that is."

"One of his eyes didn't focus right either," said Martha.

With sense of foreboding, Tony reached into his pocket and produced a copy of the most recent mug shot of Sammy Samson. "I don't suppose that either of you have ever seen this man?"

"That's him." They looked quite pleased with themselves. "Do you know him? He didn't tell us his name."

"His name is Sammy Samson. Not only is he heavily involved with drugs, taking them and selling them, but he shot Sheila and intended to kill her. He's probably the person who bashed Nellie Pearl in the head, and he might have killed the preacher." Tony mentally pulled out the last strands of his nonexistent hair, but he found the stupefied expressions on their faces somewhat gratifying. "Now tell me, what day and what time did you see him? Exactly." He wasn't smiling when he asked his questions.

Martha had the sense to keep her mouth closed,

Jane responded as if she was checking off the ingredients for her favorite recipe. "Mm? Today's Sunday, so it was the Friday before last Sunday." Jane beamed at her youngest child, but she was careful to keep her eyes from meeting his. "We went out there after I got off work and it was already almost dark."

Tony wanted to cry.

The day improved. The Cubs won. The boys didn't fight, and the three of them managed to play catch and do a little batting practice in the park. For dinner, Theo cooked his favorite casserole, and he got almost a full chapter written in his novel set in the old west.

Tony checked his calendar. Only one more month until they would fly to Montana for a brief visit. Theo would teach in Billings for a few days before she headed to Paducah. He planned to go along for a bit of a vacation and to do some research. So far he had a list of about sixty things he wanted to see in four days. He suspected that something would have to be thrown out, but he was content to lean back in his chair, eyes closed, and contemplate a break from his everyday routine.

CHAPTER TWENTY-TWO

First thing Monday morning, Tony and the county prosecutor, Archie Campbell, decided to have little visit with Sammy Samson. Returned to Park County for his formal arraignment, they hoped spending some time in jail for shooting Sheila might make him a bit more conversational. Tony doubted it, especially if he had been involved with the now-deceased Harold Usher Brown. The two men shared several indisputable connections besides their former status as cellmates. Both had been at the old motel, they had both touched the Focus and they both possessed more than a small stash of drugs.

A couple of nights in the Sevier County Jail couldn't touch serving time in prison.

Tony carried coffee in a mug with a lid. Archie carried an open mug. The tag on his teabag swayed with each step. At last, they settled into the greenhouse with Sammy's attorney.

When Kate Wyatt parked her silver BMW in the parking lot, she attracted admiring glances. Inside she drew even more, at least from the males. Kate fit the television image of a well-groomed woman making it in a man's world. For her, success meant driving a Beemer and wearing a five-hundred-dollar suit. Forest green and fitted to perfection, it complimented Kate's freckled complexion and flame red hair. So many of the residents of East Tennessee lived in poverty that her attire screamed that she did not. Sammy's bank account had to be full to pay for this woman's services. Maybe someone else was footing the bill. But who?

"How did you come to be Sammy's lawyer?" said Tony. He kept his tone conversational. "Somehow I doubt that he's a personal friend of yours. He doesn't look like your type."

"I thought he came from Atlanta." Archie interjected before she could respond. Archie's smile was frankly admiring as he lifted her fingers to his lips and checked her left hand for wedding rings. There were none and his lips pulled away from his teeth, exposing their dazzling whiteness. "How did he end up with one of the finest defense lawyers in East Tennessee? Not to mention that you are easily the most beautiful one in the state."

"I'm not sure who is paying. His attorney in Atlanta contacted my office and presto chango, here I am." Kate graced Archie with a warm smile even as she eased her hand out of his. Tony might not have been in the room for all the attention she paid to him. This woman was not going to waste her ammunition on a married man.

"Have you already met with him or do you need some time to do that?" Archie was going into total meltdown.

Tony thought he might ooze down into his socks. His close-cropped gray hair had been almost the same color as Kate's only a few years ago. His freckles were less distinct than hers were because over the years, he spent enough time outside to develop a permanent tan. If he smiled any wider, he would look exactly like a shark, lots of teeth in a really big mouth. "We can give you a few minutes to confer with your client."

"We've already talked." Sammy's arrival interrupted them. "I don't believe we need any privacy."

There was an almost desperate quality in her expression as she took a step closer to Tony. Her freckles had either gotten darker or her milk white skin had gone about three shades lighter. Two more steps and she would be standing behind him. *Interesting*, thought Tony.

Dressed impeccably in the Park County issued orange and white striped jumpsuit, Sammy shuffled into the room in handcuffs and leg irons. While he barely glanced in the direction of the sheriff and the prosecutor, his eyes focused on Kate's chest.

"Hey there, sweet thing. I was lookin' forward to seein' you again." He headed toward her.

Lank, medium-brown hair covered one eye. The eye Tony could see was mud brown surrounded by bloodshot white. His mustache grew a shade darker than the rest of his hair, including the stubble on his unshaven cheeks. Untrimmed, it extended from his nostrils to cover his lower lip. He parted it in the center to expose his teeth. They were huge, square teeth that looked like he had stolen them from a horse. He licked his lips without disturbing the tiny bits of food clinging to the strands. Rising onto his toes, he used the extra height he gained to peer into the vee of flesh exposed by Kate's tailored lapels.

Tony made a bet with himself that the next time she met with Sammy, Kate would be wearing a turtleneck.

Archie jumped to pull a chair away from the table for Kate. He acted as if they were arriving in an expensive restaurant instead of a room that resembled a bunker. Sammy plopped onto the chair next to hers.

"When do I get out?" Sammy addressed everyone in the room. "I don't want to stay in that hick jail any longer, and I don't like this one any better. Everyone around here acts like that bitch cop is something special."

Kate looked as if she would like to slap her client if she could do it without actually touching him. She had to settle for poking him with her pencil and hissing in his ear. "Shut up." The words bounced around the room. "You will not say one more word unless I say you can."

Tony and Archie were speechless. The level of Sammy's

stupidity amazed them. Even the dullest mind seemed capable of grasping the serious problems created by bragging about shooting a cop. For a couple of stunned minutes they just sat and stared at him.

Archie recovered first. "Those charges are not why we are here today." Blinking furiously, he shuffled around in his briefcase. Since the papers he needed were already on the table, this was clearly a stall. "We are here to decide what charges relating to the death of Harold Usher Brown and what drug-related charges we intend to add to your indictment."

"Who is Harold whatever you said?" Sammy's eyes returned to Kate's chest. His shackled hands rested on his crotch. He smiled.

Kate moved her chair nearer Archie's.

"You can't have forgotten your old cellmate? I think you must remember Hub?" Tony leaned forward. "Your fingerprints were found, along with his, at the old motel where you probably slept in one of the old cabins. They were also on the car where his dead body was found under some peculiar circumstances."

"Never called hisself Harold." Sammy looked a bit shell-shocked but didn't deny anything. "What was that peculiar circle thing?"

"His death was odd," said Tony.

Sammy seemed to understand that. "I don't know what happened to him. I didn't have nothin' to do with it."

"How did your fingerprints get on the door of his car?" said Tony.

"He give me a ride." Bobbing his head up and down, he leered at Kate, as if checking to see that she was impressed by his speedy answer.

"Where did you go?" Tony toyed with the pages of his notebook, flipping back as if to check a previous notation and returning to the blank page. He sat with his pen poised.

"Around." Sammy grinned as if he was proud of his quick wit.

Tony didn't return the smile. "What day was that?"

"Dunno. There was a couple of times."

"Did he show you where Quentin hid his stash of drugs and money, or did you find that on your own?"

Kate thumped her client with the pencil she held. When he looked at her, she shook her head. His lips slammed together like a door blowing shut.

"Okay, let's try this." Tony would have been stunned if Kate had allowed him to talk about the scene of his arrest. She had the reputation of being an excellent attorney. "Why were you camping out in that motel cabin?"

Uneasy, Sammy watched Kate, eyeing her pencil with suspicion. Only after she nodded her consent did he answer. "Didn't cost nothin'. Hub said it would be okay."

"Did you tell your parole officer in Atlanta that you were leaving the state?" Unsurprised, Tony watched Sammy shake his head. "I had a little chat with her this morning. She did not sound pleased to hear that you have been up here shooting my deputy. In fact, I heard her say she would check on how many violations of your parole you committed before you even left Georgia. I have to tell you that she said that she would love to research if she could nail you for possession of a firearm in another state." Tony picked up his pen and stared at Sammy. It pleased him that Sammy's attitude improved. "Now tell me, how long have you been staying out there?"

Sammy glanced at Kate. "A few days." Shifting around on his chair, he rattled his chains. "How long before I can leave? I answered everything you asked me, didn't I?"

No one said a word. Tony and Archie stared at him for a minute and then leaned together, conferring over the papers in Archie's file.

Sammy scooted his chair closer to Kate, creating a loud, scraping sound of metal on linoleum. The noise brought everyone upright. "Don't I get bailed out?" The rising whine of his voice was worse than the scraping. It rated right up there with the fingernail-on-the-blackboard sound for fraying nerves. "I didn't kill nobody."

"We're on our way to the hearing right now." Archie jumped to his feet and as he picked up his files, he gave Kate a courtly bow. "We'll see you in there." He didn't bother looking at her client again.

Tony paused at the door and glanced back at them, but he directed his question to Sammy. "Then tell me why did we find your fingerprints on the handcuffs?"

The expression on Sammy's face was easy to read. The man was simply not an actor.

"I guess I must of touched 'em when I lifted his cell phone." The sharp point of Kate's pencil drew his attention and he turned to face her. "It wasn't like he was going to be making any more calls on it."

As they made their way to the courtroom, Archie kept frowning. "I thought that there were no fingerprints on the handcuffs?"

"There weren't." Tony held the door open for the prosecutor. "I lied, but now we know what happened to the cell phone."

Carl Lee met them on the sidewalk. He smiled as if he'd won a lottery. Standing with him were a stocky young man in a navy blue business suit and a middle-aged woman dressed as his twin. Badges appeared.

The Feds had arrived.

"I don't suppose you're here for the biscuits and gravy over at Ruby's Café?" Tony could only hope. The expression that the agents shared meant more paperwork for him.

As if reading his mind, the woman stepped forward with a

sheaf of papers. "Your case against Samson will go on, of course, but we get him next."

"Why would you want him?"

"I hear your deputy is doing well." Sunglasses covered her eyes, but her lips lifted in a luminous smile. "I presume your question means you are interested in our charges against him."

Tony nodded, even as he reluctantly added more papers to his stack. Ruth Ann would not to be happy to see these. "Is this the reason Quentin is still living the good life in our little jail?"

Head bobbing, Carl Lee stepped forward. "I merely suggested that they might be interested in Quentin's testimony about the theft of certain prescription drugs that were later transported into our state from Kentucky." He looked at the agents. "Isn't that the interstate transport of stolen items?"

They nodded.

Tony smiled.

It would be worth the tons of paperwork needed to send Sammy to the Feds. Between parole violations in Georgia, the laws he had broken since his arrival in Tennessee and now the Feds, Sammy would never again see the unobscured light of day.

Unfortunately, Tony believed that Samson had nothing to do with Hub's death.

CHAPTER TWENTY-THREE

Theo wasn't sure why one of her designs simply didn't work. The math seemed right. The drawing looked possible. The damned thing would not fit together.

Nina had called three times already this morning trying to explain where it went wrong. Taking a copy of the pattern she had given to Nina, Theo tacked it up on her bulletin board and pretended that she had never seen it before. By the time she worked half way through the process, she had a pile of discarded pieces of fabric at her feet.

"I can't believe this won't work. It worked just fine the first time." She kicked the bits of what she called trial-and-error fabrics around the room. Rather than simply discard a fabric that turned out to be a dog, one that no one would buy, not even to use on the back of a quilt, Theo used it to test her patterns for accuracy.

"Is this a bad time to ask a question?" Jane stood in the doorway.

"Yes." The glare that her daughter-in-law gave her might have frozen the blood in her veins if she hadn't had developed an immunity over the years. It was nothing personal. Theo just hated distractions when she designed.

"Yes." Theo repeated the word and gave the scraps at her feet another good kick. Zoe, the kitten, bounced up the stairs behind Jane. The flying scraps looked like a gift to her. Dashing across the room and pouncing on the little bits, she made a funny little sound between a hiss and a purr. It brought a smile to Theo's face and made Jane chuckle.

"Okay, both of you. What's up?"

"I wondered if I might be able to take some time off this summer." Jane looked very uncomfortable.

"Of course." Theo's reply came instantly. She couldn't believe that Jane was wringing her hands. Asking for time off couldn't be that hard. "You aren't really a slave, you know. I just treat you like one."

"I'm thinking more like taking the whole summer off."

Theo stood, openmouthed, staring at her mother-in-law. Jane rarely took a single a day off. She went to work for Theo the first day the shop opened and had been there through thick and thin. In spite of her initial misgivings, Jane hung in there when they adapted the business for Internet shopping. Theo wondered if maybe Jane had some catastrophic illness. "Are you sick?"

Her turn to be stunned, Jane's mouth dropped open. "Where did you get that idea?"

"Well, I don't know." Theo chuckled. "It jumped into my head. I couldn't imagine why else you would suddenly ask for so much time. So, you tell me what's going on."

Jane started blushing like a schoolgirl. "I . . ." she stopped. "That is we, Martha and I, want to do a little something different this summer, something we have wanted to do since she moved here after college. Back then, I had a husband and a family and then it wasn't long before she married Frank." With a sigh, she shrugged her shoulders. "Time just got away from us."

Since Theo knew that Martha recently turned fifty, their plans had certainly been on hold for a long time. That pair sure kept their share of secrets. First there had been the purchase of the motel. What had possessed them to buy that old thing and start making plans to turn it into a museum? "Does this have anything to do with your museum plans?"

"Not directly." Jane's flushed face grew brighter.

Pushing her glasses higher up on her nose, Theo leaned forward. "Spit it out then," she said. "Your mysterious activities are making me nuts."

"We used to be a sister act." Jane's answer came out so fast that it sounded like one word. "I played the piano and Martha sang. We started when she was just a tiny little tot. She always had a voice that sounded mature, you know, kind of like Charlotte Church. We performed at every opportunity we could find, from the Sunday school pageants to the local radio show." Jane's voice slowed and finally halted.

"So you and Martha are going on the road?" Visions of Tony's mother and aunt singing in smoky roadhouses, the entertainment between bar fights, flashed into her brain. A sense of dread grew in the pit of her stomach. Hollywood could not have produced a more lurid picture. Theo hoped Tony didn't have a stroke when he found out. He might be the youngest of the siblings, but he felt responsible for his mother's safety. It was just that simple.

"I'm afraid Tony would have a stroke if he heard it put that way." Jane's words echoed Theo's thoughts to perfection. "For that matter, Gus and Callie would too. Even Virgil would get involved, and he never gets involved." Her eyes flashed. "Not that it's any of their business, but we sent a bunch of demo CD's out and from them we got offered a summer job at a little place near Chattanooga. We drove down a week ago last Saturday and took a look and we're in." Her grin looked like she had just hit the game winning home run.

"You've been planning this that long?" Gaping at Jane as if she had transformed herself into a little green Martian, Theo collapsed onto the chair in front of her sewing machine. "You don't just get a CD made and mail it out and get a job over the weekend. What about your museum project?"

A rush of words poured from Jane like water released from a dam. They buffeted Theo's ears and brain. She did manage to hang on to enough of them to determine that something the mayor's wife had done would delay the museum project indefinitely. Since that had fallen through, neither sister wanted to say anything about the singing project for fear of jinxing it. Superstitious, but true. The last bit of information Theo grasped was the name of Jane's summer replacement. Gretchen Blackburn, Ziggy's wife.

Theo almost groaned out loud.

Gretchen was a sweetheart and Theo loved her, but, she could talk the nuts off a Jeep. On the plus side, everyone liked Gretchen, probably because she laughed constantly.

Raised in Ohio, Gretchen went to Indiana University to major in vocal music. Built like a Wagnerian heroine, Theo thought she would look at home armed with a spear and shield and her long blond hair in braids. But, ten years ago, she was singing at a gospel music convention in Pigeon Forge when she met Ziggy. Two weeks later they were exchanging vows in the Heartland Wedding Chapel in Townsend. Nine months after that, she presented Ziggy with twin daughters. She might have given up on her dream of singing arias at La Scala, but she became the mainstay of the Baptist choir.

Her quilt-making skills were so-so, but each quilt she made was better than the last. In the years since she had taken the beginning class, she had come to Theo's shop at least once a week, sometimes daily. She probably knew the inventory as well as Jane did.

After giving it some thought, Theo smiled. Maybe this would be a change for the better. At least she wouldn't be worried about her mother-in-law wearing out while working for her. Gretchen would have no difficulty carrying several bolts of fabric at a time.

Tony sat behind his desk, pouring over the printout of the cell phone records of the late Harold Usher Brown. The man must have spent most his time dialing or talking. The bulk of his calls were to the Atlanta area, but he had made some to almost every state east of the Mississippi River.

On the night he died, he made four calls between the time his preaching ended and the time his life ended. One call was to Atlanta, one to Knoxville and two to Park County numbers. Tony recognized the mayor's home phone number. He dialed the other, but no one answered. It didn't take him long to find out that it belonged to one of the pay phones outside the Okay Bar and Bait Shop. That one would have to wait.

Just to see what would happen, he dialed the Atlanta number. An artificial voice informed him that the number he dialed was not in service. The Knoxville number was only slightly more productive. At that number, a recording of a real voice gave him a list of the movies playing and the times they would be shown.

He debated with himself whether or not to wander over to the mayor's office, situated in another wing of the city building or to arrive, lights flashing, in front of his house. Maybe he could get a search warrant and then he could enlist every deputy, even those off duty, to help him comb the mayor's house. It was a lovely dream but he decided to go casual. After all, receiving a telephone call from a snake-handling, drug-smuggling preacher just minutes before he died was not a crime. An ugly coincidence, to be sure, but not a crime.

With the printout in hand and Wade trotting along beside him, Tony marched out the front doors of the Law Enforcement center and over to the main doors of the City Building. He chose that route because he felt like doing something petty, and this route was much more public than using the tunnel system.

If the mayor didn't remember the phone call, Tony could still use the patrol car and lights to visit with the Missus. Queen Doreen was six times more annoying than the mayor. Tony wouldn't mind causing her a little embarrassment.

Justifiably, the town of Silersville refused to pay the salary for a full-time secretary for a part-time mayor. Marigold Flowers Proffitt took his telephone messages and did occasional typing on his official stationary when she wasn't tied up with her real job, which was taking care of the city's finances. If Marigold had too much to do, by her standards, the mayor did his own typing.

Like her younger sister Blossom, Marigold had been gifted with very little hair. Instead of taking Blossom's approach of doing the best she could with what she had been given, Marigold had long ago shaved her head. She owned an array of wigs and turbans that she wore, changing them with the rest of her ensemble. Today Marigold was coifed in a wig of short russet curls. Tony thought it looked exceptionally nice with her stylish navy dress and red high-heeled shoes. They added four inches to her height. Marigold had lovely legs and knew it. She made sure that they were always on display.

Tony could probably count on one hand the number of times she had worn slacks to work. She had been overweight as a girl, although never as heavy as Blossom, and had worked tirelessly to change that. Someone once mentioned that Marigold's husband ate three meals a day at Ruby's because his wife didn't allow food in her house.

At the approach of Tony and Wade, she looked up from her computer screen and gave them a big smile. Her teeth were perfect, small and pearl-white. Tony thought they were probably not original equipment.

"Morning, gentlemen."

After a brief exchange of pleasantries, Marigold informed

them that the mayor was indeed in his office and that if he was busy, it was most likely not because he was working on city business. Calvin's mayoral duties were mostly ceremonial. Only on rare occasions did the office require actual work. A combination of wanting more business for his wife's gift shop and the need to show the voters that they ought to keep such a paragon in office fueled his current campaign to enhance area tourism. After all, it was an election year.

Tony knocked on the mayor's door. He didn't wait for an answer but strolled on in.

Calvin's head swiveled as he looked from him to Wade and back again, sending his mop of blond hair into his eyes. If the pinched expression around his mouth meant anything, he wasn't pleased to see them. "What can I do for you, Tony? Deputy? Come on in and have a seat." The words were pleasant enough, but the tone was as sour as unripe berries.

"This is official business, not social." Tony sat but Wade merely propped a shoulder against the doorframe and watched, his arms crossed over his chest and his fingertips pressed against the underside of his biceps. The pose made his bulging muscles bulge even more. No doubt about it, Wade made an impressive bodyguard.

Tony said, "*I'm* a busy man so I'll get right to the point." He enjoyed the mayor's frown as he caught the intentional dig. "I want you to tell me all about your relationship with the late Harold Brown, also known as John Mize?"

"There's nothing to tell." The mayor's answer was immediate and a little too loud. "I'm positive I never met the man."

"Really?" Tony didn't need to look at the printout again, but opened it and made quite a production of silently reading it. He held the paper so that he could watch the mayor without lifting his eyes. Judging by the way Calvin was craning his head around to see what Tony held, it was clear that curiosity was burning the man alive. Tony looked up. "You have talked to him though."

"No. Don't believe so." Failing in his attempts to read around corners, the mayor adopted a more casual pose, leaning forward in his chair, his hands stacked on his desk. He graced them with his campaign smile. "Can't imagine why I would want to. Snakes give me the creeps and I am, after all, a lifetime member of the First Baptist Church. I don't hold with these fly-by-night churches."

"I'll accept that, for now." With a nod, Tony folded the printout and put it on his lap. "Maybe you wouldn't mind telling me where you were last Wednesday evening?"

"Wednesday?" Calvin's head reared back so quickly that it was amazing that he didn't give himself whiplash. His face went red and blotchy and it looked as if he'd swallowed his lips. Stuttering and gasping, he couldn't seem to catch his breath long enough to answer the question. "I, uh, I went to church, of course."

"And afterwards?" Tony wasn't much of a fisherman, but he knew better than to try to set the hook too soon. He made it sound like an idle question.

"I, uh, I was at home, uh, that is I went home afterwards, and uh, there I was, that is, at home." Babbling, it took him a moment to realize his statement was incoherent. He fell silent at last, but his breathing was still ragged. No longer red and blotchy, his face had turned chalk white.

Tony recognized panic when he saw it, and the mayor was going into full panic mode. Interesting. Lifting an eyebrow, he waited. From the look of things, the mayor would start pleading for mercy, or crying, at any moment.

"I didn't know him." Calvin bolted from his desk chair, running toward Wade and the doorway. When he saw Wade's hand move toward the holstered gun resting on his hip, he raised his hands and stopped dead in his tracks. Craning his neck, he peeked around the deputy, looking into the reception area.

Tony could see that Marigold's back was just a few feet away from the doorway. Her russet head moved as if she was listening to music.

"Close the door." Calvin mouthed the words but made no sound.

Stepping inside, Wade did.

It brought the deputy even closer to the mayor. Calvin made no attempt to move. The mayor was the taller of the two but Wade wasn't short. He was a powerful young man whose hand hovered near his gun.

Calvin flinched and swallowed hard as he half-turned and addressed Tony. "If I swear I had nothing to do with that man's death, wouldn't my word be good enough?" Calvin shook as if he had palsy. His eyes were glued to the gun. "Can't we just leave it at that?"

"Not even close." Unable to hear clearly, Tony left his chair and moved across the room. He stopped inches away from the mayor.

"Does this have to be spread about? I'd like to keep this private, you know, just man to man." There were tears in his eyes. He wasn't talking but he was begging nonetheless.

Tony relaxed. Mayor Calvin Cashdollar had a dirty little secret, but it was probably not murder. "If it's criminal, everyone will soon hear about it. If it's just criminally stupid, it will stay in this room."

The mayor released his breath and went back to his chair. "A man called me at home. He said that he knew I was the mayor and that if I didn't want the community to learn about . . ." he paused to cough. "A certain, indiscreet meeting I had in Knoxville, that I should get five thousand dollars in cash and he would tell me later how to pay him."

"Let me get this straight." Tony couldn't believe his ears. The most self-righteous, holier-than-thou prig in all of Tennessee was confessing to an improper liaison. "You want me to believe that you were stupid enough to have an affair, and not just to have an affair, but to have it only sixty miles away from home. Hell, man, you might as well have been fornicating on the courthouse lawn. Have you ever gone to Knoxville and not seen someone you know?"

Shaking his head, Calvin didn't say a word. His shoulders rolled forward as if to protect his chest. A tear did escape and roll down one cheek.

"So someone saw you and recognized you and thought to make a profit from it and gave you call?" said Tony. What was wrong with the people in this community? Calvin Cashdollar continued to be elected. He'd heard of towns that had elected a dog to the position and was about to decide that they were on the right track.

"That's right. I didn't recognize the voice and he didn't give me a name or a place to meet. He just said to get the money together and expect him to call again." The mayor managed to get to back to his chair and he collapsed onto it, sending it sliding across the plastic carpet cover. "Please don't tell anyone."

"So, did you get the money?" said Wade.

"Yes." The mayor opened his desk drawer and pulled out a fat manila envelope. "Would you like to count it?" His hands trembled as he offered it to each man in turn. Neither of them touched it.

"When Blossom found a dead man in that car, did you have any reason to believe he was the same man who called you?"

Calvin shook his head in denial. "If I had, I would've put this back in the savings account before Doreen noticed that it was gone." He coughed into a fist. "Lucky for me, she only likes to spend it and prefers to let someone else to do the accounting."

Tony believed him. No one would make up such a stupid story.

"Do you own any handcuffs?" said Wade.

The way the mayor's face blanched and then flushed made Tony wish that he had thought to ask that question himself. Calvin's head nodded the slightest amount.

"I did have." His long fingers toyed with the manila envelope, tearing the flap into confetti and exposing a fair sized stack of currency inside. "They're missing."

"Since when?"

"I don't know." The flesh of his face pulled against the bones, making him look like a cadaver. His pale eyes drifted toward Tony's face before dropping to the star-shaped badge and up to the ceiling. "I, um, ordered them some time ago and left them in my car, because, I didn't want Doreen to find them."

Tony could barely hear his last words. "When did you notice that they were gone?"

"After I heard about the handcuffs on the guy in the car, I looked for them and they weren't under the seat any longer."

"Why did you look for them?" said Wade. "Did you have any reason to believe they were yours?"

"No." He lifted his eyes. "I swear that I have no idea what became of them. I haven't seen them for weeks."

THE THIRD BODY OF CLUES

Sew together Unit 1's and Unit 2's. Place a 2 (flying geese) right side up with the arrow pointing left. Place a Unit 1 onto it with wrong side of triangle in upper right. Sew 1's to 2's using 1/4" seam, along long right edge. Open. You should have a 4 1/2" square. Press seam toward 2's. Sew 48.

Divide these blocks into two equal stacks. Place one stack right side up with arrow of goose pointing left. Place the other stack, wrong side up with arrow of goose pointing down. Using 1/4" seam sew these together along right edge. Press toward 1's. Sew 24.

Divide into two stacks. Place stack right side up with arrows pointing left and down. Place the other stack, wrong side up with arrows pointing down and right. Pin upper edge to hold center aligned before sewing with 1/4" seam. Center triangles will form pinwheel of fabric (B).

Before pressing, turn to wrong side and use your fingers to pop the threads in the center so that it opens and you can press each side toward unit 1's. The center on back will look like a tiny pinwheel and will lay flat.

Each block should measure 8 1/2" by 8 1/2". Make 12.

CHAPTER TWENTY-FOUR

Tony liked the Okay Bar and Bait Shop. The blue-collar establishment operated more like a clubhouse than a bar. Its regulars were mostly single men with few prospects, monetary or social. They liked to hang out together, watching television, drinking beer, playing pool and having an occasional fight. The Okay had no dance floor, in part because of space limitations, but more because men did not come here to socialize with women. A few women stopped in on a regular basis, but like the men, they didn't come looking for a date.

Sitting at the far end of the parking lot, away from the highway, the building itself resembled a cube. Its flat walls and roof bore no decorative touches, and the peeling paint exposed more wood than it covered. Kudzu spreading from nearby trees had established a toehold on the west end of the building. By the end of summer it would probably cover that whole section.

Tony had always thought that the front resembled a ghost face, the illusion created by a pair of small windows of black glass that flanked the black steel door. A group of volunteers had constructed a crude deck of rough-cut boards and attached it to the back. Donated plastic lawn chairs were arranged so that the large-screen television behind the bar was visible to those seated outside as well as those inside.

The Okay hadn't stocked bait for years.

The pay phone dialed from Hub's phone sat on a short pole, next to the road. From the first moment it was installed, it proved to be popular. Residents of the small houses and trailers nearby walked over and used it rather than pay for home service. Due to popular demand, a second phone had to be placed next to it.

Caroline "Mom" Proffitt took over the Okay when her husband died in a freak accident as he was taking down a dead tree in their front yard. Not quite five feet tall, Caroline had made two necessary changes in the bar when she went to work there. She had her brothers build a platform on her side of the bar so she could see over it. When they finished, she installed a playpen in her new office.

Mom raised her two boys and a fair number of her current customers with love and common sense. All customers had to give her their keys when they arrived and were given a claim check if they felt they needed one. Most of the men didn't bother with them but a couple supplied their own markers, just for fun. No one complained about Mom's policy, and anyone who didn't get his keys back got a ride home.

Her nickname provoked a fair number of jokes combining her with Pops Ogle. The probability that Pops would have a stroke if he ever walked into a tavern made the whole scenario priceless. A few beers contributed to the entertainment value.

In contrast to the faded exterior, the interior received regular scrubbings, keeping it spotlessly clean. Powerful air filters removed any smoke as soon as it was exhaled. As Mom often explained, she wasn't going to tell her customers not to smoke, but that didn't mean that she had to breathe the stuff.

"Hey, Mom." Tony greeted Caroline. He wished every bar had the same key policy and had told her that many times. "Can I have my regular?"

"Hey, to you too, Sheriff." Caroline's greeting sounded warm and genuine. "You want a drink, you give me those keys." She laughed at her own joke as she handed him a tall glass of ice water.

At this time of the day, there were only a couple of customers in the Okay, and they weren't drinking. Perched on the edge of a pair of wooden captain's chairs, the two watched a soap opera on the television. Clearly irritated by the two making distracting noises, they frowned and glared. One cleared his throat loudly and uncrossed and recrossed his arms.

Mom and Tony moved to the side.

The only other person in the bar was a young black man cleaning the wood paneled walls. Tony recognized Daniel, Ruth Ann's baby brother. When Daniel spotted Tony, he ambled over to visit.

Tony grinned and slapped the young man on the back. "I didn't know you were working here, and I would swear your sister has told me every other move you've made in the past few years. How'd you enjoy Army chow?" When Daniel enlisted, he had been a little overweight and now he looked extremely fit.

"Not bad." Daniel laughed. "I'll bet it was better than the stuff the Navy was eating."

Once a Navy cook, Tony shook his head in mock despair. "You out of the service now?"

"Yeah, and I don't start at the University until summer and Mom said she needed some help." His voice lowered. "She didn't tell me that I would have to scrub the walls or I might have re-upped. She might be tiny, but she's ruthless."

They all laughed at that outrageous lie. Tony could remember seeing Daniel doing odd jobs for Mom from the time he grew strong enough to lift a bucket. She had been one of his most vocal fans when he played sports in high school, sitting side by side with his mother and sister. His picture hung on the "sports wall," along with those of every other local athlete who ever played any game well.

Tony drained the water from his glass. "Were you both here last Wednesday night?"

"I came here after church." Mom propped her elbows on the bar. It looked like it took all of her willpower not to ask why he wanted to know. "It was a quiet night and I went home about ten."

Daniel nodded. "I came in about two to clean and tend bar while Mom went to church. A few regulars came in and ate and watched the tube for a bit. They were mostly gone when Mom got here."

"Anybody come in that you didn't recognize?"

He rubbed his chin as he thought. "It doesn't seem like there were any strangers. You know, all the guys sat together and talked. After they left, nobody else came in here so we closed early. Why?"

"Can you see the pay phones from behind the bar?"

"Real well in the daylight." Mom waved him onto her platform. "Not as good later on. Even though there are lights on the poles, they usually cast funny shadows on everything. At night everyone looks as short as me and their faces get all distorted."

"Damn, you are short." As tall as he was, Tony had to fold himself almost in half to see the view that Mom would see. In the lot outside, he saw Wade photographing the area. "I know your phones are always busy, but did you notice any unusual activity or someone you don't know hanging around? Someone getting calls? Anything odd at all?"

Daniel and Mom watched Wade for a few moments and then looked back to Tony.

"I've been gone so long that I don't recognize everyone who comes here any longer," said Daniel. "There was a couple of guys I didn't know out there but nothing that I'd call suspicious looking."

It took Mom longer to respond. "Seems like there was something odd that happened that night, but I'll swear that I can't put my finger on it." She wiped an invisible smudge off the bar with the side of her hand. "You know how it is when something is just out of reach. It'll probably come to me about three in the morning."

Wade joined them inside, still carrying his camera. "Do you remember anyone out of the ordinary who stopped out there that night?"

"Oddly enough, I do," said Mom. "When I pulled into the parking lot after church, I saw Queen Doreen's car parked near the phones. Now that I think about it though, I guess I didn't see her."

Tony added that to his notes. "Anyone else?"

"Well, Quentin Mize and Claude Marmot. Those two are quite a pair." Mom's eyes widened and her mouth rounded as it dropped open. "Now I remember! I saw that pretty little Sligar girl. It seemed awful late for her to be out, but she was definitely making a call."

"Prudence's daughter? Karissa?" said Tony.

Mom nodded.

The boys' favorite babysitter, Karissa was maybe twelve years old. It had to be two miles from her house to the Okay. "What time was that? Was she alone?"

"Late, maybe midnight." Mom leaned forward.

"She couldn't have been alone or I'd have gone out there. A car waited for her, but I didn't recognize it. It wasn't parked right next to the phones, but it was running and the headlights were shining on her. That's how I could recognize her."

A frown creased Tony's forehead. He flipped back in his notebook. "Didn't you just tell me that you left about ten?"

Mom nodded.

"Then how did you see her at midnight?"

Mom's mouth opened and closed a couple of times before she made a sound. "Don't make much sense, do I?" Her face flushed and she looked miserable. Fanning herself with her hand, she studied the surface of the bar. "I'm sure it was Wednesday. I went to church and then I came back here." She wasn't really talking to the men, but seemed to be trying to make sense of it herself.

"We closed early. I went home about ten. I saw Quentin and Claude about half an hour before that. I fell asleep in front of the TV during the news at eleven." She straightened and grinned. "Now I remember. I woke up a little while later sweating like a pig and took a cold shower. This menopause stuff is pretty wild, you know." There was no response from the men, so she barely paused. "Anyway, after the shower, I was wide awake again. I wanted to read and remembered that I left my book here, so, I jumped into the car in my bathrobe, zipped down here, used the back door and was home again in two shakes of a lamb's tail."

"What's the book?" said Tony.

"It's the new one by Jeffrey Deaver. I don't remember the title right off, but that man sure can tell a story. I couldn't go to sleep until I finished it."

A couple of rough looking men wearing dirty jeans and t-shirts with the sleeves ripped out strolled through the doorway and handed Mom their keys. She set a couple of bottles of beer on the bar and expertly flipped the caps into a small trashcan. "Guess that's why I forgot my little trip back down here. I kept trying to figure out who the bad guy really was and what was going to happen next."

"Makes sense to me." Tony might have said more, but Wade's radio crackled, drawing everyone's attention and sending the deputy outside. He watched Wade's expression change from curious to mildly concerned. When the young man looked at him and beckoned with his head, Tony joined him.

"Darren just found Possum Calhoun face down in a shallow ditch." Wade led the way to the cars. "Word is that the body looks like he's been dead for a while. He called Doc Nash. One of us has to drive by the clinic and lead Doc up there."

"Can we at least hope that Possum died of natural causes?" Tony couldn't believe that someone else had died. Ziggy's story about Sally asking about insurance money jumped into his mind. He didn't want to think about it. In the few years since he'd taken office, the body count had jumped. Not that many people died in Harvey's last ten years as sheriff.

Tony could already picture Winifred's next editorial on the high incidence of death by unnatural causes in Park County during his first term as sheriff. By the time election rolled around in August, she would be flying low on her broom, offering free advertising to anyone who would run against him. If the workload continued to increase, he might encourage her efforts.

The moment he saw Doc Nash climbing out of his car, Tony knew the doctor was not a happy man. He didn't need to be Sherlock Holmes to figure that out.

"Maybe I ought to quit my practice and just follow you boys around all day, or maybe I should just set up housekeeping in the jail." Furious brown eyes glared at them over the top of Doc's glasses. "I can't believe you dragged me out here. I really don't care how or why Possum is dead. Good riddance. The man was an abusive bully." Doc sucked air into his lungs and exhaled sharply, his expression unchanged. "Not only that, but he was stupid. I'm surprised he lived this long."

Tony couldn't tell which of Possum's myriad sins irritated the good doctor more, but he agreed wholeheartedly with Doc's assessment. If it wasn't his job to investigate, he would probably be inclined to shrug and mumble, "Good riddance to bad rubbish," but he couldn't.

Possum's body lay, face up, on a patch of red mud. Drag marks surrounded it, showing how it had been pulled from a drainage ditch.

The moment they arrived, Darren began apologizing. He blathered continuously about his moving the body. "I knew he had to be dead, but I swear my first instinct was to try and save him. I'm really sorry."

"It's okay, Darren, I understand." The anger that the deputy sensed did not stem from his good intentions. Tony's anger went deeper. It made him mad that men like Possum ever walked the earth and madder still that now he had to deal with his death. Even dead, Tony thought the man looked mean and stupid. His narrow features and protruding teeth were more reminiscent of the rodent family than that of humans. Flaps of skin hung from his knuckles. The lack of scabs indicated that he might have injured them shortly before his death, but they could have been older and the scabs had dissolved. Someone else would have to determine that. Knowing Possum, Tony guessed he slugged someone to cause that kind damage to his hands.

Tony wondered if they could find out who or what suffered those punches. Although Possum didn't limit his violence to her, Sally usually received the lion's share.

Possum hadn't smelled pleasant when he was alive. Now, coated with mud and insects, his decomposing body was not an improvement. It was obvious that he had been dead for some time. He could have died before the rain.

Wade started taking pictures as soon as he climbed out of the car. He began with the overview and worked his way toward the corpse. It didn't take long before he had to make his customary pilgrimage to the far side of the road.

The doctor squatted near the body, making the most cursory

observations into his pocket tape recorder. When he stood up, he glowered at Tony as if blaming him personally for his troubles. "I'd say he has been dead for at least three days, probably longer. I'd also say that he didn't drown."

"How can you tell that?" Wade paused between heaves and looked over at the physician.

"Damn, boy, but you have got the weakest constitution I ever saw. You a vegetarian?" Doc's lips lifted in a wide grin as he looked at Tony. "Bet he can't even deal with a dead goldfish without puking."

"Do you know what killed him?" Tony breathed through his mouth.

"Looks like a knife wound, here," said Doc, pointing to the side of the corpse's neck, just beneath the jawbone. "Someone inserted a great big knife here. Something with a wide blade, not one of those little paring jobs. I'd say he probably bled to death, but until the autopsy, we won't know much more than that."

"He didn't die right away?" With his stomach empty, Wade moved to look more closely at the body.

"Naw." The doctor backed away. "I'm just guessing for now, you understand, but it might not have even killed him if he had received immediate medical help. I should be able to tell that during the autopsy."

Tony squinted, looking around to see if he could tell where the body might have washed down from. There were many small trees and dense vegetation right down to the edge of the ditch where the body had stopped. The ditch itself ran parallel to the road, and this stretch of road was pretty level.

Tony stared uphill. "If he was stabbed near his house, I don't think he would have washed down here. His place is almost a mile from here and there just wasn't enough rain to move him that far."

"Maybe he walked," said Doc Nash. "It's pretty easy to stumble downhill."

"Let's check around and see if we can find a trail. Maybe if we just go back toward his place we'll be able to find out something," said Wade.

Doc Nash planned to stay until the ambulance left with the body and then he would follow it to town.

Darren, Wade and Tony fanned out and began walking in the direction they guessed Possum traveled. It was the most direct route between his home and the road. About a half mile from the body, Darren spotted a knife in a patch of trampled weeds.

Not a kitchen knife, it didn't look like the average hunting knife either. It was a dagger. The eight-inch long blade was thick and heavy and tapered to a sharp point like a miniature claymore. At some point, the hilt had been wrapped with silver duct tape. Since that time, wear had exposed the threads inside the tape. The guard was missing and the blade worn from countless sharpenings. Something that resembled dried blood encrusted both the blade and most of the handle.

Wade photographed it before anyone touched it. Then he carefully bagged and tagged it.

No one found anything suspicious between the knife and the Calhoun shack. They saw no signs of broken plants, no blood, and no signs of a struggle.

Sally's face appeared in the window that faced them. Expressionless, she stared through the filthy, cracked glass, but made no move to join them.

Tony approached the cabin. The narrow porch was covered with worn carpeting that looked like fake grass. Afraid that knocking on the rickety door would knock it off its hinges, Tony rapped on the wooden frame.

Sally came to the door and opened it just a crack. "You can't come in, Sheriff. Possum won't like it if he sees you inside."

"If you don't want me to come in, I need you to come outside, Sally." Tony spoke softly. Even in the diffused light, he could see that greenish-yellow bruising darkened the left side of her face. "It's important."

After a moment, Sally pulled the door open just wide enough to slip outside. Wearing baggy jeans and a dirty T-shirt, she paused to tie a frayed apron with a large center pocket around her waist. With her fingers, she combed her stringy brown hair forward in an obvious attempt to cover the bruises. When Wade and Darren came around the corner, joining Tony, her eyes widened and she took a step backward. "Possum won't like findin' y'all here."

Tony couldn't decide the best way to approach her. Telling friends and relatives bad news was the absolute worst part of his job. "How long has Possum been away?"

Sally gaped at him for a moment, then her chin jutted forward. "Didn't say he was away, did I? Possum just don't like visitors."

"How about you, Sally? This is your home, too. Do you like visitors?" Tony watched her expression. He doubted that anyone had asked her what she liked in years. He knew for a fact that Possum took great pride in not "letting the wife waste good money on soap," because he'd heard the man spouting off about it.

"Whatever Possum likes is fine with me." Sally's eyes did not meet his but moved constantly.

Tony wasn't making much headway and decided on the direct approach. "I've got some bad news for you." He looked around the yard and saw a tree stump that would make a reasonable seat. "Why don't you come and sit down?"

"Bad news?" Sally's hands began shaking and she crossed her arms over her stomach and gripped her elbows, but she refused to sit. "What kind of bad news, Sheriff?"

"We found Possum's body down near the road." His eyes didn't leave Sally's face. A flash of something unidentifiable moved across it. Was it fear? Relief? Curiosity? "It looks like he's been dead a while."

"Dead?" Sally swayed on her feet.

Tony extended a hand, offering it but not reaching for her. She grabbed his forearm with both of her hands and dug her fingertips into the muscle. He was grateful she didn't have long fingernails.

"You must have wondered why he didn't come home." Tony led her to the stump and she sat at last, but did not release his arm.

"I did."

As she watched Wade and Darren moving about in the yard, Tony realized that under the coating of grime that always seemed a part of her, she was quite pretty and younger than he expected. Framed with extravagant dark lashes, her eyes were large and a clear blue-gray. He suspected that, if clean, her hair would be a rich brown. He looked at the hands still gripping his arm. The knuckles of each finger were twisted, red and swollen. Countless fine scars crisscrossed every inch of her chapped skin. Some scars looked old, other fresh.

Anger surged through him, but he kept his tone neutral. "What did you think happened to him?"

"I thought he might have drowned. The water got awful high." Sally's voice was a monotone. "I ain't supposed to leave the house without him."

"You didn't call my office." The total lack emotion in her face and voice chilled him to the bone. She might have been reading a grocery list.

"Possum, he keeps the phone with him, you know, for safekeeping, and I only asked that insurance man 'cause I seen him down by the road." She released his arm and shoved her hands into her apron pocket, cradling the slight bulge of her belly. "I figured he'd know and if Possum come home, he wouldn't like it if he learnt that I'd been talkin' to you."

After watching the changes in Theo's body during her pregnancies, he'd swear that Sally was pregnant. He signaled for Wade to approach. "Have you got that knife with you?"

Wade pulled the evidence bag from his carryall and handed it over.

Tony watched Sally.

Sally watched the knife as it changed hands. Her expression could be described as haunted, but why? Was the sight of her husband's knife the sign that her beloved husband would not return? Would fingerprints on the knife prove that she had wielded this knife and killed him? If so, why after all these years?

"That's Possum's."

"It's not a hunting knife." Wade lowered the bag again.

"No." Sally turned and pointed to a small shed that bore two heavy padlocks on the door. "He keeps his hunting stuff in there."

"Do you have the key?"

"No. It's all his stuff." Sally looked surprised that they would ask.

"What did Possum use this knife for?" Tony thought he could guess. When she tried to cover the fine scars with her hands, he knew.

"I know you think he was bad, Sheriff." Her voice barely made sound. "It was my fault that I provoked him. He didn't want to hurt me."

Tony shook his head. How could he convince her that what Possum had done was wrong? He hoped she hadn't turned on him with his own knife or, if she had, she hadn't left any evidence. "He was a mean bully, Sally."

"No." She shook her head. "You're married, right?"

Tony nodded, wondering why she asked.

"You should understand or don't your wife provoke you?"

Tony suppressed a snort. Theo provoked him every day of the year, usually without trying, but he'd never lay a hand on her. He guessed he provoked her as well, maybe even a lot. It was part of marriage. He doubted that Sally would understand. "I would never hit her, or slice her arm with a razor sharp knife. She only has a black eye if she has an accident. A real accident."

Sally's eyes went wide but her expression remained blank.

The world that he described must sound like a lunar landscape to Sally. He decided to change directions. "Was anyone angry with Possum? Did he have any enemies?"

"Well, Possum kept mostly to himself." She held up a hand to stop him from speaking. "There was a man. I don't rightly know his name but Possum did squabble a while back with that snake guy. You know who I mean?"

Tony shook his head. Did she mean Stan or Hub or someone else? "Did you see them argue?"

Sally nodded. "He had him a pickup the same color yellow as daffodils."

Stan, he thought. Who else would match that description? "What did they argue about?"

"Dunno." She started to laugh. "It was awful funny, seeing that fat little man jumping up and down, screaming at Possum. We was stopped down the road a piece, you know, where old man Ferguson sells boiled peanuts. His face turned as red as anything I've ever seen."

"Did Possum say anything to you about it?" said Tony. "You know, later on."

Sally just shook her head slowly, as if that little movement sapped the last of her energy.

It looked to Tony as if she might faint. "Would you like for us to take you somewhere? To stay with a relative? A friend's house?"

"I think I'd best stay here. Possum don't like me to go nowhere without him." Speaking in a soft monotone, she swayed, almost falling from her perch. "Me 'n' my sister Pinkie ain't talked in years."

Her blank expression chilled Tony to the core. She had no friends and she probably hadn't seen a relative since her wedding. Possum had dominated her life so totally, she seemed not to understand that he wasn't coming home. Tony didn't feel he could leave her alone up here.

"I know just the place for you to stay tonight."

CHAPTER TWENTY-FIVE

Satisfied that he made the right choice, Tony left Sally in Ruby's office. He thought that Ruby took one look at the pitiful woman and recognized her former self. Within minutes, she had Sally wrapped in a clean apron, sipping a glass of milk. A nod of Ruby's head sent them into the hallway.

"If she needs a lawyer, Sheriff, I'll pay for one." Ruby's voice sounded calm, but her hands trembled. "Are you going to arrest her?"

"I don't know that she's done anything wrong, Ruby. We'll just have to wait and see what evidence turns up." He pinched the bridge of his nose. "You seemed the most likely person to get her through tonight. I hope it's not an imposition."

"No," said Ruby. "It's time for me to give someone else the same help I received. Sally will have to make the changes, and she will have to decide for herself the kind of life she wants. I can only offer support."

Ruby's words replayed in his head as Tony stood in the deep purple doorway of the Klip 'n' Kurl Beauty Salon. Prudence, the complete opposite personality from Sally, stood behind her client, apparently gluing pieces of aluminum foil in the woman's hair. She wore a denim jumper that didn't quite disguise the bulge of her latest pregnancy.

As he glanced around the room reading labels, Tony discovered myriad brands of tubes and jars and bottles of stuff that could be rubbed on, sprayed onto or washed in or out of hair.

He wondered what they did. Since he had begun serious hair loss while still in high school, he hadn't spent much time in such an establishment.

The haircuts he remembered receiving were administered in the barbershop. The barber wielded a pair of electric clippers and never asked how his customer wanted to look. As Tony recalled, he had either been sheared like a sheep with all of his hair cut the same length or clipped like a hedge with the top left a bit longer.

He sniffed the air. The mostly floral scents of the shampoos and lotions brought a smile to his face. After the aroma of the decomposing Possum, the beauty parlor smelled a little like heaven. He thought Sally would be as lost in here as well.

Prudence paused when she saw him stroll in. "Sheriff?" She held a square of foil and a comb. She paled.

He smiled reassuringly. "Could I talk to you for just a minute, Prudence?" Tony backed outside and waited on what had been the front porch of the old house. The parlor had been converted into the salon. The rest of the house was her home. The hot pink walls hurt his eyes and he turned to look into the street.

Prudence trotted out right behind him, all but running into his back. "Has something happened to Darren?"

"No. He's fine." Tony took time to reassure her. Any time he arrived in an official capacity to the family, or, in this case, the fiancée of one of his officers, he made sure their concern was eliminated as thoroughly and quickly as possible. "I saw him just a few minutes ago." He didn't fill in the detail of seeing his deputy standing over the decomposing body of Possum Calhoun. "I actually need to talk to Karissa."

Concern, mixed with a touch of anger, suffused the woman's lovely features. "What's she done?" Even as she glared at Tony, she led the way to a pair of lavender metal lawn chairs. With a grateful sigh, she sat down and buried her hands in her hair, elbows lifted, and began massaging her scalp. "Some days she's as wonderful as they come, and then the next day she's a real little pill. The joys of motherhood are seriously strained by puberty."

Tony nodded. "As far as I know, she hasn't done anything bad, but it is my understanding that she might have been out fairly late Wednesday night. I just wanted to ask her a couple of questions about something she might have seen," he said. "That is, if you don't mind. You're welcome to stay while I talk to her."

"That's fine." Prudence looked relieved. "She's already grounded for that little escapade and now I have her ironing for penance. She'd probably welcome a break and some fresh air right now." A definite sparkle rose in her bright green eyes. "I can't very well put bars on her bedroom window, you know, just in case there is a fire. But, I can sure make her think twice about sneaking out."

"Ironing?" Tony smiled. As far as he knew, Theo never ironed anything but her quilting fabrics and Sunday clothes. He had long ago learned to iron his uniform shirts or pay someone else to do it.

"She hates it." The corners of Prudence's mouth tilted up. "So, of course, I told her that she has to iron every piece of laundry for two weeks. That includes the kitchen towels and the boys socks." A timer inside the salon buzzed. "I'll send her right out." She dashed up the purple steps.

Minutes later, watching as Karissa strolled around the corner of the hot pink house, Tony couldn't help but think that the girl would be drop-dead gorgeous by the time she reached high school. If her family didn't come to terms with her looks, personality and the effects of peer pressure, Prudence and Darren would be miserable. Right now, Karissa resembled a thoroughbred racehorse with long legs and sleek lines and a mass of red-gold hair pulled into a ponytail. It bounced and swung from side to side as she approached. Only the smattering of freckles on her nose and the mouth full of braces kept her looking like an almost teenager from a tiny Tennessee county and not a high-fashion model.

"Mom said you wanted to talk to me?" Karissa dropped into the chair that her mother had recently vacated.

Tony detected a hint of rebellion in her soft brown eyes as they met his. She stared at him briefly before her eyes dropped to examine the knees of her jeans. The "I'm an angel" design on her yellow T-shirt might not have been truth in advertising. Judging from her expression, he knew she had guessed that this was not a social call.

"I need to ask you a few questions about Wednesday night." He watched as bright patches of color rose in her cheeks. She looked disappointed more than surprised.

"Did my mom call you and ask you to come over and give me the lecture about how stupid I was?" In the blink of an eye, she turned as prickly as a hedgehog. "Maybe it was 'Darling Darren'?"

"You don't like him?" Tony didn't respond to her question.

The girl sat staring into space for a while. "He's okay, I guess." The flash of rebellion seemed to ease. "It's just weird, you know, 'cause Mama didn't marry my father or the boys' fathers either. I just never thought she'd get married."

"Have you talked about this with your mother?" What Tony really wanted to ask was if she knew her father; and if so, what was his name? He would never have the nerve to ask her that.

Karissa nodded. "She says she *loves* Darren." She examined her knees again. "The boys think that he is wonderful, and he really is good about playing with them."

"I imagine it will take a while for everyone to adjust." Tony offered. "Tell me about Wednesday night."

"Well," she said, dragging the word into three syllables. "Me and some of my friends planned to meet at ten-thirty and just hang out over behind Tommy Anderson's house. There's this kind of field back there. We packed flashlights and a portable CD player, and one of the girls said she could get some beer and another was bringing some cigarettes." Her thin shoulders pulled forward and she slid down in the chair until she sat on her spine. "We just wanted to see what it would be like and figured that Wednesday would be easier than sneaking out on the weekend."

"I'm guessing that it didn't turn out to be much fun on a cold evening." Tony gave her credit for confessing the whole plan.

"It was awful." Tears rose in her eyes, magnifying them. "I took two sips of a beer and smoked half a cigarette and then just wanted to throw up and go home. I never thought they'd taste so awful. I can't imagine why anyone would try that twice."

Tony managed to keep from smiling. "How did you get there?" The Andersons lived maybe half a mile from the Okay, which would make it about two and a half miles from her home.

"Rode my bike." After a glance at his expression, she elaborated. "I climbed out of the window because the door always squeaks, and I left my bike outside before I went to bed. I could see the road okay because of the moonlight, but since I don't have a headlight on it, I had a lot of trouble seeing the bumps and potholes."

She showed him a vicious looking bruise on her elbow. It was a monster, red and purple with tinges of green, covering most of her forearm.

"I finally had to walk the last part. Anyway, we stayed for about an hour and none of us was having much fun so we started home. About the time I got to the pay phones at the Okay, I thought I was going to die and wanted to die at home."

The tears finally overflowed their banks and trickled down her cheeks. "Mr. Smith stopped and offered me a ride home, but only on the condition that I called my mom first and tell her where I was and how I was getting home. He put my bike in his trunk and waited until I got off the phone. I've never heard Mom say half of those words before. She was really mad."

"Was there much traffic around the bar?" Tony leaned forward. "Did you see anyone else using the phones or hanging around while you were there?"

As she considered his question, she wiped the tears from her face with the heels of her hands. "I saw Mrs. Proffitt inside the bar. At first, it was all dark inside, and then the light came on. She had on her bathrobe. I thought that was pretty funny." Like the flicker of a firefly, a grin illuminated her face and then vanished. "I think the parking lot was empty, but there were several cars going both ways. Sure surprised me."

"Why's that?"

"I didn't think anyone in this one-horse town stayed up later than the eleven o'clock news." She leaned forward, her expression more mischievous than concerned. "There's lots of programs that come on after that, but I don't think anyone but me knows about them."

Tony had to laugh. Even on a busy night, Silersville was quiet. The girl was bright and a little feisty. "No wonder Chris and Jamie like it when you're their babysitter. You know what's going on."

"Hey, you've got fun kids. I like them." Karissa's face lit up. "Oh wait, I just remembered something." Since she had confessed to everything that she'd done and the dreaded lecture from the sheriff had not come, the girl seemed to relax again. "First a motorcycle and then a pickup truck drove out of the parking lot, just before I called home. The truck was some dark color and had flames painted on the front, you know what I mean?"

Tony nodded and immediately thought of both Quentin's truck and the one that he saw parked at the motel office/church on Thursday night. "Did it have lights on the roof?"

Karissa shook her head, sending her ponytail bouncing. "I really don't remember. I just tried not to barf and wanted to get home again. I barely even noticed the truck at all. I just remember seeing the flames. It was moving fast."

CHAPTER TWENTY-SIX

Pops Ogle looked like he had aged forty years in the past few days. His posture had changed from upright to pulled in. When he greeted Tony, his eyes lacked their usual sparkle. "Sheriff?" Pops stood next to his desk in the county clerk's office. "Have you found out what happened?"

Tony shook his head. The changes in Pops alarmed him. "Are you all right?"

"I'll be fine. This whole business has taken a toll though." Pops slid onto his chair and rested his hands on his desk. The fingers that usually seemed to play music of their own accord lay still. Pops sighed. "Since you came out to see us, I have heard some horrible stories about Mr. Mize, er, Brown. Do you think they could be true?"

"I'm afraid he was not the man he pretended to be. My guess is that he fooled lots of people." Tony didn't know how much of the truth about Hub had made its way to Pops ears.

"Is it true he was married to that sweet little Miss Ruby?" Pops was concerned and disillusioned. His head clearly vied with his heart. Even as he asked, his head moved from side to side as if he couldn't bear to hear the answer.

"Yes." Tony slipped an antacid tablet into his mouth. "I don't suppose he ever mentioned having a child or where his next of kin might live?"

Pops slowly shook his head. "That nursing home story was a lie, I know that now." He paused. "Doesn't Quentin know?"

"I really came here about another matter," said Tony. He didn't feel like explaining that Quentin barely knew the man. "Can you tell me who drives the little pickup I saw at the Thursday meeting? The one painted with flames and sporting the rack of roof lights."

"Sure can." Pops smiled for the first time. "That's me."

"You? I thought you were a Saturn kind of guy."

"I am." The twinkle came back into Pops's eyes. "And strictly a brown one at that." He watched Tony and grinned when he saw the answering glint in Tony's eyes.

"And the truck?"

"That belongs to my sister's youngest boy, Matthew. She took it away from him until he gets his grades up and I just drive it from time to time to keep it running." He leaned forward and lowered his voice like he had something embarrassing to confess. "It's a lot of fun to drive."

"I'll just bet it is." Tony leaned back in his chair. "Were you driving it on Wednesday night?"

Pops stopped smiling and closed his eyes. He seemed to be the picture of concentration. "Can't say that I remember for sure. Why do you ask?"

Theo was thinking about Jane and Martha even as she prepared dinner. She still couldn't quite believe that the pair of them planned to leave Silersville for the summer and try to start a singing career. Martha was a late baby and she was fifty now. Jane's carefully guarded age had to put her in low to mid seventies. She couldn't wait much longer.

The pair had guts. Theo had to give them credit for that, and she hoped it would be a positive experience, but at the same time she couldn't help but wonder how long it would take before Gretchen knew her stuff. Jane would train her replacement, but still, it would take time for all of them to adjust.

Chris and Jamie sat across from each other at the kitchen table working on their homework. Jamie had a map to color and Chris worked on a book report. He tried to keep his paper neat but since he was left-handed, his papers usually had pencil smudges all over them.

Daisy emerged from under the table. Tail wagging, she trotted toward the front of the house signaling Tony's return. After one woof, she went quiet except for the sound of her toenails clicking on the hardwood floor of the front hall. If a stranger approached the house, Daisy would bark a deep, warning bark.

After the front door opened and closed, Theo expected to hear the closet door open. Tony preferred to leave his pistol in the gun safe before even greeting the boys. The distinctive scraping, squeaking sound of that door opening didn't come. Curious and still clutching the dishtowel, Theo left the kitchen. She found Tony slumped against the front door, his back pressed to the wood, his eyes closed. "Tony?"

"I'm fine." He lifted one eyelid. "Or at least I will be after a few minutes of peace."

Without another word, Theo stepped closer to him and pressed a kiss on his cheek before returning to the kitchen. If he hadn't already heard about his mother's plans for the summer, she sure wasn't going to mention them until he was feeling stronger.

A short time later, she heard the opening and closing of the hall closet door, and then Tony joined them in the kitchen.

After dinner, Tony pitched a game of home run derby in the park. Chris and Jamie pounded the whiffle ball with an oversized plastic baseball bat, sending it soaring through the trees. Daisy raced after the ball, bringing it back, soggy but intact. Later, Tony settled into his favorite chair. Theo and the boys joined him for story time. Not until the boys were asleep did he bring up the subject of his day.

He didn't even flinch when she told him the latest plan hatched by his mother and aunt.

Rested after an uninterrupted night's sleep, Tony spotted Doc Nash's flame red Corvette parked in front of the tiny morgue. It drew him like a beacon. Inside, he saw that the doctor was almost done with Possum's autopsy and wondered if Doc ever had a decent night's sleep.

"Okay, Doc," said Tony as he perched one hip on a stainless steel table. "What happened to Possum?"

Doc's eyes narrowed as he gazed out the window. With obvious reluctance, he turned back to face Tony. His eyes flickered to the gold badge and away. "Nothing that he didn't deserve."

"Agreed." When the doctor didn't continue, Tony cleared his throat and leaned forward. "Now then, what are your official findings?"

"The cause of death was massive blood loss from a knife wound that nicked the left carotid artery. It was not cut all the way through." He fidgeted with the edges of his papers. "I saw no signs of a struggle. No defense wounds."

"What about his knuckles?"

"Those scrapes were at least a week old. His own knife caused the wound in his neck and it was found in his vicinity. It fit exactly." He focused on Tony's eyes, his own bloodshot and bleary. "Unless you have some other evidence, I'm calling it an accident. While running downhill, he tripped and stabbed himself."

Tony stared at the doctor. "There were no clear prints on the knife, and the position of the body is consistent with that scenario, but . . ." Tony's words trailed away to silence. "Someone killed him and I can't prove it."

Doc's lifted eyebrows were the only reply.

"Two things don't add up." Tony sucked on an antacid tablet

while he watched Doc processing his statement. "The first is that I can't imagine Possum actually running. That would require more effort and energy than I have ever seen in the man."

"And the other?"

"I don't think it was muddy enough."

"What wasn't muddy enough?"

"The body." Tony pulled a photograph from the doctor's file and tapped his finger on the image of the back of Possum's shirt. "Assuming he *was* running and fell, slipping in the muck, shouldn't he have rolled over onto his back at least once or had a snoot full of mud?"

"I did wonder about that, but he didn't die right away so he could have walked there in a more or less orderly manner." He lifted his eyes from the photograph. "If I call this a homicide, what will happen?"

"It will create lots of paperwork and leave the file open. I sure don't have any evidence to make an arrest. Just because I think someone ought to have killed him, doesn't make it so." His words trailed into silence.

"What do *you* think happened?"

"I think Sally is pregnant." Tony rolled his shoulders. "I think she wants this baby enough to fight back, to take his knife from him and stab him to protect it. If that's what happened, I doubt that Archie would charge her with anything."

"Unless you have some strong feelings to the contrary, I'll call it an accident." Doc cleared his throat. "If you want to talk to Sally, she told me she's going to stay with Ruby until her baby is born."

CHAPTER TWENTY-SEVEN

Tony disconnected the phone and went looking for Wade. For a change, the eager-beaver deputy wasn't hovering around his desk.

Ruth Ann sat at hers, talking on the phone. Using a tiny tool, she decorated her freshly painted, baby-blue fingernails with microscopic decals of leaves and daisies. Her voice carried clearly to his ears, so he knew that she wanted him to hear her side of the conversation.

"Marigold, I think you've been into the hooch in the mayor's office. You're telling me the mayor is suggesting that the sheriff ought to be impeached?" Her eyebrows lifted as she watched Tony approach. "For what reason? Proving that the mayor is an idiot and a lazy one at that?"

Tony couldn't hear Marigold's response, but Ruth Ann's grin let him know it was something not quite complimentary about the mayor. The fact that the mayor continued to be reelected each year assured Tony that his own impeachment was unlikely. A town whose citizens thrived on doing everything the same way things were always done was not likely to get out and vote to impeach the sheriff.

Frankly, he thought, he'd be surprised if he could lose an election. People were known to vote for the dead in some elections. When former sheriff Harvey Winston retired, he talked Tony into running as his replacement. Tony wondered who he'd con into taking the job.

Wade sauntered down the hall, carrying a large bottle of Sprite.

"Ready for a little adventure?" Tony asked. The young man's expression was not encouraging. In fact, Tony thought Wade looked closer to being frightened away than being intrigued.

"Dull would be nicer." Wade swallowed half of the contents of his bottle. "I have had enough adventure lately to last me for the rest of the year. Between the bodies and the autopsies, I'm ready for something duller. I've lost five pounds the hard way." He burped, a long rolling belch that seemed to echo in that small space, and grinned. The gleam in his eyes as he smiled showed a clear appreciation of his accomplishment. "Maybe I could handle a week of being the school crossing guard, followed up by a lot of paperwork."

There was more sympathy in Tony's heart than he hoped showed on his face. He shook his car keys. "I think it's dry enough now that we can put the Blazer into four-wheel drive and make it up Quentin's driveway. You might remember that we still have a search warrant to execute. I think we might as well take care of that before he gets released, don't you?"

Wade grumbled like an old bear, but his eyes were starting to sparkle.

As they drove past Nellie Pearl's house, Wade turned to Tony. "How's the old lady doing? Is she making any progress?"

"I heard earlier today that she is stabilized but still unconscious." Tony's hands tightened on the steering wheel. "I'm afraid if she doesn't come out of it pretty soon, she won't."

"Is that what the doctors say or just your opinion?"

"My opinion," Tony replied. "It's based on what the doctors are not saying. They don't want to climb out on that limb, but I've seen and heard a fair number of discouraging forecasts and I'd have to say theirs is pretty severe."

After a last lingering gaze at Nellie Pearl's house, Wade turned and concentrated his attention on the road ahead. "You think we'll make it up there?"

Tony wasn't sure. Ahead of them, the long driveway to Quentin's house was scored with newly eroded areas. The mud and trash, carried from the hills above the road, had accumulated in long tangles caught by the trees. "That stuff looks fairly dry to me. If we stay away from the puddles, we ought to be able to make it up." He put the vehicle into four-wheel drive. "If this doesn't work, we'll ride up on mules."

Wade flinched. "It's easy to see that no one has been on this section of road since the rain. A butterfly would leave tracks in this stuff." Wade slipped his sunglasses down on his nose and grinned. "Do you suppose the lovely Angelina has been baking cookies for our visit? You know, for a married man, you certainly have your share of admiring women. Blossom and now Angelina."

Tony hands jerked on the steering wheel and his stomach lurched. He had forgotten about Quentin's repulsive girlfriend. "You don't think she's still up there, do you? I assumed she left the area." Knowing that he sounded childish didn't bother him half as much as the prospect of spending a moment in her company, even with a burly chaperone.

"You mean you *hope* that she's gone." Wade's shout of laughter boomed inside the Blazer. "She did rather take to you. Aren't you concerned that Theo will hear about your new friend and get jealous?"

Another shudder ran through Tony. "I do believe she is the sluttiest woman I've ever met, and that's saying something."

"Considering that you worked vice in Chicago for a while, I expect you do have some fine examples to compare her to." Wade frowned. "I never thought I would say this, but Quentin's way too good for that woman."

"At least Quentin's got a few good qualities."

As they came around the last curve before reaching Quentin's house, they almost skidded into the passenger door of the flame-painted pickup. It rested at an angle blocking the drive. Muck and mud were spattered up to the roof and half-covered the windshield. Its tires were embedded in mud and garbage up to the axle. Under the crumpled hood, a small tree sprouted between the engine and the radiator.

"Oh, man, that's not going anywhere for a while." Wade's voice was almost a whisper. "Quentin's not going to like what she did to his baby."

"That's no joke." Tony's thoughts were dark as he looked at the depth of the ruts and the small footprints leading uphill from the truck. "Unless she walked down through the trees, Angelina's still up here." He thumped his chest as if to emphasize the need for body armor. "If she's been up there cooking meth and using it all this time, who knows what she's liable to do when we knock on the door."

Nodding his wary agreement, Wade checked his equipment.

They left the Blazer on the downhill side of the pickup and walked up to the house. A careful study of the outside showed no signs of Angelina.

She didn't come outside to greet them. Tony presumed she had been using so many drugs, she would find it difficult to recognize her own mother.

Giving Wade enough time to make his way through the piles of garbage to the back of the home, he knocked on the door. It shuddered with each knock. There was no response. No dogs barked. Tony didn't see them outside. He couldn't imagine her taking the dogs for a walk. Knocking louder, he called out, "Angelina!"

At length, he heard a rustling and banging inside. It sounded as if a cow had been locked in the building. Finally, the door flew open. Angelina looked even worse than she had the first time he'd seen her. She wore only an oversized T-shirt. It might have been white before it became a combination of napkin and drop cloth, and to Tony's eyes it did not come close to being a satisfactory cover. The combined aromas of rotting food and her poor personal hygiene sent him reeling backward about two steps. She stared at him without apparent recognition.

He addressed her in English and then in his best high school Spanish, explaining what he planned to do. The search warrant held no interest for her. She accepted it from him and let it fall to the floor. It didn't require a medical degree to see that she was drugged to the point of being comatose, mentally if not physically.

"Sheriff?" Wade's voice came from outside.

"Come around to the front." Tony didn't take his eyes off of Angelina for more than a couple of seconds. No one else seemed to be in the house, but he didn't want to take any chances. He didn't recognize the hound of dubious breeding that wandered by, pausing on its way outside to hike his leg and pee on the woman's leg. She didn't react.

"Sir, I've found something here that you should see," said Wade.

"Angelina?" Eyeing the open sores on her arms, Tony pulled on a second pair of gloves before taking her elbow with his left hand. "Why don't you come with me? A little fresh air might make you feel better." As he pulled, leading her, she moved slowly, as if sleepwalking.

Wade stood near the shed. After an assessing glance at Angelina's condition, he turned his head and avoided looking directly at her. "It's definitely a meth lab. I'm surprised it hasn't exploded." He shook his head. "There's enough matches and white gasoline in there to blow up half of the mountain."

Tony peeked inside and nodded. "I warned them. Call it in to the district. Tell them we need it cleaned up soon." He pulled

Angelina away from the shed. Cleaning up a meth lab was not for amateurs. It was dangerous and expensive.

"Mine!" She began to struggle. "Lousy sons of beeches. Don't touch nothin'! You bad." Her English seemed to desert her about then and she filled the air with what sounded like curses in Spanish.

Not amused, Tony slipped one bracelet of his handcuffs on her right wrist and read her rights to her in English and Spanish. Leading her around to the porch, he found a railing that he judged sound enough for his purpose. He slipped the second bracelet between rails and attached it to her other wrist. Someone had discarded a long-sleeved plaid cotton shirt on the porch. Tony grabbed it and tied the sleeves around her waist so that she wore it like a skirt. To thank him for his consideration, she kicked him in the thigh, missing her target. Luckily for him, her legs were short. As he and Wade went into the house, the sound of her swearing followed them.

Tony stopped cold just inside the doorway. Trash covered every surface in the house. The amount of garbage surprised him. He assumed that the yard looked bad because they threw their garbage out there, but now he realized what was in the yard was just the overflow.

It would take a little while to become accustomed to the smell. The worst thing he could do would be to go outside for a breath of air. "I don't know why they haven't just up and died in here."

"Man, oh, man, I think something did." Like Tony, Wade pulled a second pair of gloves over the first.

Tony looked around. They stood in the main room of the trailer, a combination kitchen, eating and living room. It was a decent sized room that held a couch, a couple of recliner chairs and a table with five chairs. A narrow hallway led to the bedrooms. He hoped that one of the bedrooms was Hub's.

"Man, oh man," said Wade. It was becoming his mantra and Tony didn't blame him. Rotting food covered the counters and the floor. Wade stepped in something that, by the look of it, indicated that the dogs were not constipated. "Ah, hell." He paused to scrape the refuse off his boot with an empty soup can. "How are we going to know what belongs to Brown and what belongs to Quentin or Angelina?" Wade gestured to the hodgepodge of litter.

"I vote for grabbing any piece of paper that has either of his names on it." Tony held up a North Carolina newspaper with a mailing label. The addressee was Harold Brown. It had been delivered to a post office box.

Soon they had a sizeable stack of papers belonging to John Mize or Harold Brown. Some empty plastic grocery sacks they found on the counter were pressed into service.

The largest bedroom was littered with men and women's clothes. "You think this stuff belongs to Quentin or Hub?" Wade held up a pair of long, narrow jeans.

"Definitely Quentin. Mr. Brown hasn't got the legs for those." Tony didn't see anything in the room that looked like it might belong to Hub. "Let's check the other bedroom."

Surprising both of them, the second one smelled better. Still, it was a mess. Piles of things filled the corners and spilled from open drawers.

Wade pulled a chair out of the corner near the door. A warning rattle met his ears along with the ominous sound of something slithering across paper. It was dark in the corner and old clothes were piled into a heap.

He froze. "Sheriff?"

Tony turned, alerted by the quaver in Wade's voice as much as by the sound of the rattle. He drew his pistol and aimed in the direction of the deputy's horrified stare. He couldn't see anything but trash. "It's probably in a box, but we'd better be certain." Inching his way closer, he looked for a tool. Leaning against the far wall, he saw a broom. "Hang on. I'm going to grab that broom and move some stuff. You get ready to shoot the damned thing."

"Quentin owns a broom?" Wade's voice still shook, but there was a touch of humor in it. "Who knew?" His right hand inched his pistol from the holster.

A couple of careful steps resulted in Tony being armed and able to check the snake's habitat. Holding the broom just in front of the brush, he poked the handle into the corner and lifted away a pair of worn jeans. Without the muffling effect of the cloth, the rattle grew louder. The geometric markings of a gray and black rattlesnake were in shadow but still plainly visible.

Tony held his breath, watching it even as it watched him. Coiled, tail erect, its rattles vibrated but all Tony could hear was the sound of his own heart.

"Jeez, it's loose!" Wade flipped the safety off and took aim, arms extended. He held the Glock with both hands, his aim steady. "You're in my way."

Tony stared at the snake. Its tongue flicked in and out, the forked tip easy to see. The snake seemed to coil more tightly. The sound of the rattles intensified. Tony stayed motionless as he considered his options.

"I've got no place to go. You back up." The words were no more than out of Tony's mouth than he realized that there was another snake working itself into a coil only two feet to their right. It looked just as mad as the first one.

"Wait. Do you see it?" He whispered. He had no way of knowing if the sound of loud voices irritated snakes or not, and he certainly did not want to take any chances.

Behind him, Wade did not seem to be breathing. A faint, "Yeah" was the response.

"On three, I'm going to hit snake one with the jeans and you take out snake two. I'm going left. Maybe you can get number one then." He stared at the snakes. "Okay?"

"Yep." Wade gradually swiveled his upper body, leaving his feet and legs still, and took aim at the second snake.

"One." Tony tightened his grip on the broom. "Two." He squinted as he visually measured the distance to the snake. "Three." He swung the broom and jeans at the snake and jumped to the left. The blast of Wade's shot was deafening in that small space. Something caught his right ankle and he looked down. The jeans had hit the mark, pushing snake number one out of the way. Stunned, Tony stared at the creature attached to the outside of his leg. "Damn! Wade!"

Pivoting, Wade pulled the trigger and hit his mark. Two shots into snake number one. "Don't move." The first two snakes dead, Wade turned toward Tony.

Tony didn't even breathe as he waited for Wade to fire. It was a half-second that felt like a lifetime. At the moment he heard Wade's fourth shot, he felt the bullet pierce the snake's body. Only the flawless accuracy of the shots meant that the snake was dead and Tony's leg was untouched by hot lead.

The slow-motion effect of the entire event allowed Tony to consider that if he, or any of his deputies except Wade or Sheila, had taken those same shots, two out of three snakes would be rolling on the floor, laughing too hard to slither anywhere. At the same time, Tony would be seriously injured. He shuddered to think how the impact of a bullet that size hitting the flesh and bones of his lower leg would feel. It would be devastating from that range. "Damn, you're good."

"Wow! I didn't see that one." Wade was checking for more snakes. "Where did it come from?" He didn't wait for a reply but babbled on. "It was hanging from your pants. Did it get you, Sheriff?" He picked up the discarded broom with his left hand, holding the pistol ready with his right and began to work his way through the debris, inch by inch. There was a broken snake box in the corner. A pile of papers stuck out of the false bottom.

"I think so." Tony leaned against the doorframe to examine his ankle and found a pair of small holes in the bottom of his khaki pants leg. Without the light shining through them, they would go unnoticed. Lifting the pants, he saw dark spots on his khaki socks just above his shoe. He was certain that he had been bitten, but had to push down the top of his sock to see.

A double puncture wound was right next to his anklebone. One hole seemed slightly smaller than the other one. The heavy leather of his shoe must have deflected it. Blood oozed from the injury. "Grab those papers. We're leaving." He pulled his sock back up. "We'll call Doc on our way."

Wade scurried to add the papers from the box to the ones they had already bagged.

Tony walked outside, just ahead of his deputy.

By the time Wade caught up, Tony had refastened the handcuffs in front of their prisoner. It reassured Tony that he felt little pain. Wouldn't it hurt if it were bad? He'd heard of snakes biting people and not releasing any venom. With any luck, that would be what had happened to him.

Angelina bombarded them with a constant stream of invective. Swearing in two languages, she disparaged everything from their ancestors to their manhood.

Neither man paid any attention to the obscenities she screamed at them. They hustled her down the drive and around the bend, heading for the Blazer. Quentin's truck didn't look any better from this angle.

"Just as a matter of curiosity," Tony inquired as he pointed to the crumpled truck. "When did you do that?"

Angelina's reply sounded like another curse. She didn't look remorseful at all. She was still squawking when Tony helped her into the back seat and shut the door.

"Sorry I asked." He tossed Wade the keys and climbed into the passenger seat and reached for his phone.

This side of the mountain had terrible cellular phone reception. After one attempt to use the phone, Tony radioed Rex. He didn't bother to tell Rex much more than that they were bringing in Angelina, before he asked to be patched to the doctor's phone. It took only seconds to get Doc Nash on the line.

When the doctor wanted verification about the type of bite, Tony was offended.

"I'm damned sure that it was a rattlesnake, Doc," he barked in response to the doctor's question. "It bit me. Wade killed it and there were rattles on its damned tail. Noisy rattles. Now there's a pair of bleeding holes in my ankle and it's starting to swell."

"Does it look bruised? How much is it bleeding?" Doc's words boomed through the radio.

Tony pushed the sock down. "Yes. It does look bruised, but it's not bleeding very much." He glanced through the windshield and then back at the swelling. "We're at Nellie Pearl's and moving fast," he said. "I don't think it's necessary, but Wade's got the lights and siren on. Where do you want us?" His ankle didn't feel bad, but he'd swear that his tongue was swelling and his lips felt numb.

"You sound funny." Doc's voice crackled in his ear. "How do you feel? Do you have the snake with you?"

"Muh wips and ton are bitting mum." Tony was pleased that he was able to answer clearly because his thoughts were a bit jumbled. "No snake. Neber wad to see that snake again. Oh, man, it's really starting to hurt."

"Tony, can Wade hear me?"

Tony nodded.

Wade spoke loudly, not quite shouting, "I hear you Doc. The sheriff is getting worse."

Tony could hear Doc's voice. It looked like the sound was coming out of Wade's mouth. Fascinated, Tony heard Doc say, "Come straight to the clinic. I'll meet you in the back."

Wade drove fast and carefully, pulling up in back of the building that served as doctor's office, emergency room and next to it, the county morgue. From there emergency patients were sent home, driven to Knoxville or air-lifted to Knoxville. The parking area doubled as a helipad.

Doc was by the door with a gurney and a nurse. The two men maneuvered Tony onto the gurney while he mumbled about his tongue.

"Damn, he's big. Couldn't we have elected a ninety-pound weakling?" Doc complained as they wheeled him into the treatment room. "Tony?" He examined the pair of puncture wounds. "When was your last tetanus shot?"

"Dog blow." Tony watched the doctor's face, looking for signs of concern. Doc looked as inscrutable as ever.

Nurse Foxx slipped an IV needle into a vein in his arm. She attached it to a container of saline solution. Satisfied with her work, she proceeded to set him up with an oxygen mask.

"Dog blow, huh?" Doc Nash grinned. "Excellent diction, I must say. I can check your record for that but in the meantime, we're going to inject this serum under the skin. We're checking you for allergic reactions."

The doctor proceeded to measure both of Tony's legs around the ankle and the calf. After prodding the flesh with his gloved finger and determining where the swelling ceased, he drew a line on the leg and wrote the time on it. "How long did the snake hang on?"

"Bade bot it." Tony was pleased with his ability to answer the doctor's questions clearly and distinctly. "Didn' hurd. Hurds now. A lot."

The doctor didn't seem very impressed by his speech and turned to Wade for the answer. "How long?"

The deputy shrugged. "I have no idea. It was still hanging on by a fang when I shot it, but the whole thing only took seconds." He shifted from foot to foot. "I was thinking more about getting rid of it without shooting my boss."

By now, the doctor, his nurse and the receptionist had gathered in the treatment area. Each one held a small bottle and carefully rolled the bottles back and forth between their palms, gently mixing the contents.

The pain continued to worsen. Tony felt like something corrosive had started crawling through his veins.

The doctor turned his attention to his patient. "Since you've had no reaction to the serum we injected under the skin, Tony, we're going to start giving you some anti-venom." He held up a vial. "We don't like to use it if we don't need to, but it looks like it's time to begin."

Doc looked up at Wade. "Why don't you call Theo and tell her to come hold this big brute's hand. And while you're at it, move your vehicle. It's blocking my drive. The helicopter won't be able to land."

Wade's eyes widened. "Oh, dammit to hell, I've got a prisoner in the back seat." He bolted from the room like someone dropped a firecracker down his shorts.

As he ran, he dialed Theo's shop.

Theo heard the shop telephone ringing, but she had her hands full with a customer. She decided to let Jane and her trainee answer it.

Gretchen handed Theo the portable phone. "It's Wade."

Theo listened for a minute, moving away from the others, pressing her hand over her free ear. Her fingers tightened around the phone and she could feel the blood leaving her face. "Thanks, Wade."

She disconnected and dropped the phone on the counter and looked at the faces around her. "Gretchen, you're in charge. Jane, come with me." She wasted no time giving anyone an explanation.

Once they reached the sidewalk, she decided that it was faster and safer to walk to the clinic than to drive. As they walked, she told Jane what she knew about Tony's condition. They were hurrying down the street when Theo spotted Tony's Blazer headed toward them. Wade stopped it in the middle of the street and rolled down his window.

Holding Jane's hand tightly, Theo approached the vehicle. She could see Angelina in the back seat. The woman sat there spouting a constant stream of curses in Spanish and English. A glance was all Theo needed before she focused her attention on Wade's face. There was an edge of pallor to his features, but his smile was warm as he greeted her.

"Has there been any change?" said Theo.

"What's happening?" said Jane.

"It looks like they're going to have to give him the serum." Although he tried to maintain a stoic demeanor, Wade's eyes betrayed him. He was deeply concerned. "Doc says for you to just go on past the desk to the treatment room."

It only took another minute for them to reach the front door of the clinic, but it felt longer. Theo's heart pounded as if she had run there. The reception desk, normally occupied by Rose Flowers Walker, was empty. An elderly couple sat in the waiting area holding hands. Theo and Jane didn't pause, but walked straight through to the back.

Rose spotted them first. She smiled as she waved them forward.

For Theo, seeing Tony's uniform, vest and duty-belt piled in a heap on the floor was almost more traumatic than the sight of him stretched out on the gurney in a hospital gown, with an IV attached to his arm. She knew he would never abuse his equipment like that if he could do otherwise. Theo remembered seeing it treated like this before, while they prepared him for surgery in Chicago. That day, Tony's partner, Max, had collected it and taken it away.

Next to her, Jane made a moaning sound. Doc Nash must have seen the stricken expression on her face because he hurried to her side. With the ease of apparent practice, he eased Jane onto a chair and pressed one hand on her upper spine. "Take a moment to breathe, Jane. You know that big lummox is tough."

He looked up from his examination of Jane's color to wave Theo toward Nurse Foxx. "Go on, Theo. I promise it's not as bad as it looks."

Theo wouldn't have been surprised to learn that Sarah Foxx had been a nurse on Noah's Ark. Even when Theo was a child, Sarah had worked for the doctor of the time. The woman had more medical experience and information than most physicians, and Doc Nash had always respected that.

Sarah met Theo's arrival with a wide smile and a beckoning wave. "Here's someone to see you, Sheriff."

Theo thought Tony looked way too big for the small bed. His head was raised, but his feet extended well off the bottom. Sarah bustled around the bed, measuring Tony's ankles and calves. The two legs were clearly not equal in size or coloring. The swollen one had dramatic patches of angry color. Drawing lines on his skin with a black marker, Sarah wielded a yellow measuring tape with the skill of a Hong Kong tailor. "This stuff doesn't wash off so he'll have zebra stripes for a while." The elderly nurse seemed to find it amusing.

Doc Nash came up behind Theo with Jane in tow. "The

ambulance is on another call, so we are going to send him by helicopter to Knoxville. They'll keep him in the hospital for a little while and use up some of their plentiful supply of anti-venom." He patted her shoulder. "I'm guessing that he'll be home tomorrow."

Relief flooded through her. "Thanks, Doc." Theo moved past him, pulling Jane with her, until they stopped by Tony's head. His eyes were closed, and he was clearly having trouble breathing. An oxygen tube snaked around his neck, into his nose. One monitor kept constant track of his blood pressure, while the contents of a clear bag dripped through a tube and into his IV.

When she kissed his cheek, he opened his eyes, but he seemed not to recognize her at first. They were a darker blue than usual and had a lost, vacant expression. When he lifted his hand and ruffled her hair before giving her a crooked little half smile, she released the breath that she hadn't realized she was holding.

"How do you feel?"

Tony could feel himself slipping in and out of reality. His tongue and lips were almost completely numb and his ears were a real problem. "Numb. And tingly. My ears are gone." His words were indistinct even to his own ears. When he tried to talk, he felt like he using someone else's tongue. Opening his eyes, he was glad to see Theo smiling at him. Her blond curls were flying everywhere. Just the sight of her pretty face was enough to make him feel better. He reached up and touched her hair, but couldn't feel it. Even his fingertips were numb. "Dandelion fuzz."

He focused on Theo's eyes and discovered that he could see them through the tears on her glasses. The combination of the droplets and the prescription plastic distorted everything in the oddest way. His breath rasped in his throat and his thoughts scattered. Was this how Harold Brown had felt? If he were to be handcuffed now, would he know it? Why were there tears on Theo's glasses?

As he slipped into oblivion, he realized that he was unbelievably cold. He couldn't stop shivering.

The next clear thought he had was that being in a helicopter was not much better than being in a coffin. He complained about it to the man with a full beard and pointed teeth who sat by his head.

"You must be the devil," said Tony.

At that, the devil laughed uproariously. "Welcome to hell."

PUTTING THE CLUES TOGETHER

Each block should measure 8 1/2" by 8 1/2". If yours are larger trim them to this measurement. If they are smaller, measure carefully and determine the common size.

If your blocks are smaller than 8 1/2", trim the length of the 2 1/2" by 8 1/2" rectangles of fabric (A) to 2 1/2" by that size.

Sew 4 sets of pinwheel block/2 1/2" by 8 1/2" rectangle (A)/ pinwheel block/rectangle/pinwheel block. Press all seams toward the rectangles of fabric (A).

Sew 3 sets of rectangle (A)/2 1/2" square of fabric (C)/ rectangle/square/rectangle. Press to rectangles.

Assemble by placing strips between rows of blocks. When finished, you should have a rectangular top of twelve blocks, separated by strips of (A), set with cornerstones of (C).

Measure center of pieced top from side to side. Cut 2 of the 1 1/2" strips of (E) to that length and sew to top and bottom. Repeat for sides. This is the inner border.

Repeat the process with the 3 1/2" strips of (A) for the outer border. If you have used a directional print for (A), pay attention to direction of motifs.

Reserve the remaining 4 strips of (A) for the binding.

Congratulations! You've solved the mystery to Springtime in the Smokies.

Chapter Twenty-Eight

"I brought you some papers to sort through." Wade hefted a bulging cardboard box onto the flimsy rolling table and slapped a box of gloves on top of the pile. Dust flew from the box and floated in the morning sunlight. For his efforts, he received a glare from the occupant of the bed. "It's the stuff we picked up at Quentin's. I haven't had two minutes to look at it." Wade paced back and forth at the foot of the hospital bed.

Watching him was making Tony dizzy. "What happened with our arrest?"

Wade stopped pacing and threw himself onto the chair. An accusing frown pulled the corners of his lips down. "Angelina spat a vile yellow glob of something at me. She wanted to have it land on my face." He shuddered. "Luckily she missed her target or I'd probably be in the bed next to yours, only it would be serious."

Tony frowned, moving and shifting on the bed. His fingers plucked at the sheet before moving on to test the tape that held the IV in place. Although Wade made light of it, Tony could tell it had been a most unpleasant situation. "What did you charge her with?"

"I wanted to charge her with being pond scum, but Archie charged her with assault on a police officer and several other things, including the attempted murder of Nellie Pearl. We learned that she showed Sammy the way up the hill, but left when she spotted Sheila."

"So, your engagement is off?" Tony teased, laughing at Wade's expression.

Wade ignored him. "I sent her fingerprints out and guess what? Our Angelina is wanted by the Feds for drug charges, the Arizona State Police, and the INS. We'll be rid of her real soon." Looking quite pleased with himself, he lounged on the plastic chair. "I drove Kenneth and a couple of his guys from the drug task force up to Quentin's. They're mad about the lab. Real mad. If they can find a way to level heavier charges against her because of the inconvenience of that cleanup, I'm sure they will."

Then Wade started to laugh. "Since Quentin sat in our jail at the time and her fingerprints are the only ones in the makeshift lab, they have no evidence to directly link Quentin to the crime. He'll be able to go home when they finish cleaning up the site unless we charge him with possession."

"Does he know about his truck?" Tony noticed that he could feel his lips when he smiled. That made him smile again. "Seeing it like that is bound to break his heart."

"I hated to tell him, but I thought he should know. We had to get it out of the way. I skirted around the amount of damage but I did tell him that I had to have it towed to the Thomas Brothers' Garage." Wade cracked his knuckles as he shook his head. "He and Elvis were singing the blues when I left. I believe all that practice is paying off. They sound better."

Tony lifted an eyebrow as if to ask a question and the corners of his mouth twitched. He didn't say a word.

"Yeah. Yeah." Wade grinned at the same time a flush rose on his cheekbones. "I know that it is just Quentin in there, but . . ." His voice trailed away and he shrugged. "At least he'll have his dogs. Joe Kyle's on day shift for the moment. He found both of them, plus Angelina's, running in the mud." Wade chuckled.

"I'm just glad I don't have to clean that much mud off my backseat."

Wade left the hospital with Tony's list of things he needed to accomplish.

Tony slipped down in the bed and slept for a couple of hours.

Awakening to the sound of Chris and Jamie trying to be quiet brought him peace and put a smile on his face. "Hey, boys." He sat up. "Come give me hugs." The boys readily complied and settled down to investigate the IV, the remote control that worked the television, the adjustments that could be made to the bed, all the time chattering with apparent delight about the snakes. From what Tony could gather, they considered his snakebite a positive thing. He just hoped he wouldn't have to go to school and be "show and tell."

"I hear you get to come home tomorrow." Theo smiled but still looked worried as she leaned over to kiss him.

Delighted that he could feel her lips, he kissed her again.

Theo straightened but looked happier. "What's the stuff on the table?"

"Work. You and the boys can help." He pulled on a pair of gloves and handed others to his wife and sons.

"Do we get paid?" said Jamie. He tried to blow the glove up like a balloon but failed.

"Do we get a badge?" said Chris.

"No to both of you." Tony reached into the box and pulled out a sheaf of papers. "As your mom and I go through these, I want you to put them in piles."

Theo pulled a handful from the box. "How do you want these to be separated?" She flipped through the pages. "I have a real assortment in this bunch."

"Let's start by separating them by name. You know what? Let's put all the Mize papers by that chair." He waved in the direction of an unoccupied chair in the corner. "All of the

Brown papers by the window, and anything that doesn't have a name on it or has a different name in a pile next to the chair."

"Are we looking for anything specific?" Theo pulled a couple of empty envelopes from the pile and handed one to each boy.

Watching the boys scurry to place them in the designated pile brought a grin to Tony's face. "No." He shook his head. "But if you find one that says 'meet me at the parking lot behind Ruby's at midnight,' you might separate it from the rest." Suddenly he felt so tired that he knew he would have fallen if he wasn't already lying down. His eyelids lowered and he drifted off to sleep.

Accompanied by the sound of Tony's steady breathing, Theo and the boys continued to sort and stack the papers. She read a couple of letters that made her feel unclean and mumbled to herself, "I can't believe no one has killed you before this, you rotten, creepy man."

Most of the postmarks were from places in North Carolina and Georgia. There were a few from Tennessee and one from Phoenix. The mail itself was a mixture of handwritten letters and receipts for things he had ordered on the Internet. She found receipts for everything from rattlesnakes and mice to male enhancement medications.

By the time they had everything sorted, each pile had a sizeable number of papers. After Tony dozed off, Theo started another stack. It was made of Hub's notes to himself. The bulk of them seemed to be girls' names and phone numbers. Some of his personal notations were merely lewd, and some of them were outright perversions. A few sketches detailed roads or directions.

Toward the bottom of the box she discovered a letter addressed to Harold Brown. The words seemed to grab her, jumping off the paper. "Tony, look at this." Theo's hands shook as she held the typewritten note.

"What?" Tony's body jerked as he woke up. "Read it to me." His eyes flickered open for a moment and closed again. "I promise I'm listening."

Theo read, keeping her voice low. "Someday I will deliver you to the devil or return you to hell. You have destroyed our dearest love. Since you are not capable of love, I cannot deprive you of your own. Your death will be my retribution for the wounds that can never heal. If I must accompany you to hell, it will be worth it. Only your damnation will ease any of the limitless pain that you have caused. Watch for me."

By the time she made it halfway through the reading, Tony sat at attention on the bed. Wide-eyed, he stared at Theo. When she finished, he reached to take it from her. "Was there an envelope with this?"

"No. It wasn't in one." She lifted a couple of torn envelopes and waved them back and forth. "We have a lot of empty ones that don't seem to have any letters to match."

Tony intently read the letter again. "Our dearest love? Wounds that never heal?" He carefully placed the letter in an empty file folder and left it open on his lap. "What does that sound like to you? What could never be forgiven?" His eyes searched hers.

Theo's eyes flickered to the corner where her children, having lost any enthusiasm for the project, were now making up a card game. Her stomach tightened and she could feel the color leach from her face as she turned to face him. Tears filled her eyes. No words were necessary.

Tony's heart mirrored her fear. "He took Ruby's baby." He gazed out the window.

To Theo, it looked as if he was trying to separate his emotions from the facts.

After a few moments, he announced, "It wasn't Ruby. She didn't write this."

"How can you be sure?" Theo moved to sit on the edge of the bed and leaned against Tony as she reread the letter. The solid strength of him pressed against her back, reassured her. Having her children at her feet gave her peace.

"Look. It says 'our' dearest love." He tapped the paper with his thumbnail. "If ever there was a single mother, even though she had a husband, it was Ruby. I don't know who I despise more, her mother or her husband." He rested his chin on her head as if he too needed the contact. "I would expect a letter from her to be a clear threat, you know, like, 'return my baby you scheming pervert, or else.' "

"True." Theo sighed. "There are some other notes that express a hatred for the man, but nothing else so threatening." She added a couple of papers to the file. "I can't imagine how he could hide such a ruthless side from so many people."

"Unfortunately, the price of faith is that it sometimes blinds people to the truth." Tony pulled her closer against his side. "How many times have you wondered how cheating spouses get away with it for so long?"

"That's no joke." Theo studied the letter. It looked like it could have been printed by any computer in the world. "Why would he keep this?"

"And how long has he had it?" He reached for the pile of empty envelopes and handed some of them to Theo. "Let's see if any of these have local postmarks and if so, what was the mailing date."

A handful of envelopes had local postmarks, but they were all addressed to John Mize instead of Harold Brown. At the end of their search, three were addressed to Harold Brown in care of John Mize. A couple had Atlanta postmarks and one came from North Carolina.

"I've got an idea." Tony reached for his phone and punched

the buttons that would connect him with his deputy.
"Wade, I need you to check something."

CHAPTER TWENTY-NINE

"That's it." Through the earpiece came Wade's excited voice. "You want me to pick him up?"

"Wait fifteen. I'll call and get a warrant." Tony looked up as the doctor arrived. "Hang on. I'll call you right back."

Dr. Morse examined the chart, poked at the receding swelling and finally pronounced Tony fit to go home. "You'll need to use crutches or a cane for a while, but you're not likely to improve any faster here. Stay off it as much as possible, and call Doctor Nash or myself if you develop a rash or anything new. Allergic reactions to the anti-venom can be worse than the bite. I'll see you for a follow-up visit next week."

The minute the doctor was out of the room, Tony called Wade. "Pick up the warrant from Archie and swing by my house in two hours. Don't worry, our guy's not going to run."

Theo and the boys played cards while they waited. "What happened?"

"Payback." Tony was not happy about being right.

Red Smith lived in a recently completed house just down the road from Nina. The dark green steel roof blended with the trees. The home's exterior was a combination of wood siding and native stone. A pair of young crepe myrtles flanked the front sidewalk and a clump of dogwoods had been planted near the road. The yard and garden were spotless, ready for the arrival of spring. Tony thought it looked beautiful but impersonal.

The curtains were tightly closed. Flocks of tiny birds gathered at the assortment of feeders in the yard. There was no sign of human life anywhere.

Tony struggled to walk with the unfamiliar crutches, feeling unwieldy and awkward as he and Wade approached the blond oak front door. Before they could knock the door opened.

Red invited them inside like honored guests.

They entered a tiny foyer. From it, they could see the large kitchen and small den to the left, the living room ahead and a short hallway to the right. Nothing hung on any of the walls. The off-white paint looked and smelled fresh. The floors were bare as well. There was no furniture, no sign that anyone lived here except for a small cardboard box sitting in the center of the living room.

Red lifted his empty hands toward Tony and pressed his palms together like a child learning to pray. A wry smile played across his features and his eyes twinkled. "I suspect you'd like to use your own handcuffs."

Tony almost refused, but the expression on Red's face stopped him. Red wanted this. Tony carefully explained Red's rights as he closed his handcuffs around the man's thin wrists.

Red looked at Wade. "Would you please bring the box?"

Seated across the steel table from them, Red looked so frail that Tony almost called to have Doc Nash standing by. It looked like a mere breath of air would flatten him.

"If you don't mind, Sheriff, I'd just like to tell you my story and then you can ask me all the questions you want." With trembling hands he adjusted his jacket, pulling it closer to the loose skin of his throat.

"That would be fine." Tony felt sorry for the man but couldn't let sympathy stop him. "I am going to ask Carl Lee to sit in. You might find a lawyer is a handy thing in a situation like this."

"You might as well get Archie down here." Red shifted rest-lessly on his chair. "The prosecutor ought to hear this, and I only want to tell it once, Sheriff. If you hadn't come for me, I planned to come in on my own."

Luckily, Carl Lee was not busy. Only minutes later he loped down the hall to meet with his newest client and the sheriff. "Give us a few, okay?"

"No problem." Leaning heavily on his crutches, Tony eased out the door and closed it behind him. Most days, he received great satisfaction in sniffing out the bad guys. This was not one of them. Even without knowing the details of Red's motivation, he guessed that Harold Brown had deserved what had happened to him.

Archie arrived from the prosecutor's office and sat in the chair by Ruth Ann's desk. No one spoke. Only a few minutes passed before Carl Lee opened the door and waved Tony, Archie and Wade inside. "He'd like to make his statement now."

"We read him his rights when we picked him up," said Wade. "I always like to read them again." Setting a small bottle of water in front of Red, he said, "I thought you might need this."

Nodding his thanks, Red sat quietly and listened politely as the young deputy spelled out everything he was entitled to under the law. He reached for the bottle of water and took a sip. "That was fine, Wade. Your voice gives those words a noble sound.

"I'm not sure where to start, so forgive me if I tell you more than you need to hear." He laced his fingers and rested his hands on the surface of the table. "Raeleene and I got married right out of college and settled in Atlanta. We wanted lots of children but it didn't happen. We'd been married for almost twenty years and had long since given up being parents when Raeleene became pregnant and Louise was born."

Tears filled his eyes, but his smile was luminous. "It was a miracle. She was the sweetest, most beautiful baby you ever saw. I guess everyone thinks that, but our Louise, she was just like Shirley Temple, you know, pretty and smart and sassy."

Unlacing his fingers, he spread his hands before him, holding them up as if to stop anyone else from speaking. "After high school, she still lived with us while she went to college. Raeleene said Louise was a slow bloomer and that's why she was content to stay with us. I didn't care. I loved having her there." He stopped and gazed unseeing into the distance.

"But that changed, didn't it?" said Tony.

Red nodded. "She got herself a beau. Oh, don't get me wrong. She had always been popular and there were young men calling for her all the time, but this was different. This was not a young man. He was a middle-aged man with cruel eyes and tattoos on his hands. Frankly, he scared me." Shivering in his chair, Red gripped the water bottle with both hands. "Soon she took to staying out to all hours every night, and the college sent a letter saying she'd failed her classes. Until he came along, she had been on the Dean's list." He shook his head. "When I tried to talk to her about it, she sneered and said that she didn't need to take classes any more because she'd found something better. Her eyes looked funny and her personality changed. She was my baby and I guess I didn't want to see the truth, but Raeleene found pills in her room."

Lifting the bottle of water to his lips, Red gulped down half of it. "We tried to talk to her about it, but she wouldn't hear. She was always out with that boyfriend of hers. He came into the house only once, but I saw him lots of times. Her skirts got shorter and she started dressing like trash because he liked her to. She moved out of the house. It wasn't long after that that she was arrested for prostitution and drug possession." Wiping tears from his face with the backs of his hands, he kept talking.

"He turned my beautiful baby girl into a drug addict and a hooker. One night, the man he sent her to, her client . . ." Red's lips twisted as he forced the words out. "He killed her. That man beat her and strangled her and left her to die in a filthy little room. The cops didn't know if he was on drugs like her or if he was just some sicko. They never did find him. Her so-called boyfriend didn't even come to her funeral." Suddenly he dropped his face into his hands and began to sob. "I couldn't help her."

Carl Lee squeezed his shoulder and looked into Tony's eyes. "Do you think that my client can have a moment to compose himself?"

Unable to sit so close to the agonized man, Tony nodded and stood. Wade and Archie sat motionless, like statues on chairs. Tony believed in divine retribution and sincerely hoped that the late Harold Brown had begun his stay in hell. Moving to the door, he stood with one arm propped up on the wall and stared through the tiny window into the hallway. At her desk, Ruth Ann's fingers flew across the keyboard even as she talked into the telephone.

Behind him, Red's tear-clogged voice began again.

"A few months after the funeral, we moved up here." Pulling a handkerchief from his pocket, he polished the tears from his glasses. "We had vacationed up here many times in the past and liked it a lot. Raeleene couldn't stand being in Atlanta anymore. I retired. I was willing to do anything she wanted." His expression grew haunted. "I couldn't stand our house there anymore either. I even thought about burning it to the ground, just to get rid of it, but luckily it sold fast."

He gazed at the beige walls and smiled. "After a while, we found some peace here. We hadn't realized that Raelene had the cancer when we moved. It was still a good move though. Even late into her illness, Raeleene loved to watch the birds and she spent hours staring at the feeders. Her favorites were the cardinals." He fell silent, his tears flowing.

Barbara Graham

No one spoke.

After a few minutes, Red shook his head and regained enough composure to continue. "Do you believe in fate?"

Tony shrugged, waiting to hear what Red believed.

"Only a week after Raeleene died, I went to a liquor store in Knoxville. I tried to drown my sorrow, but I can't drink enough beer because it's too filling. I was standing in the store trying to decide on my poison when Hub came into the same store and bought a case of vodka and left. I bought a case of it too, thinking that if I drank it all that maybe I'd finally get up the nerve to join Raeleene and Louise. I had an old pistol that would do the trick. I just needed a little more courage, even if it was from a bottle."

His faded eyes burned with grief and anger. "As soon as I saw him, though, I changed my mind about dying right away. Oh, I bought the booze all right, and took it out to the car and climbed in. He was parked next to me. When he pulled out, I followed him." He made a sound that might have been a sob or a laugh. "I couldn't believe it when he turned onto the Silersville Pike. It was a sign. I laughed as I followed him all the way back to town. I lost him out near the crossroad, but somehow I knew I'd find him again so I started making my plans."

The water bottle was empty. Red didn't seem to notice until he had lifted it to his lips several times. "Could I please have another?" His fingers picked at the label.

When Tony nodded his approval, Wade stood up and asked, "Anyone else?"

Carl Lee refused and Archie accepted.

While they waited for Wade to return, Tony tried to ease his sore leg. There seemed to be no position that felt good and several that felt a good deal worse than others. As he watched Red peeling the label from the bottle, Tony didn't want to consider what he might have done to Harold Brown if it had been his own family the man destroyed.

Wade seemed subdued as he handed out the bottles.

Red began to talk again as soon as he twisted the cap free. "The handcuffs were my Christmas present to myself." He looked amused. "I guess you must wonder what I had planned."

The three men nodded.

"I thought that if I handcuffed him to something, he would have to talk to me. I wanted him to tell me why he turned my beautiful baby into a hooker. I wanted him to tell me he was sorry." He stared into Tony's eyes. "And then I was going call your office and have you arrest him for pushing drugs. That cardboard box contains evidence I collected on my own. You'll find photographs of some of his drug deals and dates and times of others. I don't know if you can use it, but it made me feel better to do it."

"So what happened?" said Tony.

"How did you find him?" said Wade.

"I knew what his car looked like and this being such a small town, there weren't very many roads he could take. One day in January, I saw it zip past Ruby's and then only a few minutes later it went back the other way. Bingo! After a while I noticed that it often passed by about the same time, so I prepared to follow it. I wore a disguise." He lifted the bottle to his lips. "Eventually, he led me right to his church and from there to his home."

"Did you go all the way up Quentin's road?" Tony could only imagine the drive that would have been in Red's Buick. His thoughts must have shown on his face.

Red grinned at him. "I'm not crazy, just angry and vengeful. After all, I've lived here long enough to know Quentin and the kind of road he lives on." Suddenly the little man had a fit of the giggles.

It was so unexpected that soon everyone joined in, laughing

or grinning. It eased some of the tension in the room.

"So you followed him," said Tony. "Why did you wait so long to approach him? Weren't you afraid that he would leave town before you could talk to him?"

"I wanted him to be alone. I was willing to be patient, and after all, what else did I have to keep me going? Seems like whenever I was about to go up to him, he had someone with him or he left before I got there." He peeled away a long strip of label and rolled it into a ball. "It almost made me quit, but that night, I followed him and saw him park up in the back lot of Ruby's. It looked like he planned to wait for someone, but I never saw anyone else. It was perfect. I walked right up to the car window and tapped on it with my old revolver. He lowered it right away. You should have seen the surprised look on his face when I pointed that gun at him and dropped the handcuffs in his lap. I told him to put them on. He did."

"Why did you cuff him to the steering wheel?" said Tony.

"I didn't. He did that to himself by accident. I just wanted his hands tied together so he couldn't drive away."

"Was the car running? Were the lights on?" Although a video camera taped the interview, Wade continued making copious notes.

Red looked thoughtful. "Yeah, it was running. When he rolled down that window, hot air came out. It was like a sauna in there. I don't remember whether the headlights were on or not. The dome light was definitely on. I'm sure about that because I could see those ugly tattoos on his hands."

"Did he recognize you?" said Archie.

"Not at first, but I told him who I was. I told him that he had to pay for killing my little girl, that he'd killed her as surely as if he'd shot her." Red's eyes widened as he looked around the room. "Can you believe that he denied it? I went wild. Anyone watching me would have known that. I was flapping around and waving that gun in his face the whole time I was reminding him about the filthy drugs he had given her and the filthy things that he made her do. When I told him that she thought he was going to marry her, he laughed right in my face and said that even if he wasn't already married, he'd never marry a slut." Burying his face in his hands, he sobbed. "I wanted to shoot him, I really did, but I just couldn't."

Tears streamed down his face. "I hated him, and I hated myself for not having the balls to shoot him. I was just turning to leave when I saw those cages in the back seat. I knew that he kept snakes in them, but I figured that they were his pets. I was so frantic to do something, anything, that would upset him that I jerked open the back door and grabbed a box and shook it up good and dumped the snake into his lap and then I did another."

"Did he say anything that made you think that the snakes were a danger to him?" said Archie.

"No." Red paused and gave the question more thought. "Not really. He started shrieking at me, but I just figured he was mad at me for messing with his pets."

"And then?" Tony shivered as he recalled the horrendous sight in the car. "Did you just leave?"

Red nodded. "When I shut the door, he was screaming and squirming in that seat. He called me every name in the book and used language that was so vile I didn't even recognize all the words. I was just happy that I'd made him miserable for a little while." The shadow of a smile crossed his plain face. "He begged me to let him out just like I begged him to leave my daughter alone. A night sitting in his own car didn't seem like much of a punishment for what he did to my family."

Twirling the water bottle, he seemed fascinated by the movement of the water. Eventually he looked up and met Tony's steady gaze. "I almost fainted when I heard he was dead, but I swear I thought one of his drug connections was responsible. It wasn't until word circulated that he died of snakebite that I realized I did manage to kill him. I guess his pets didn't like him any better than I did."

Archie sat staring at the floor. Although he appeared to be giving it his full attention, Tony guessed there was nothing special about the linoleum at his feet. He was glad the sheriff's office only had to do the investigation. Now that they'd found the killer, it was up to Archie's office to decide what kinds of charges might come from this. They couldn't release him and yet, hadn't the man suffered enough?

"Sheriff?" Red's voice finally penetrated Tony's circulating thoughts.

Tony lifted an eyebrow.

"I need you to explain this to your mother. I need you to tell her that I really enjoyed the time we spent together and all." His eyes seemed to be filling with tears again. "She's a real special lady."

If Tony's thoughts weren't already scrambled, thinking about his mom dating this man sent them spinning. "Tell Mom? You want me to tell Mom?" Even to his own ears, it sounded as if his voice was cracking. Panic was too strong a word to describe his feelings, but it came close. Tony would prefer to suffer another snakebite than have that conversation. "Wouldn't you like to do that yourself?"

Red glanced at Carl Lee as if his attorney would save him. The man seemed quite involved in a serious and complicated discussion with Archie. Crestfallen, he returned his focus to Tony and made a slight upward motion of his shoulders before letting them fall. "I guess. I owe it to her to tell her myself."

Tony thought that Red looked about as eager to tell his mother as he felt himself, but his agreement was all Tony needed to hear. "I'll get you a phone in a bit and you can talk as long as you like."

Looking as if he'd just been reprieved from climbing the steps to the guillotine only to face the electric chair, Red hastened to make assurances that there was no need to hurry.

A tidal wave of fatigue hit Tony as the adrenaline rush of the arrest wore off. It made him feel so odd, almost dizzy, that he slumped on his spine and rested his head on the wall behind him just to keep it from crashing onto the table. All he wanted to do was to stretch out on that institutional gray floor and sleep for a month.

"Sheriff," said Wade. "You pass out on this floor and your wife is likely to rip my arm off and beat me with it." There was no smile on his handsome face, but definitely something that looked like fear shining in his dark blue eyes. "Someone needs to take you home. From here on, we are nothing but bystanders. Archie and Carl Lee have the ball now."

Tony nodded. A part of his brain wondered why his little old mother and his sweet wife were so terrifying to everyone. "Is Sheila still out there doing paperwork?" Tony used the edge of the table for support as he struggled to his feet. Once he was upright, he grasped the crutches. "If so, tell her that she gets to drive me home. If not, tell Ruth Ann to get her keys. You stay here."

A last glance around the room before he made his cautious exit showed him that Archie and Carl Lee looked as if they were settling in for a marathon negotiation. Red, the object of their conversation looked like he didn't care much about the outcome of it.

"I don't believe it." Jane stomped around Theo's workroom, slamming cabinet doors, dropping books onto the plank wood floor and generally making more noise than a den of cub scouts. "He couldn't have done such a thing."

Every book that fell was an insult to Theo's building

headache. She felt sorry for Jane. Her mother-in-law was always prepared to see the good in people, and now she was being hurt.

"It shocked me too when I heard he confessed to the whole thing. For what it's worth, I don't think he really meant that man to die." Theo couldn't bear to consider the horrible way that Red lost his daughter.

"It's not as if I was in love with the man," said Jane. "I did think he was sweet, and we had fun the night we went to the play." She took her frustration out on the shelf of books, pushing them off, one at a time.

Half of the books on the shelf had hit the floor by the time Theo's headache threatened to blind her. A large book hit the floor.

"Jane, my head is killing me. Could you please not slam anything else?"

"I'm sorry, sugar." Instantly contrite, Jane's voice was barely louder than a whisper. "I could get you some aspirin if you like."

"Thanks, but I took some already. It just hasn't done anything yet." Theo pressed her fingertips against her temples. "I'm the one who's sorry. You need to be able to release your emotions. It's just that I need a few moments of peace and quiet, and then I'll be right as rain."

Jane tiptoed toward the door. "I guess it is just a day for retribution. Nina's husband is back in town."

"Wait." Theo's eyes flew open. The light blinded her and she closed them immediately, covering them with her cupped hands. "How do you know?"

"I saw him sitting on a bench in front of the courthouse. I have to say that he looked awful, but I couldn't find any sympathy for the man."

Theo sneaked a peek. Jane stood so straight, it looked as if she had swallowed a ruler.

"If Nina takes him back, she's a fool," said Jane.

"Did you talk to him?" Theo knew that Jane was too sweet and too well-bred to snub the man. It just wasn't in her nature to be rude.

"No." She was subdued. "Well, not really. I just said hello and asked when he got back into town."

"And the answer was what?"

Jane looked at her watch. "About two hours ago now."

Theo waited for Jane to leave before she then bolted for the telephone. Headache or not, she had to talk to Nina. Her friend answered on the second ring. "Good news. People will have to quit assuming that the body in your woods is your creep of a husband."

"Why? What happened?" Nina sounded wary.

Theo relayed the story from Jane. As soon as she got off the phone, she would call Tony and fill him in. She knew he couldn't help but wonder what had happened at the Crisp house.

"That's good." Nina's sigh came through the phone. "People at the Food City were starting to point and stare. If they are going to do that, I should at least have the satisfaction of being a widow."

Theo moaned. "I can't laugh. My head is splitting open."

"I might have some news that will help that. Good news in exchange for wonderful news." Nina's voice softened. "I was just getting ready to call you because all the tops are finished and all of the patterns are perfect. You're good to go, kid. You can box it all up and send it to your publisher."

"Bless you, Nina."

"What about my baby?" Ruby's dark eyes looked black in her swollen, tear-stained face. "Did you ask Red if he knew anything about my Anna?"

Tony felt only slightly better now than he had when he'd heard Red's confession. He insisted on telling Ruby what he learned before heading home. Sheila paced in the hallway, rattling her keys.

His heart ached for this young woman. One of her hands clutched a soggy tissue and the other held Mike's hand in a death grip. His fingers looked like wax where she'd squeezed the blood out of them. It was the first time he'd seen her look like she hadn't combed her hair.

Mike cleared his throat. "I've got some vacation due, Sheriff." With his free hand, Mike reached into his pocket and handed Ruby his handkerchief. He pulled the soggy tissue from her fist and tossed it into the trash. "If there is any clue at all, I'll pursue it."

"I thought that might be your plan." Tony rummaged through a pile of papers on his desk. Finding the ones he sought, he handed them to Mike. "Obviously, I cannot give you the originals, but these are photocopies of an envelope and the letter I found inside. They were mailed from North Carolina."

Mike held them at an angle so that Ruby could share with him.

"Do they talk about Anna?" Ruby's whole body trembled as she tried to read them through the cascade of tears.

"Not exactly, and definitely not by name, but I called the sheriff over there. He said that this woman is Hub's sister." Tony massaged the back of his neck while he considered what else to tell them. "He also said that he doesn't know of her having a girl of the right age, but she lives pretty far off the beaten track. She might or might not know anything."

"It's worth a try." Mike lifted his eyes from the envelope. "That's just on the other side of the mountains. We can drive there in a few hours."

★ ★ ★ ★ ★

That evening, Tony leaned back in his recliner and checked the swelling in his leg. It looked better than it had earlier in the day, but he was so tired that it took the last of his energy to pull the flannel quilt over himself.

He had not heard from Mike and Ruby. Did that mean they had found Hub's sister? If so, did she know the whereabouts of little Anna?

He yawned several times, fighting to stay awake. At least Daniel Crisp had returned. That cleared up the problem of where he was and freed Nina from the musings of suspicious minds.

Tony couldn't help but wonder if they would ever know whose body Theo had found. The state lab had not reported anything. He doubted they would have had time to do more than assign a file number the remains. Maybe he'd give them a call sometime soon.

His boys were playing some private game that included plastic dinosaurs, lots of blankets and Daisy. It seemed to produce lots of giggling. They blocked his view of the television, but he wasn't even tempted to tell them to move or to be quiet. The moment of cooperation between brothers wouldn't last, but it was a joy for the moment. He forced his eyelids to stay up. It wouldn't be long before he lost that battle.

Theo sat in her nearby chair quilting. Although she appeared to be paying attention to nothing but her needle and the part of the quilt that was in the hoop, Tony knew she was keeping up with the program on TV and what the boys were doing. She turned and smiled at him.

"I meant to tell you earlier, the hospital called to tell you that Nellie Pearl regained consciousness." She pushed a ringlet of hair behind her ear. "They think she will be fine and that she claims she is ready to testify against Samson."

"That *is* good news." Tony grinned, only halfway paying attention to what she said.

For a change, he was wise enough to keep his thoughts to himself as he watched Theo. She sat between two lamps, and all that light shining on her hair proved one thing. It really did look like dandelion fuzz.

ABOUT THE AUTHOR

Barbara Graham began making up stories in the third grade and immediately quit learning to multiply and divide. Her motto is "every story needs a dead body and every bed needs a quilt." Most of her early stories involved her saving the world. Fortunately for all involved, she and her heroic skills have never been put to the test.

A prize winning quilter and partner in a pattern company, her quilts have been in calendars and magazines, as well as displayed in shows. Married to a wonderful man who can do math in his head and as the mother of two perfect sons, she lives in Wyoming.